FERAl

Book 2 of the Dı

C. S. Churton

Cover by May Dawney Designs.

Other Titles By C.S Churton

Druid Academy Series
DRUID MAGIC

FERAL MAGIC

PRIMAL MAGIC

TalentBorn Series
AWAKENING

EXILED

DEADLOCK

UNLEASHED

HUNTED

Available Soon

CHIMERA

Chapter One

I leaned back against the old oak tree and stared at the ball of fire between my hands, idly making it bigger, then smaller, and bigger again. The flames twisted and flickered between my palms, responding instantly to my will. With a sigh, I released the flames and before I drew my next breath, they had burned themselves out. I wasn't here to play with fire.

The new academic year was starting the day after tomorrow, and I had a whole heap of work to get done before they sent a portal for me. I'd be lying if I said I hadn't spent the entire summer focussing on my practical work, because let's be fair, magic is freaking awesome. Less awesome was all of the theory work my professors had set me to do over the summer, even after I'd scraped a pass in all of my exams.

I opened my worn old backpack and pulled out a pad of paper, and wrote across the top, 'Practical Uses of the Solerium Sithum Leaf in Modern Magic', then paused and chewed the top of my pen. I'd been putting this one off for weeks because I didn't have the slightest idea where to begin. Honestly, I didn't even know what the Solerium Sithum *was*, and it was hardly as if I could just jump online and look it up. After a few more moments of chewing and staring at the blank sheet, I tossed it aside.

I'd do it tomorrow at the academy, with a little help from Kelsey – the druid/werewolf/genius I called my friend. No point in me guessing and getting it wrong when I could just hold off for a day and make sure I had the right answers.

Pleased with my logic, I stretched out against the tree again and conjured some more flames, this time letting them lick harmlessly along my fingertips. It always fascinated me how the same flame that could reduce a log to ashes in seconds never left the slightest mark on me. Knowing a conjured element couldn't harm its maker was one thing; seeing it in effect was another entirely.

I encouraged the flames to trickle up my arm, spreading past my elbow and leaving my entire lower arm wreathed in bright orange. And then a wisp of smoke caught the corner of my eye. Shit. I let the flames go and looked down at the singed sleeve of my t-shirt. Another one. Great. I was going to have no clothes left at this rate. The flames couldn't hurt *me*, but my clothing was another matter entirely.

If there was one saving grace for my lapse, it was that there was no-one around to see me almost turning myself into a human torch. Again. One of the perks of the grassy clearing I was sitting in. Not only was it one of very few beautifully green spots in the grey little town of Haleford, it was a druid grove – an area accessible only to magic users, meaning there was absolutely no chance of mundanes stumbling across me playing with fire and accidentally exposing the entire magic community. And since I was the only magic user in Haleford, I always had the place to myself. Most people had to share with the other druids in their town – their families, at the very least. *Family.* I grunted and plucked a blade of grass from beneath me, toying with it between my fingers.

I shook my head and chased the thought from my mind. It was a beautiful day, and tomorrow I'd be back at the academy, and, ridiculous assignments notwithstanding, I couldn't wait. Now wasn't the time for self-pity. I was a freaking *druid*, and I had a future in a whole world I'd never even known about this time last year. I'd be crazy not to be completely thrilled. That was the reason I spent most of my waking hours at the grove. Not the other thing.

I grabbed my discarded notepad and pulled it onto my lap again. I should probably at least take a crack at it before I got back to the academy. But I'd barely written the first sentence before a rustling in the bushes distracted me. I looked at them, cocking my head to one side. There were no animals here – the druidic protection charm kept *everything* that wasn't magical out, furry friends included. Last year a wampus cat had visited a lot, but since he turned out to be a dark druid and tried to turn half the academy into zombies, this whole town had been warded against him. And there was no way he could have found a way through Professor Talendale's wards. Right?

My breathing hitched in my throat and my eyes locked onto the bushes, staring at the spot where I could see them moving. Suddenly, they parted and a figure burst through. A man. I scrambled back and collided with the tree behind me, the book still clutched in my hands. The man was easily six-foot-tall, with dark hair cropped short, and lean muscle that I could make out through his t-shirt. He was wearing jeans and trainers, and as he moved I saw he was dragging one leg behind him, like he could barely put weight on it. Even from here I could make out the dirt encrusted under his fingernails, and the grubby state of his clothing.

He grunted in pain and his hands trembled, and then started to blur around the edges. A gasp slipped from my lips, and his head pivoted to me. I sat, frozen, as he advanced on me in his lopsided gait, his eyes locked onto me. Eyes that kept shifting from almond-shaped to round, and back again. He wasn't one of us. He was a werewolf.

"W…What are you doing here?" I stammered, my voice barely a squeak.

He stopped moving and cocked his head to one side, then gritted his teeth. His eyes returned to their human shape. He couldn't be much older than me. But I'd never seen him before. There were no werewolves in Haleford.

"Easy, druid," he said, keeping his weight on his uninjured leg. "I come in peace and all that crap."

"You better," I said, conjuring a flame. Smoke rose up immediately, and the flames flared more brightly than I'd intended. I glanced down and saw the flames lapping at the notepad I'd forgotten in my hands. Shit. I groaned and put the flames out. My visitor smirked.

"Nice show, hot stuff."

I glowered at him. I was pretty sure I could set *him* on fire easily enough.

"Relax," he said. "I told you, I'm not looking for trouble."

"Then what are you doing here?"

He gestured to his leg.

"Well, you might have noticed, in between setting everything on fire, I'm in need a of a little help. I was hoping for some healing."

"Funny way of asking for help," I said, eyeing him reproachfully, "coming in here, insulting me. Anyway, I can't heal."

He frowned.

"What do you mean, can't heal? You're a druid, right?" He glanced around him, as if confirming where he was. "This *is* a druid grove, even if it is a little small."

I pushed myself up from the ground, because I was getting a little sick of staring up at this jackass. Come in here and call *my* grove small, would he?

He held his hands up in mock surrender.

"Size isn't everything, right? It's very…" He looked around again, as if trying to find the right word. "Quaint."

"I'll give you bloody quaint."

I had absolutely no idea how I was going to kick a werewolf's backside in a fight, even an injured one in his human form, but I was pretty sure that I was going to find a way if he kept insulting my grove.

"Why can't you heal, druid?" he asked again.

"Because I'm still in training, not that it's any of your business." I narrowed my eyes at him. "Why can't your pack heal you?"

"It's complicated."

I waited for him to expand until I started to get the sense I'd be waiting all day.

"Fine. Don't tell me." Flashes of shifter sociology from class were starting to come back to me. "Shouldn't you just… like, heal on your own or something?"

He rolled his eyes and gestured to the single, rustic bench in the clearing.

"Do you mind if I sit, if we're not going to fight? Because this hurts like a bitch."

"Who said we're not going to fight?"

He hobbled over to the bench and perched on the edge without waiting for permission, which made me wonder why he'd bothered to ask in the first place.

"I did. You're a druid, I'm a werewolf... it'd be really bad for inter-community relations." He shot me a grin. "And once I kick your ass, there'll be no-one around to help patch this up."

"And just what makes you think you'd win?"

He snorted and started rolling up his jeans' leg on his injured side.

"Werewolf, remember?"

I considered conjuring another fire ball to remind him he wasn't the only one round here with powers, then I remembered my smouldering notepad and decided against it. The last thing I needed was to set light to my clothes with him watching.

He'd rolled his jeans up past his knee, and I caught a glimpse of the wound that was the source of the blood saturating his clothing. The skin was marred with jagged tears, like it had been bitten or clawed. There was so much blood that I couldn't tell which. Already the skin was inflamed around the wound, and tinged a grey-ish colour.

He prodded at the torn flesh and winced, then leaned back on the bench with his armed stretched along its back. He'd have passed for casual if it wasn't for the way his hands were blurring. I eyed him carefully from where I stood, because if there was one thing I'd learned from Kelsey, it was that young werewolves were dangerous until they had full control of their powers. After a moment, he seemed to get his pain under control, but he didn't touch the wound again.

"I'm Leo," he said.

"Like the lion?" I blurted before I could stop myself. "Except you're a wolf."

Oh my God, did I really just say that? My mouth had no filter. Leo rolled his head to look at me with a less than amused expression.

"Very original, druid. Yeah, like the lion. Are you going to tell me your name?"

I considered it for a moment, then gave a shrug. He was inside my druid grove. What difference did it make if he knew my name?

"Lyssa. Lyssa Eldridge."

"Well, Lyssa Eldridge, it's lovely to meet you," the shifter said, with a voice that could have been genuine, but I suspected was leaning more towards sarcastic. "I'd get up, but…"

He gestured to his torn leg, and my eyes flicked to it once more of their own volition. Shredded would be more accurate.

"What happened to you?" I asked, pretty sure that I didn't want to know the answer. His hands blurred and he looked away from me for a second until they stopped.

"A dog," he said eventually. "I was cutting across some farmland and a guard dog got the drop on me."

"Mauled by a common dog? And you couldn't fight it off, seriously?"

"Suggesting violence against animals? What sort of druid are you?"

"A shit one, apparently."

I edged closer, watching him carefully but he seemed to have himself back under control.

"Anyway, I'm new to all this. I didn't even know about any of it until last year."

"Well, that's just great," he said, and this time there was no mistaking the sarcasm, either in his voice, or on his handsome face. "Exactly what I need. Tell you what, why don't you just ask your alpha—"

He must have caught the confusion on my face because he screwed his up in thought and amended,

"—wait, mentor, right? Just ask him to come down here and heal this up, and I'll be on my way."

"I don't have a mentor."

"Fine, your parents, or whatever."

"My parents don't know magic."

Leo leaned forward, staring at me, then grunted as he accidentally put weight on his injured leg.

"You don't have a mentor, and your parents don't know magic?" He looked around him at the grove again, frowning. "You're definitely a druid, right?"

"Yes, I am a druid," I snapped, scowling at him. "And yes, this is *still* a druid grove, before you ask. I– I'm adopted."

The words were harder to get out than they should have been. It was nothing to be ashamed of. Just because we weren't related by blood didn't make them any less my parents, or make Holly any less my sister. And the fact that they hadn't told me until I found out for myself – thanks to the unexpected appearance of my magic – didn't mean they loved me any less.

"Oh. I'm… sorry?" Leo sounded confused, turning the statement into a question, but he seemed sincere enough. I remembered from my studies that pack and family were important to shifters, especially wolves.

"Don't be." I shrugged it off. "Anyway, I don't know anyone who can help. And term starts soon, and no-one other than me comes here, so you're going to need to find another grove. Another druid."

He looked at me like I was crazy, which was rich considering he was the one who'd come bursting into *my* grove, and then shook his head.

"Sorry, that's not going to work, druid girl. The nearest grove could be fifty miles away, and I'm not going anywhere on this leg. We'll have to make do. You're a fire element, right?"

"Yes, I'm a fire element." Obviously. "Wait, what do you mean, 'make do'? What do you expect me to do? I already told you I can't heal."

"You can use your powers to cauterize the wound and burn off the infection. With any luck that'll keep it in check until I can get somewhere safe."

"Yeah, and you seem like the luckiest guy alive. Hold on, cauterize the wound – as in, burn you?" I shook my head. "I can't do that."

"You can," he said, "and you have to. Look, it's easy." He reached out and took my hand, positioning it over his leg. "Just hold your hand here, and think about how much I piss you off."

I snatched my hand away.

"No!"

He cocked his head and gave me a mocking look.

"Is the little druid worried about hurting the big bad werewolf?"

Getting less worried by the second. I squatted down next to his injured leg – it really was a mess, the gouges were deep and smeared with dirt and blood, and underneath it, the grey-ish tinge seemed to be spreading.

11

"Maybe you should go to a hospital," I said doubtfully. He snorted.

"Maybe you should just stop being squeamish and cauterize the damned wound."

I rocked back on my heels and glared up at him.

"You know what? Maybe coming in here insulting me and my grove isn't the best way to ask for help, did you ever think of that?"

He looked down at me like he genuinely hadn't – I mean, seriously, didn't they cover basic etiquette in shifter school? – and then burst out laughing.

"You're still upset I called your grove quaint, aren't you?"

"So what if I am?"

I had absolutely no idea why I felt so defensive about my grove – it was perfect as it was, thank you very much – but I was getting pretty sick of people laughing at it for being small, or rustic. It was mine, and it had everything I needed. So what if it wasn't as big or grand as some of the groves in more populated areas? I was a freaking *druid*, we didn't care about big or grand.

"Okay, I'm sorry, I'm sorry," Leo said when his laughter finally died down. "It's positively the most impressive grove I've ever seen, even the Pack of the Seven Suns would have been honoured to tread its sacred ground."

He snorted again, so I slapped his knee just above the wound and he gave a satisfying yelp.

"I don't know who the pack of the seven whatevers are, but if they're as irritating as you, they can stay away from my grove."

"You've never heard of the Pack of the Seven Suns? Seriously? What are they teaching you in druid school?"

"Well, duh, *druid* stuff."

"Not much of it, apparently, if you can't heal yet."

"You know what? I changed my mind. I would love to burn the hell out of your leg."

"Finally!" He clapped his hands then rubbed them together, leaning forwards in anticipation. "Let's do it, then."

But, for all my bluster, I really wasn't sure I wanted to do it. I'd never used my powers on another person before. Not a living one, anyway. Leo was an arrogant prat, but even so, I didn't want to hurt him. Not that badly, anyway. I squinted up at him – the sun had snuck out from behind the clouds, making it hard to see his face.

"You do know this is going to hurt, right?"

"Just… make it hot. I don't want to do it twice."

Yup, he knew it was going to hurt. There was more going on inside his thick werewolf skull than he was letting on. I drew in an unsteady breath and lifted my hand, pushing it tentatively towards him, then jerked to a stop.

"Come on, druid girl, don't wuss out on me now."

I gritted my teeth and tapped into the anger inside me – this idiot called my grove *quaint* – and my hand flared red. I could feel the heat pulsing out of it, though it didn't hurt me.

"Ready?" I asked the shifter. He sat back and stretched his arms along the back of the bench, curling his fingers over the edge, and then nodded.

"Do it."

"On three. One, two–"

And on two, I jammed my hand into his wound, channelling all the heat into his ragged flesh. His back arched and he howled in pain, the sound half-human, half-animal. His muscles all locked up and I could see the veins standing out in his neck. The stench of burning, putrid flesh stung my nostrils, and his right foot gouged a hole in the green earth, but between his will power and my grip, his injured leg stayed still. It only lasted five seconds, but it felt like at least twice that. I was pretty sure it seemed a whole lot longer to him.

When I moved my hand, he sagged back into the bench, eyes still closed, panting and drenched in sweat. The wound had stopped bleeding, and the flesh around it was dark and burned. The hint of grey seemed to have disappeared from his skin, but it was hard to tell with all the damage.

I sat back on my heels while he recovered – as much as he was going to, at least, given that I'd burned rather than healed him. Something caught my eye and I pushed myself to my feet, and stalked round behind the bench. When I was halfway there his eyes opened, and he rolled his head round to follow me.

I gasped, staring down.

"What the hell?"

"Sorry," he said weakly.

"Do you know how long this bench has been here? Look at it!"

There were huge chunks gouged from the wood – long, finger width groves an inch deep in the top two planks.

"Well, it was that or your neck, which would you have preferred?"

My hands fluttered up to my throat of their own volition, touching the smooth skin there.

"Yeah, that's what I thought," the shifter said, flexing his leg and wincing. "What happened to three? They didn't teach you to count at druid school?"

"I figured it was best to get it over with."

I bent over, examining the damaged wood. As far as I could tell, the bench had grown itself right out of the ground, and the wood was solid. Hard enough that it had me wondering how badly I'd have been hurt if Leo *had* turned on me. At Dragondale, the professors healed the students all the time – particularly the ones who, like me, rode surly hippogryffs in their spare time for fun. Out here, and alone in a druid grove no-one in this town could enter, I'd probably bleed to death. A shudder ran through me. That didn't sound like a whole lot of fun.

When I looked away from the wood, it was to find myself inches from Leo's face, with his dark green eyes staring right at me. My breath caught in my throat beneath his feral gaze, then I jerked my eyes away and straightened up with an awkward cough.

"I better go. I'm, uh, I'm not going back to dru- I mean, Dragondale Academy until tomorrow. They'll send a portal for me, but you can stay until then. If you want to, I mean. While you're getting better."

He let out a throaty chuckle.

"Thanks. Promise not to chew the furniture."

"You better not. I don't know how to grow another bench. It's not like this place came with a manual."

I headed back over to the tree where my backpack sat, abandoned, and rummaged inside it. After a moment I turned up an apple, and a bottle of water, and tossed them both to Leo.

"I know you guys prefer meat, but…"

"This is great. Thanks. Really. For everything."

I looked away, cramming my burned book back inside the pack, and swinging it up onto my shoulder.

"Good luck," I said to him.

"You, too, druid girl."

Chapter Two

I half expected to find the werewolf still in my grove the following morning, but when I got there an hour before the portal was due, there was no sign of him. The damage he'd done to my bench unfortunately hadn't done the same vanishing act as he had, but one out of two wasn't bad.

The portal arrived dead on time, as you'd expect from an academy whose headmaster was as obsessed with punctuality as Talendale, and I wasted no time grabbing my bags and stepping through. Directly in front of me were the closed gates of a massive castle, with grounds stretching further than the eye could see. I glanced up, running my eyes over the castle's many towers, until I picked out a dark shape circling it. A dragon. A smile tugged at my lips. It was good to be back amongst my own kind. No more hiding my magic for the next ten months.

The first time I arrived here, I was running late because I'd wasted time arguing with Rufus – one of the academy's recruiters, responsible for making sure first years find their way here – whether this whole thing was a hoax, and which of us was the insane one. We'd gone right up to the gates, hurried through, and barely made it for the headmaster's greeting speech in the main hall.

Today, I was on time, having stepped through the portal as soon as it arrived, and there was a queue twenty or so students waiting to get in. Arrivals were staggered, so as to avoid hundreds of druid students trying to check in at once, and the first years would arrive last, once the rest of us were out of the way. Less intimidating, apparently – though from experience I'd have to say they missed the mark on that one.

I joined the end of the queue, hauling my heavy bags with me, before dropping them to the floor with a sense of relief. I rolled out my shoulders as I idly watched a student at the front of the line give his name to the goblin in his waist-high gatehouse, and then step inside.

"Lyssa!"

I turned around, and grinned as I saw the figure hurrying towards me, with several heavy bags slung effortlessly over one shoulder. I snorted softly. Werewolf strength.

"Kelsey! It's great to see you." I hugged her. She tossed her bags next to mine and looked me up and down.

"How are you? How was your summer? You're looking really well." She grinned and clamped her mouth shut for a second, then opened it again. "Am I talking too much again?"

19

"Nope," I said with a shake of my head. "Just enough. I've got loads to tell you." I glanced around. "But later."

I wasn't quite sure why I didn't want to talk about Leo out in the open, but it didn't seem like a good idea.

"Oh look," a scathing voice cut across our reunion. "It's the charity case and her loser friend."

I pivoted on my heel. A tall blonde was standing behind us, her too-perfect face turned up in disgust as if she'd caught a bad smell.

"Hello, Felicity," I said, trying for sweet but not quite pulling it off. "Didn't manage to acquire any class over the holidays, then?"

The two shorter girls standing on either side of her – Paisley and Cecelia – glared at me while Felicity continued to sneer.

"I'm surprised they even let you back in," she said. "Dragondale *used* to be a little more... exclusive."

"I guess they decided they'd rather have talented druids than cheating, petty little daddy's girls."

"We'll see who's got the talent," she snapped, stalking off to the front of the queue, no doubt to bully someone into letting her cut in front of them. Paisley and Cecelia followed on her heels, carrying her bags as well as their own. I shook my head as I watched them go.

"I guess some things don't change around here."

"You shouldn't let her get to you," Kelsey said, but she was staring at her feet.

She'd been an outcast her entire life and hanging out with me didn't exactly make things easy for her. She'd always been a little sensitive about her heritage – and no surprise, given how most of both the druid and the shifter communities felt about inter-breeding – but she seemed even more subdued than usual. I guess her first summer amongst the pack was a rough one. At least no-one here knew what she was, other than me, Sam, and a couple of the professors. Felicity and her ilk were bad enough without the added ammunition.

"Girls!" The voice boomed out from behind us. "Did you miss me?"

"It's offensive to call us girls," I said as I turned around to greet one of my best friends with a smile on my face. "We're women."

"Don't I know it?" Sam looked us both up and down with the most pervy expression he could muster, and I gave him a slap across the shoulder for good measure. He laughed and wrapped me in a bear hug.

"You're setting feminism back about fifty years," I complained. He grinned and reached over to hug Kelsey.

"Let's go for a century."

"If you try to kiss me, I'll turn you into a toad," Kelsey threatened from within his arms.

"Yeah, yeah, you don't know how." He carefully untangled himself and looked at her cautiously. "Right?"

By way of response, she just grabbed her bags and shuffled forward as the rest of the queue moved. There were only two people in front of us now, and I could make out the grey-green face with yellowish eyes peering out from the small hatch set beside the gate. Goblins, as Rufus had told me last year, were not to be trifled with, and all of the students knew it. The guy at the front gave his name without a hint of impatience at having to wait to get into the school, and thanked the creature as it let him inside.

A few more moments and I grabbed up my bags, groaning under their weight, and shuffled up to the hatch that was level with my knees.

"Name?" the creature asked with a grunt.

"Lyssa Eldridge."

His eyes vanished from the gap, and returned a moment later.

"Lyssa Eldridge. Not late this year."

"Uh… no."

Apparently, goblins had good memories. Or good notes.

"Well, hurry up then. Haven't got all day."

I looked up with a start and saw the gate had swung inwards.

"Um, thanks."

I hefted my bags and shuffled through the gate before it swung shut, waiting on the far side for the other two to join me. I wasn't sure what would happen if someone tried to rush through the gate without permission, but I was certain it wouldn't be pretty. Wisely, Kelsey and Sam both waited their turn before slipping through, and making for the large, oaken entrance door. I lagged slightly behind them, dragging my bags with me. Why were books so *heavy*?

"Here, let me," Kelsey said, plucking the straps from my hands and lifting the bags as easily as if they'd been full of feathers. I didn't get why everyone was so hung up about half-breeds. It seemed pretty cool to me. Too bad I couldn't find someone to bite me and turn me into one. It sure would be nice to have super strength and super senses. And if it meant struggling to control myself on a full moon and when my temper got the best of me, well, that didn't seem like such a bad price to pay. Then I thought of Leo and the gouges he'd left in my bench while trying not to attack me. On the other hand, I was probably better off just as a druid. Self-control was hardly my strong suit as it was.

We made it as far as the Fire element common room door before we all shared an awkward look.

"Um, anyone know the password?" I ventured. Both of them shook their heads. The massive wooden door was enchanted, and could only be opened by pulsing our fire magic against it in a distinctive pattern. But since we'd just got here, and hadn't seen our head of house yet, I had absolutely no idea what it was.

"Are you planning to stare that door into submission?"

The voice came from behind us, and I turned to see a tall, handsome guy with short dark hair standing behind us, already in his uniform, and with a dusky red cloak hanging loosely over his shoulders.

"Logan! How's it going?"

Logan Walsh was the captain of the Itealta team, the crazy sport druids played for fun, involving trying to put a ball through a hoop whilst riding at high speeds on the back of a hippogryff.

"Good, thanks. We're doing try-outs this afternoon. Hope you kept sharp over the summer."

He reached past us and pressed his hand to the middle of the door. His palm flared bright red for a long second, then one short pulse, three more long pulses, and one short. I made a mental note so I wouldn't be stranded in the hallway again, then frowned at his words.

"You know I don't have my own gryff. I haven't ridden since last term."

"Bummer. I'm going to get some early practice in after Talendale's speech. Why don't you join me?"

"Sure, it's a da– I mean, I'll be there."

He grinned, and disappeared into the common room, leaving me with a face almost as red as his cloak. I'd had a massive crush on him last year which had rendered me incapable of acting like anything other than a hormonal teenager. Apparently, I hadn't managed to shake it over the summer.

"Hello, earth to Lyssa?"

I blinked Sam back into focus, to see him waving a hand in front of my face.

"And you think *I'm* setting feminism back," he muttered.

Oops.

"Sorry, what?"

He rolled his eyes at me.

"I said, we should dump our bags and head down to the main hall."

I nodded, and we moved inside the common room. Behind us, the door swung shut with a soft thud, and sealed itself. Unlike the first time I'd stepped inside the massive common room, it was almost empty, with just a couple of students heading to and from their dorms, lugging bulging bags behind them. Most of the students must have left their bags for the helpers to move, and headed straight for the main hall. Probably a smart move – it wasn't a good idea to be late for Talendale's welcoming speech.

I hurried through the room, paying scant attention to the many sofas and armchairs, or the many now-familiar banners and tapestries hanging from the stone walls, but I still couldn't help admiring the strange way vines and twigs wound through the stone walls, leaving a trail of earthy brown against the grey.

High above us, fireballs hung all around the room, floating just below the ceiling, though the massive windows set into the walls made their light redundant at this time of day.

We reached one of the corridors leading off from the hall, Kelsey and I taking one to the girls' dorm, while Sam headed off to the boys'. Dragondale was old fashioned like that. Our old dorm was exactly how I remembered it – four plain wooden beds, with warm bedding and welcoming pillows spread across them, and a roaring fire set into one of the walls. Across another wall, several wardrobes took up most of the length, and I dumped my bags next to one of them.

We stuck around just long enough to toss on our uniforms – a skirt and a blouse, which I knew I'd just have to change right after the gathering if I was going to ride, and a red cloak over the top, denoting our elemental house.

I was still wrestling with my clasp – this cloak was new, and it turned out they took a bit of breaking in – when Kelsey started tapping her foot by the door.

"Hurry up, we're going to be late."

"Alright, alright, I'm coming."

As it happened, we made it to the hall in plenty of time to grab a seat with Sam, after finding him amongst the several hundred students scattered around the main hall, seated in rows of chairs facing a stage. Talendale wasn't standing at the podium yet, which meant we wouldn't be starting the semester with black marks against our names. That was progress.

Around us, students chattered loudly, trading summer stories and admiring new haircuts, new clothes, and new attitudes, all swathed in cloaks of one of four colours. Earth elements wore green, air elements wore yellow, water elements blue, and of course fires wore red. This was the first and last time this year we'd all be mixed like this – when we took our meals here for the rest of the semester, dozens of tables would be split between the four quarters of the room. But for today, we presented a united front. Some sort of academy tradition, according to Kelsey, who was the expert on all things Dragondale.

There was a loud cough, and I pulled my eyes away from the tiny dragon made entirely of flames that Sam had conjured, and looked up at the stage where a man with short dark hair, the tips of which were just starting to go grey, was now standing, wearing a multi-coloured cloak and a haughty look. His face had a few more wrinkles than last year, but his eyes were as sharp as ever as they swept over us. Several first years shrunk away from his gaze.

"Greetings, students," Talendale began, to utter silence in the hall. "And welcome to the Dragondale Academy of Druidic Magic, or welcome back, those of you who graced us with your presence last year. As many of you know, I am Professor Talendale and I am your headmaster. It is to me you shall ultimately answer should your efforts in your lessons prove... insufficient – though of course I know you shall all strive to make your academy, your houses and yourselves proud."

Or, in my case, to avoid flunking every class, getting expelled, and having my magic bound. The rest of it? Well, I'd never been much for team spirit. I zoned out for a little bit while Talendale droned on about the elemental houses and the noble history of Dragondale. If I missed anything important, Kelsey would fill me in. My mind was already on the gryffs out in the academy grounds. I hadn't seen Stormclaw in nearly two months. Leaving him had been one of the hardest things about going home for the summer – not least because he had a tendency to bite anyone else who went near him. I hoped he hadn't maimed anyone too badly.

"Finally," Professor Talendale continued, jerking me out of my daydream, "I must remind you that the Unhallowed Grove remains off limits this year."

I shot a little grin at Kelsey – her tendency to erupt into a giant wolf each full moon was the reason the grove was off limits. It wasn't a good idea to run across her in that form while she was still learning control. I mean, I'd done it, but it's not something I'd recommend making a habit of for anyone wanting to keep all their limbs.

"Further, the academy grounds are off limits after dark to all students."

A loud muttering swept through the hall, and I shared a look with Sam and Kelsey.

"Since when?" I whispered. "I thought it was only first years who couldn't go out after dark."

"Failure to observe this rule will result in expulsion," Talendale continued over the top of the noise, and it quickly died away. "Classes will begin tomorrow. You may spend the rest of the day getting acclimated, and should you have any questions, your elemental heads will be able to assist you. You are dismissed."

Chapter Three

I stopped by my dorm for long enough to swap my skirt for a pair of leather-lined jeans – because saddle chafing is no joke – and headed straight down to the massive red and gold on-campus barn to catch up with my favourite non-human.

When I got there, I saw two figures already outside. One was Logan, who flashed me a smile when he clocked my riding jeans and saw I'd taken his advice to get some practice to heart. The other was a kindly looking, middle-aged lady with ruddy, wind-chapped cheeks, draped in a worn red cloak.

"Good morning, Professor," I greeted her. Professor Alden was our Supernatural Zoology lecturer, and was also in charge of the many magical creatures kept here on the campus grounds. She knew each of the creatures in her care, from the bizarre to the beautiful, but none were more dear to her than her herd of hippogryffs. Except, perhaps, the gryphon that had sired half of them, but as far as I was concerned, the less said about Ares, the better.

"Ah, good morning, Lyssa. I thought I might expect a visit from you today. Can I count on your assistance again this year?"

I nodded. I'd spent last year working for Professor Alden because, coming from a mundane family, I had no druid currency, and I hated having to rely on the academy stipend to buy my supplies. I'd always paid my own way, despite Felicity's many gibes – and it helped that my job meant I got to spend most of my spare time with the magnificent gryffs.

I peered over Alden's shoulder into the barn, where I could see over a dozen beaked and feathered heads leaning over stall doors. My eyes ran along them, looking amongst the stunning beasts for the familiar face I hadn't seen in weeks. My smile slipped a little from my lips and I turned back to Alden.

"Um, Professor? Where's Stormclaw?"

The professor heaved a sigh, and my stomach tied itself in knots. I searched her face, looking for answers.

"I'm afraid he hasn't been the most sociable of creatures over the summer. Of course, he's always been temperamental, but he's become almost feral. No-one has been able to get anywhere near him."

"But he's okay?"

"Well, physically, yes."

Relief bubbled up in me, untying the knots in my gut.

"But, Lyssa, I should warn you, you're going to need to find another gryff to ride this year. He's not safe."

31

Another gryff? I frowned. No. I couldn't do that. Stormclaw was the whole reason I was even on the team. I didn't want to ride just any gryff. I wanted him.

"He'll behave for me, I know he will."

"Lyssa, more than one of the groundkeepers have had to have their fingers regrown in the hospital wing. And they weren't even trying to touch him at the time. He just charged them. Someone could have been killed. We've had to isolate him in a shielded paddock for everyone's safety. The headmaster has ordered us to have him destroyed."

I gasped in horror. Talendale wanted to kill him? And keeping him in a shielded paddock? A cage is what she meant, limiting how far he could run, how high he could fly. And in total isolation, no wonder the poor boy was acting out. Gryffs were social creatures. And so what if he bit a few people? It only took Madam Leechington minutes to grow fingers back.

"Please, Professor, let me at least try? I don't care if he tries to bite me."

Alden looked me up and down for a long moment, and then nodded.

"I was hoping you might say that. You're his last chance. Grab that bucket. Logan, I'll leave you to get Dartalon out. Be a dear first and let Madam Leechington know that we might need her services shortly."

I grabbed the steel feed bucket before the professor could change her mind, and while Logan scrambled back up towards the castle with a grin on his face, we headed deeper into the grounds. It seemed like a long walk, taking us past the rest of the herd cavorting in the paddocks and snatching fish from the stream, and then further past the enchanted dragon enclosure, which looked like little more than a stone shack from outside, but when you crossed the threshold you found yourself in a protected enclosure covering hundreds of acres.

Eventually, we reached a smallish paddock edged with post and rail fencing that in most cases were purely decorative, as the gryffs could just fly over the top of them and roam the grounds as they pleased. This one, I knew, was different. If I looked carefully, I could just about make out the faint blue shimmer occasionally catching the sun – the shield preventing anyone entering or leaving the paddock. At the far side of the paddock, I could see a black and gold horse-like figure standing listlessly, head down, completely ignoring our arrival.

The professor handed me a headcollar, and with a muttered incantation, created a gateway in the shield. I stepped through and climbed into the paddock, rattling the bucket and sloshing its contents as I went.

Across the field, the creature lifted its head, and let out a bird-like screech of rage. He threw himself forward, from stationary to a flat-out gallop in the blink of an eye, flapping his wings out on either side of him in anger and running straight at me. I threw a glance over my shoulder at Alden, wondering if I should run, but there was no time – it would take him only seconds to cross the length of the paddock, and I could see the muscle rippling under his feathers as his front talons tore at the ground beneath him, and his rear hooves powered him forwards. He tossed his head, screeching again.

"Stormclaw!" I shouted, though his hearing was so acute I could probably have whispered. "Stormclaw, it's me."

He continued to gallop right at me, head tucked down like he was going to butt me with his huge, curved skull.

"It's Lyssa."

His feathered ears twitched, and he tossed his head again, and then he was right in front of me. I tensed up and squeezed my eyes shut, bracing myself for his massive bulk to hit me – and I wasn't sure even Madam Leechington could repair the damage being hit by a tonne and a half of angry gryff would do.

I heard another snort – this one right in front of me. I held my breath for another second before I registered that I wasn't in the dirt with a hundred broken bones. Cautiously, I prised one eye open, to see the magnificent creature towering over me, head cocked as he stared down at me.

"Hey," I said, opening the other eye to get a proper look at him. "How you doing, boy?"

He snorted again in what I thought might have been admonishment, and pawed at the ground with one scaled talon.

"It's not my fault. I wanted to see you, but the academy was closed for the summer. I'm back now, though."

He tossed his head and rustled his wings, flashing the gold-edged black features in the sunlight, and clacked his beak at me in something that was not an entirely friendly gesture. But he hadn't trampled me, so that was something.

"Here, want a fish?"

I reached inside the bucket and pulled out a fish head. He snorted again and tossed his head, then stamped a rear hoof.

"Guess not." I sighed and tossed the head back in the bucket. It was mackerel, too, his favourite. He really was in a foul temper. But no surprise, if he hadn't seen his own kind in weeks, and the only people who'd visited him had just dumped his food and left before he could get near them.

"I'm sorry," I said, looking up into his shining black eyes. "I missed you."

I stretched out a tentative hand towards his hooked beak, pausing a few inches from it and watching him. After a moment, he shook out his feathers and pushed his head forward, butting his beak gently into my hand. I rubbed my palm over its smooth keratin surface, and he crooned softly.

"Good boy. Good boy," I crooned back, stretching up to scratch him between the eyes. "Thanks for not eating me. Shall we get out of here?"

It took only a moment to slip the headcollar over his face, and then I led him from the paddock, past a beaming Professor Alden.

"Well done, Lyssa, well done!" she enthused as she walked along beside us – but not, I noticed, so close that Stormclaw could kick her or reach her with his beak.

When we made it back up to the barn, Logan was already mounted on Dartalon and circling through the air. There was a spare saddle and adapted headcollar hanging on the fence rail, which I recognised as Stormclaw's riding tack. I guess Logan had a little more faith in my ability to calm him than Professor Alden.

"Right, I'll leave you to it," Alden said with a satisfied nod. "I've got fourteen other gryffs to get ready for this afternoon's try-outs."

I led Stormclaw over to the fence and wasted no time tacking him up – not the easiest thing in the world since he was so much bigger than me, and the massive leather saddle wasn't exactly light, but Stormclaw obligingly stood still while I scrambled up the fence and hauled it onto his back. After triple-checking the girth strap was tight enough – because no-one wants their saddle to slip round to their gryff's belly when they're flying at high speeds – I slipped his riding headcollar on in place of his normal one, checked the reins were properly attached, and vaulted onto his back. He immediately pranced a few steps sideways, tossing his head and snorting. My stomach lurched and I gripped the reins more tightly. He'd never acted this way with me on his back before. He stamped a rear hoof, clearly unhappy about something. And if he decided he wanted to throw me off, there wasn't likely to be much I could do about it.

I sucked in a deep breath, gripping more tightly with my legs, and Stormclaw lurched sideways again, ruffling his wings in what I knew was an expression of displeasure. *Please don't throw me off.* I really didn't want to end up in the hospital wing having bones repaired on my first day back. I'd be the laughingstock of the whole academy. And, you know, broken bones hurt.

Across the paddock, I was vaguely aware of Logan bringing Dartalon back to the ground and glancing over in our direction, but my attention stayed on Stormclaw, prancing on all his feet now, and swishing his tail. What was wrong with him?

But really, what *wouldn't* be wrong with him, after being locked up all summer? He'd been bored, and lonely. He'd been betrayed by the people who were supposed to care for him. I needed to earn his trust again. And I only knew one way to do that. Taking another deep breath and blowing it out slowly, I relaxed my legs and dropped the reins.

"Alright, boy," I said, stretching one hand down to stroke his shoulder. "I'm listening. Let's do this together, okay?"

I felt his shoulder muscle twitch under my hand, and then he set off at a walk, following the fence line. I sat back and let him take me wherever he felt like going. He wasn't going to throw me. He'd looked after me last year, he would look after me again.

"You okay?" Logan shouted as we passed. I nodded and flashed him a thumbs up, not wanting to risk shouting in Stormclaw's ear.

"We're fine, aren't we, boy?" I murmured, smoothing the feathers on his neck. I felt his taut muscles starting to relax under me, and then he jumped forward, picking up speed into a bouncy trot that threatened to throw me from the saddle. I gripped the huge saddle horn – a tall lump of leather at the front of the saddle generally used for holding onto with your legs when you were leaning out of the saddle to grab a ball from the ground – and pulled myself deeper into the saddle, but before I could mutter a complaint about the uncomfortable gait, he lurched forward again, this time going into a smooth canter, and then a gallop. A laugh bubbled up inside me as the fences became a blur.

"Are we good, then, boy?" I asked, picking up the reins. He flicked an ear in my direction, and I grinned. "Alright then, let's fly!"

At my word, he sunk his haunches for just a second, then launched himself upwards, spreading his wings as his feet left the ground and giving two mighty flaps. The ground fell away beneath us as we soared through the sky. I squeezed the rein in my left hand with the lightest of pressure, and Stormclaw banked to the left.

"Atta boy. Faster!"

He beat his wings harder, sending us through the air even faster. Somewhere below, I heard Logan whoop with delight.

"Let's give him something to really cheer about. Show him what you've got, Stormclaw!"

I leaned forward over his shoulders and fixed my eyes on the ground in front of Logan. Stormclaw reacted immediately to the shift in my weight and tucked his wings against his sides behind my legs, sending us into a sharp dive towards the ground. If we hit too hard, it would mean broken bones for sure. But Stormclaw knew what he was doing, I just had to trust him. I held the reins in one hand and wrapped my other around the horn, holding myself in the saddle as the ground rushed up to meet us. A split second before we collided with the grass, I released my grip on the horn and hooked one knee around it, leaning as far out of the saddle as I could. My fingers stretched right out to the ball lying on the floor in front of Dartalon's feet, and snatched it up by one of its four metal handles.

The second Stormclaw's rear hooves hit the ground, he sunk his back end and launched himself upwards again. The force threw me back into the saddle, the ball safely hanging from one hand.

Logan cheered again, and applauded loudly as I brought Stormclaw back to the ground, and circled him around to face the team captain with a grin on my face. I tossed the ball to Logan and vaulted down from the saddle, glancing around for the water trough.

As we took a step towards it, Stormclaw's legs trembled and he snorted loudly, his chest heaving. Something wasn't right.

"What's wrong, boy?" I said, then spun round to look up at Logan. "What's wrong with him? Is he hurt?"

Logan shook his head.

"No, he's not hurt. He's unfit. Untack him, he can't do any more today."

"But what about the tryouts?" We had to make the team, we had to show everyone he was safe, otherwise Talendale would have him killed for sure.

"That *was* your tryout," Logan said with a smirk. "Get him fit again, and you've got your spot on the team."

Chapter Four

I didn't even bother watching the proper try-outs — I'd find out who'd made the team soon enough. Instead, I spent the rest of the afternoon with Stormclaw in one of the back paddocks behind the barn, painstakingly working dead feathers loose from his coat, and brushing out the black hair on his hindquarters until it shone in the sun. His stunning feathers — black, and trimmed in gold — were still dull and lifeless, but only good food and regular exercise would fix that. At least there weren't any more dead ones jabbing his skin each time he moved.

"You've really let yourself go, you know that?" I said, as I found yet another stray feather, this one somehow tangled in the matted mess that was his tail. I worked it loose with a combination of tugging, combing, and threats to incinerate the damned thing if it didn't oblige. Eventually it budged and I tossed it with the rest, and got on with tackling the rest of the knots. While I worked, Stormclaw stood patiently, making a low thrum of contentment in his throat. Apparently, I was forgiven for abandoning him all summer. If only getting Talendale to forgive *him* for attacking half the staff was going to be that easy.

It was evening by the time I was done, and led Stormclaw back down to the main paddock. I figured Alden wouldn't mind me returning him to the rest of the herd now that he'd settled down a bit. Besides, he wasn't going to get any better standing in a field by himself.

"So don't blow this," I warned him, as I slipped the headcollar from around his face. He thrummed and tugged at a strand of hair on my head.

"Yeah, I know," I sighed, leaning against his huge shoulder and scratching his withers. "Now, go on, get out of here. Go play with your buddies."

With a squeal, he took off across the field, kicking up his legs in delight as he went. I watched him for a moment longer, then headed back to the castle.

I stopped by the common room long enough to wash the worst of the grease and grime off, then made for the main hall. As usual, it had been totally transformed for mealtimes, with dozens of wooden tables divided into the four quarters of the room – one for each elemental group, and at the front of the hall, where Talendale's lectern had stood, was a counter with a man standing at it, handing out food to a line of hungry students.

"Lyssa, over here!"

I glanced round to see Kelsey leaning out of the dinner line, waving to me. I hurried over to join her and Sam, earning myself a glare from the Air element queuing behind them. We shuffled forwards until we reached the counter.

"Hey, Aiden," I greeted the guy serving with a bright smile – because if there was one person in the entire academy you wanted to be on good terms with, it was the kitchen mage. He didn't cook, as such, but you placed your order with him, and so long as the raw ingredients needed were in the storeroom, he'd instantly turn them into whatever you desired. Or slop that tasted like old boot if you upset him – according to Alex, at least.

"Hi, Lyssa," he said. "What can I get you?"

I'd worked up a pretty good appetite working with Stormclaw, so I skipped the healthy option and went for a burger and fries. Kelsey, of course, opted for a steak with all the trimmings – werewolf appetite – and Sam played it safe with a lasagne. As soon as Aiden muttered a few words and the food appeared fully cooked on our plates, I knew I'd made a horrible mistake. That lasagne looked amazing. I eyed it enviously as we made our way to one of the empty tables in the fire quarter and grabbed some seats.

For a while, we were all too busy eating to say anything – no-one cooked like Aiden did. It was the best burger I'd ever eaten, lasagne be damned. Food envy was for people who didn't already have the most incredible food in the world on their plate. Don't get me wrong, my mum was a good cook, but she had nothing on our Aiden. Hell, Gordon Ramsay probably had nothing on Aiden. Swore less, too.

"So," Sam said, swallowing a steaming gulp of lasagne as I lifted my burger for another mouthful. "I take it you're back on the Itealta team?"

I set the burger back on the plate without taking a bite. From the corner of my eye, I saw him share a look with Kelsey.

"Or not?" she ventured, setting her knife and fork down.

"No, I am. I mean, I think I am. It's not that. It's Stormclaw." I lifted my eyes to meet theirs, and even I was surprised by the anger in my voice when I spoke again. "Talendale wants to have him killed."

"What?"

"Why?"

Their horror-struck faces stared at me over our ignored food.

"He got aggressive over the summer. Attacked a couple of people. But," I added defensively, "he's fine now. He was just lonely. I'm not going to let them hurt him."

"Well, when Talendale sees how much better he is, he'll have to let him live, right?" Kelsey said, and her voice got faster and faster as she spoke. "I mean, they can't blame a hippogryff for being a bit sharp, that's just what they're like. We all know Stormclaw isn't really nasty. They can't kill him. They just can't."

I smiled weakly. Kelsey only spoke that fast – and for that long – when she was nervous or upset. She cared about Stormclaw too.

"She's right," Sam said, when he could get a word in. "When Talendale sees Stormclaw back on the team, he'll have to admit he's fine again."

"Yeah, well," I said, stabbing one of my fries with more force than necessary, "there's a problem with that. They kept him isolated all summer. He's completely unfit. If I can't get him fit again in time for the match, Logan will have to play a reserve instead of us."

"You can do it," Kelsey said. "I know you can. You know more about gryffs than anyone in our year."

"But when? Our workload is going to nearly double this year, all the professors have been saying it, and Talendale's banned anyone leaving the castle after dark. If this carries on, the only chance I'll have is at weekends."

I stabbed another of my fries and bit it in half with a savagery that would have made Kelsey's inner-beast proud.

"Why did Talendale have to put that stupid ban in place, anyway?" I grumbled. "He's never done it before."

Kelsey leaned closer to us and lowered her voice to a whisper.

"I think I know."

She glanced around, but no-one was paying us any attention.

"You know about... my mother's family."

I nodded. Kelsey's mother was a werewolf, and her father a druid. Relationships between shifters and druids weren't forbidden, as such, but they were strongly discouraged. Kelsey didn't dare reveal her heritage to the rest of the academy; doing so would make her an outcast. Even more than she already was for hanging around me, that was. As far as I knew, she was the only shifter-druid hybrid to come to Dragondale in generations. And the prejudice went deeper than just inside the academy's walls. Kelsey's mother's family had refused to have anything to do with them for years, they'd been outcasts from their pack. I don't think they'd ever forgiven Kelsey's mother for choosing a druid over them, knowing what it would mean. But over the last year, they'd grudgingly allowed Kelsey and her mother to visit.

"Well, I visited them over summer. Most of them still don't want anything to do with me, but I heard things. Rumours."

"What rumours?" My voice slipped out as barely more than a breath. Kelsey almost *never* spoke about that side of her family. Not in the academy where anyone might hear.

"That a werewolf has been illegally creating other wolves."

"What do you mean, illegally?"

Kelsey sighed in exasperation.

"Don't you ever pay attention in Law?"

"I try not to."

"Under the Mundane Protection Act of 1629, shifters are prohibited from making other shifters by biting ordinary humans."

"You mean…" My burger sat in a heavy lump in my stomach. "Someone's been *biting* people?"

"Not just any people," Kelsey continued in a hurried whisper. "Unwilling people. Mundanes who knew nothing about our world. Biting them, and then leaving them, without telling them anything about what they are."

Kelsey shuddered.

"No pack, no training, no clue of how dangerous they are. If the rumours are true, all the south of England packs had to work together to stop us being exposed."

"What are you guys whispering about?"

The three of us jumped as one as Dean set his plate on the table. Sharna pulled out the chair next to his.

"We were discussing whether you two are finally an item," Sam said, without missing a beat, while my face worked its way from crimson back to its usual pale colour.

Sharna took Dean's hand shyly in hers.

"No need to whisper about that," Dean said with a grin that stretched from ear to ear.

"He's only with me for my history notes," she said.

"And potions," he teased, then silenced her with a kiss.

"Eugh," Sam said, wrinkling his nose. "Sorry I asked. Spare us the public displays of affection."

Sharna flushed pink, but didn't let go of Dean's hand. Dean only laughed and leaned in for another kiss.

"I reckon that's our cue to leave," Sam said, standing up. "Catch up with you guys later."

Chapter Five

L ife started early at Dragondale, with our first lesson of each day taking place before breakfast. It wasn't so bad, once you got into the routine. Of course, that depended on what your first lesson actually was.

"I can't believe we're starting the semester with Atherton," Sam groaned as we found our seats in our spellcraft lecture room.

"Well," Kelsey said, opening her bag and pulling out the highly originally named 'Second Year Spellcrafting' textbook, "at least the year can only get better from here."

She wasn't wrong about that. It was bad enough that Fire had to take this as a joint lesson with Air element, which included Felicity and her cronies, but that alone I could have lived with. Professor Atherton had taken a dislike to me from the moment he laid eyes on me, and I spent most of last year getting kicked out of his lessons for stupid reasons – with the result that I'd barely scraped a pass in my exams, and only then because Sam and Kelsey had broken the rules and helped me practice in secret. Of course, as second years we weren't subject to those same rules, which was just as well, since I was bound to need just as much help this year as last.

"Daydreaming already, Ms Eldridge?" a voice cracked, sharp as a whip, from the front of the room. "I would think one who received such poor results as yours last year would resolve to pay more attention in my lessons."

I heard a few scattered cackles – airheads, for sure – and jerked my head up to glower at Atherton. He was wearing his citrus yellow robes that marked him as an air element. Short, jet black hair topped his wiry frame and cruelly amused eyes.

"Something you wish you say, Ms Eldridge?" he asked, arching an eyebrow. There was no mistaking the challenge in his voice. I was *not* going to give him an excuse to chuck me out this early in the year. Dammit, he taught really cool stuff, even if he was a total bastard.

"No, sir," I ground out, dragging my eyes from him and pulling my book out of my bag.

"Well then, if you're through interrupting my class, perhaps I may begin my lesson?"

I was smart enough not to answer that one – if only because Kelsey chose that exact moment to stamp on my foot. As if I was the one causing the disruption.

"You will open your textbooks to page seven," he said, watching us imperiously from behind his desk. He was silent for a moment as half the class grabbed their books out, and we all flipped to the correct page.

"Today, we will begin our work on piercing glamours. I trust you are all capable of recalling what a glamour is – even those of you who chose not to attend most of my lessons last year? Yes, Ms Hutton."

He nodded to Felicity, and she stood with a toss of her long, blonde mane of hair.

"An illusion cast on one's appearance. Experienced magic users can see through them, but mundanes and–" she broke off for a beat to shoot a glance at me, "–inexperienced druids can't."

"Yes, very good."

Felicity sat back down with a smirk.

"There is no spell, as such, to allow you to pierce a glamour. Rather, the technique relies upon your ability to recognise a glamour, and your determination to see through it."

"Well, that's me out, then," Sam muttered under his breath. I was careful to keep the smile from reaching my lips. Atherton's philosophy seemed to be that if I was smiling, I was probably doing something I should be punished for. Then again, he felt the same way about me breathing.

"You will pair up. One of you will assume a glamour, the other will attempt to pierce it."

I glanced round the room hopefully, trying to spot a Fire who hadn't paired up with anyone, before one of the airheads could try to make my life even more of a misery. No such luck. There was an odd number of Fires, and Felicity was already wearing a smirk as she headed our way. I sighed as I turned to face her and squared my shoulders. Might as well meet my doom with some dignity.

Sam stepped in front of me and beamed at Felicity.

"Looks like we're working together today."

He shot me a wink over his shoulder as she glowered at us, clearly furious but unable to find any real reason to object. I gave Sam a grateful smile, hoping Atherton wasn't watching, and made a mental note to put in a good word with Alex for him – he'd been crushing on her hard since last year.

When I turned back to Kelsey, her hair, usually long and red, was settled around her head in grey curls.

"Rocking the old lady look, huh?" I said, and she gave me a tight smile in return. Okay. I could do this. I took a deep breath and furrowed my brow, staring at her glamoured hair. *It's not real*, I told myself. *See what's real.* Her hair stayed resolutely grey.

I let out the breath and shook my head.

"Try again," Kelsey urged.

This time, I clenched my hands as I glared at her hair with all the focus I could muster, willing it to go back to its usual red. A gasp slipped from my lips. Her hair was red again… but was it always *that* red?

A few heads turned in my direction at the sound of my gasp, and a sharp voice cut over my excitement.

"The objective is to pierce the glamour, Ms Eldridge," Atherton sneered. "Not cast a counter glamour. The rest of us should still be able to see the original illusion."

My face reddened until it matched Kelsey's new hair. I hadn't *meant* to glamour her. Hell, I didn't even know I *could* glamour someone else. Scowling, I found the connection between myself and the newly formed glamour – easy, now that I was aware of it – and severed the link. Her hair was grey and curled again.

"Why don't I try?" she suggested, and in the blink of an eye, her hair reverted to its natural, soft red. I nodded, and reached deep inside myself, then focussed on the magic as I exhaled, visualising a mane of long, blonde, Felicity-like hair over my own brown locks.

"Inspired by anyone we know?" Kelsey asked, almost innocently, glancing at a point slightly beyond where my natural hair ended, but the illusion continued.

"Well, I liked the thought of piercing her," I said, tossing my head and my imaginary hair with it. "Though preferably with something sharp."

Kelsey smothered a chuckle, and then straightened her face and stared at my pseudo-blonde mane. Her brow furrowed just slightly, and a second later, her eyes relaxed with a grin.

"Already?" My mouth hung slack, and Kelsey immediately looked guilty about her success. "Well done," I added belatedly, trying to look genuinely pleased for her. I mean, I was pleased, it was just... well, it was a little frustrating spending so much time with someone who was such a natural.

"Want to try again?" she asked. I nodded, because I figured I might as well make the most of the fact Atherton hadn't thrown me out yet. This time, she made her eyes change colour, maybe figuring I'd find it easier to pierce a smaller glamour. She'd have been wrong, though – by the end of the lesson, no matter how many variations she tried, and how hard I tried to see through them, I hadn't managed to pierce a single of her glamours. On the plus side, at least I'd managed not to get booted from Atherton's lecture room for an entire lesson. That might have been a personal best.

After breakfast, we headed for one of the least interesting classes here at Dragondale: Law. It wasn't that Professor Dougan didn't try to make the lessons engaging, it was just there was only so much you could do with such a dry subject. Truth be told, I found anything that wasn't heavy on practical work a bit dull, and Dougan had spent the whole of last year teaching us the many, many laws we were expected to abide by, and the punishments for breaking them, most of which seemed to involve having your magic bound – stripped – as if that would solve the problem of someone being a bit of a dick. Then again, it was apparently a pretty effective deterrent. Nearly all druids were raised in magical families. The thought of being without their powers was enough to keep most of them in line. I was the odd one out, having not even known magic existed until last year. All of which boiled down to the fact I had a lot of catching up to do – in Law as much as any area.

Dougan was a tall, gaunt man, with a thick Scottish accent and heavy lines starting to set in his face. In his mid-fifties, he'd worked for the Enforcers before coming to teach at Dragondale. A career chasing druidic law breakers had left him with lightning fast reflexes, and an even faster sense of humour. Too bad not even that could make Law interesting.

"Alright, everyone, settle down," he said, tossing his red cloak onto a hook behind the door. "Time fer another rivetin' lesson."

I fished my textbook and a notepad from my bag, and sunk deeper into my chair, wondering whether anyone would notice if I drifted off to sleep for a while. I'd spent the whole of last night tossing and turning, worrying about Stormclaw and Talendale, and a two-hour lecture in

Dougan's hypnotic accent was exactly what I needed to send me off to sleep.

"Binding yer powers is the primary form of punishment fer most crimes," he began, and I felt my lids getting heavy. "Tell me some crimes that'll earn yer such a fate. Liam."

From the corner of my eye I saw the Earth element lower his hand and say,

"Risking exposure without reasonable cause."

"Aye, good. Reasonable cause almost exclusively meaning tae alleviate immediate endangerment of life. Another. Janey."

"Assault on another druid using magic."

"Excellent. Depending, o' course, on the severity of the assault. One more. Anyone? Lyssa, how about you?"

I jerked my head up, moments from drifting off, and tried to conjure one of the other laws to mind. There were so many... but I'd never been good with everyone staring at me.

"Um... uh... Getting expelled?"

He laughed.

"Okay. Nae a crime, as such, but yer right – failing to graduate means yer magic being bound. Good."

He perched on the edge of his desk and looked out at us.

"That's nae the only punishment wrong-doers face, o' course. There are lesser sentences… and greater ones."

A quiet whispering started up along the rows of tables throughout the room.

"Aye," Dougan continued. "I'm speaking of Daoradh, reserved fer the very worst of us. A druid who finds him or herself convicted of, say, murder, will be incarcerated in the underground prison, stripped o' their magic, and locked within a warded cell. Very few who enter the walls of Daoradh will leave again – at least, not as the same person as who they entered."

The entire class stared at him, rapt – Daoradh was spoken about only in whispers. Few people really knew what went on there, and those who did rarely spoke of it.

"Escape is impossible. There are no doors, no windows. The only way t' leave is through magic, magic that the incarcerated druid no longer has access to."

"Please, sir," Dean said, from two tables behind us. "What's stopping someone else breaking them out?"

"Other than the dozens of highly skilled enforcers stationed there day and night? There are over a hundred wards placed on each cell, each spell designed to neutralise a type of magic that might be used to breach security. No portal can be opened within ten miles of Daoradh, and its location is kept secret from all but a few. Very hard to break someone out if you don't know where they are. In fact, there has never been a single breakout in the whole of Daoradh's history. There are those who say that death is preferable to a lifetime of solitary confinement in a small cell buried beneath the earth."

I shuddered. I was definitely one of them. Why would any druid risk breaking the law, knowing the fate that awaited them? Or a werewolf, come to that.

"Of course, capital punishment was outlawed in 1702 – write that down – several hundred years after Daoradh was built."

"What about other magic users?" I blurted, without meaning to. Dougan turned to look at me and my face reddened, but I continued anyway. "Like shifters, for instance?"

"Excellent question," he beamed, and I flushed again. "Shifters generally enforce the law on their own kind, preferring more… archaic punishments. In their society, execution is not outlawed. Though, o' course, as druids we are responsible for overseeing all magical communities, and the council will step in and enforce the law if they feel proper punishments are not being meted out. Whilst in theory a shifter may be incarcerated, in practice I have nae heard of it being necessary, nor do I think the shifter community would take particularly kindly to it. They have always been resistant to outside interference, and t' interfere without good reason would cause further friction between our community and theirs. Some might say their justice system is more primitive than ours. Others might say it is more effective. But now we're stretching into the realms of politics, and I'm afraid that's far beyond the scope of this class. Textbooks open, please. Page nine."

I shared a glance with Kelsey. If she was right, and there was a werewolf out there biting academy people, and that was the reason we weren't allowed to roam our own school after dark, then the shifters would have to act quickly to apprehend him. I couldn't see the druid enforcers turning a blind eye for much longer, not if he – or she – was a risk to the students. The truce between the two communities had always been tentative at best, but in the last decade it had become more strained than ever. One of the reasons you didn't get many druid-shifter hybrids. It seemed like even our world wasn't immune to xenophobia.

The question was, how much more pressure could the truce take before it broke down completely? And what would that mean for my half-werewolf best friend?

Chapter Six

It was still light when we finished our last lesson of the day, so I ate a hasty dinner, then changed into my riding clothes and hurried down to the animal barn.

"Ah, Lyssa," Professor Alden greeted me, pulling her hand out of a bucket of something I didn't care to identify, but which appeared to be a lumpy, pinkish slime. "You'll be here to check on Stormclaw, I take it?"

I nodded, with a glance at the barn's open door, though I couldn't make out Stormclaw's distinctive face amongst those bobbing over their stall doors.

"How's he been today?"

Alden wiped her hand across her thick apron, leaving a trail of the goo in its wake.

"Better," she hedged, but I sensed a 'but' coming. She wiped her other hand, which had been clean but picked up traces of slime from the apron, without seeming to realise what she was doing. She exhaled heavily. "But he still won't let anyone near him. He's stopped charging people, which is an improvement, at least…"

"But that's not going to convince Talendale."

"*Professor* Talendale. And no, I don't think so." She met my eye and gave me a smile that seemed forced. "But it's only been a day, so we mustn't give up hope yet."

"I'm not, Professor," I promised. I wasn't going to let anything happen to Stormclaw. "He's still in the field, then?"

"He is. The Air team are coming up to practice, so I can't let you use the schooling paddock, I'm afraid."

"No problem, Professor."

I grabbed Stormclaw's headcollar from the tack room and headed down to the field. I wasn't planning on riding in circles around a paddock. He wasn't going to get fit that way. He'd been in confinement for weeks. It might not have been as extreme as Daoradh, but a paddock wasn't much better for a gryff. He needed to stretch his wings, and remember that some of us were on his side. And I wasn't going to show him that by chucking a saddle on his back and trying to boss him around. We were a team, and nothing Talendale said was going to change that.

"Stormclaw!" I called as I approached the herd, scattered across the large paddock. By the river, a head lifted, glistening black and gold in the evening sun. I could just about make out a squirming shape clutched in the yellow beak, and grinned. There'd been no river in the isolation paddock, and fishing was one of Stormclaw's favourite ways to entertain himself. I watched, expecting him to toss the fish in the air and gulp it down, as I'd seen him do dozens of times before. Instead, he stretched his neck out towards a chestnut gryff beside him, holding out the wriggling fish. She – and it had to be a she, Redwing, if I wasn't mistaken – shook out her neck feathers and then took the gift, gulping it down whole.

"You old smoothie," I muttered, climbing up onto the fence. I'd call him again, but far be it for me to break up a budding romance. The chestnut nuzzled his neck with her cream-coloured beak, and he rustled his wings in contentment, and if I wasn't mistaken, a touch of smugness. Who knew wooing a girl-gryff was as simple as giving her a fish?

A gentle breeze brushed over my arms, and a moment later, Stormclaw's head went up, maybe catching my scent. He glanced back over his shoulder at me, nuzzled the chestnut one last time, then came trotting towards me with just a little more swagger in his stride than usual. I hopped down from the fence as he reached me and scratched the feathers along his neck.

"Sorry, boy, didn't mean to disturb you."

He cocked his head and made a thrumming deep in his throat.

"Fancy going for a ride?" I asked, as usual unsure how much of what I was saying he actually understood, but erring on the side of caution anyway. If nothing else, he recognised the word 'ride', because he butted his head into my shoulder with an audible thump and enough force to make me wince, then dropped into a low bow beside me. Without a saddle, I couldn't scramble onto his back even with him in this position, but we'd done this before. He stretched one claw out behind him, making a platform for me to step onto. I glanced at the headcollar in my hand, shrugged, and tossed it on the fence. Guess we were going tack-free.

I climbed up onto his back and had barely settled into place, with my legs hanging down on either side of his neck, when he stood back to his full height and shook out his wings.

"Go easy on me, boy, alright?" I said, my voice just a little breathless. "I'm out of practice at this."

He let out a loud screech that may as well have been a laugh.

"Well, just don't drop me, at least."

Before I could say anything else, he lunged forwards into a bumpy canter. After half a dozen strides, his haunches sunk, and I crouched low over his neck, anticipating his ascent. A moment later, we were airborne, his massive wings propelling us across the clear blue sky.

Wind tugged at my hair as we soared higher and higher, and I sat astride the gryff, a mere passenger as he flew in whichever direction took his fancy. It would be terrifying on any other animal, to be utterly powerless to control where we were going, and how fast, and even on

Stormclaw I felt my stomach clench and unclench as we dipped and banked, but each time he levelled out before I slid more than an inch from my perch on his shoulders. He wouldn't drop me. I eased the kinks out of my shoulders and let my legs hold me loosely in place. Below us, I could see the other gryffs relaxing in the paddock, and over by the barn I could just about make out the Air team bringing their gryffs out of the barn. But up here, we were utterly alone – and utterly free. No schoolwork, no laws, no Talendale. Just us. I could stay up here forever.

Stormclaw banked hard with a loud screech, flinging me to one side. I snatched at a handful of his feathers and my leg, half-dislodged, thudded into his neck. A scream ripped from my throat, torn away by the wind. Far below, the ground loomed, and I could feel myself slipping towards it – and certain death. My hand came away from the gryff's neck, clutching a handful of feathers. My arms windmilled frantically before I threw myself forward, desperately trying to wrap my arms around his neck, but his head was too far forward. My heart raced, pumping terror through my veins as I felt my leg slipping further. And further. I was going to fall.

My throat was too dry even to give another scream, and the wind hammered into me, buffeting me and my already-precarious grip. My leg slipped another half-inch, and I screwed my eyes shut. This was it.

Stormclaw gave another screech, then banked sharply the other way. The movement tossed me about and I felt myself thrown back across his neck. He levelled out, and gasping, I forced myself back upright again. Heart pounding painfully in my chest, I looked past his shoulder at the ground and sucked in another breath. It was okay. I was okay. I hadn't fallen.

But what the hell had made him do that? Behind us, I heard a loud screech that made my bones shudder and fear well in my stomach. I risked a glance back over my shoulder, and got my answer. Rising from behind one of the academy's spires was a dragon. No wonder Stormclaw had freaked out. I patted him on the shoulder, feeling a lance of guilt as my hand ran over a newly created bald patch. What the hell was a dragon doing out here?

I frowned, and cast another look at the dragon, and the spire it had risen from. Realisation hit me with a thud. *We* were the ones who shouldn't be here. That was the shadow tower. Beyond it was the dragon pit – the riders regularly exercised their dragons here in the evenings. We'd drifted much further east than I'd realised.

Astride the feral beast's back, a small figure looked at us, and even from this distance I could make out the horror on her face. Talia. I raised a shaking hand and flashed her a thumbs up, then leaned my weight forward, asking Stormclaw to get us out of here. I didn't have to ask twice.

He streaked across the sky, then swooped down towards the ground. I couldn't say I didn't agree with him – I didn't much fancy being in the air right now, either. Especially without a saddle or reins. I let him choose a spot to land, and it wasn't until I was sliding down from his back and planting my feet back on solid ground that I realised where he'd brought us. We were in a small clearing almost completely encircled by luscious trees with stunning foliage. Flowers crept up the tree trunks, and more of them spread across the ground in the little meadow. The grass was green and welcoming, and the branches of the trees swayed gently in the breeze. It would have been beautiful, if not for what it backed onto on one side. I glanced over at the twisted, towering trees and unnaturally dark spaces between them that could not have been more different from the summery trees opposite them, and raised an eyebrow at the gryff.

"The Unhallowed Grove? Seriously?"

He snorted and pawed the ground in what I assumed was a 'be grateful I didn't dump your ass mid-air' gesture, and I tossed it off with a shrug. I didn't fall to my death, and so long as we didn't actually go *into* the grove, I wouldn't get expelled. No problem. Unless you counted the red glow being cast over everything by the setting sun. It was going to be night soon, and if I wasn't back inside the academy's walls I'd be in just as much trouble, thanks to Talendale's ridiculous new rule. Talk about paranoid.

I patted Stormclaw's sweating neck and rubbed the patch where I'd plucked a half a dozen feathers. The muscles twitched under my hand, but he didn't try to bite me, so I figured I was probably forgiven.

"Come on, boy, let's get moving. Don't want to give Talendale any more excuses to be on your case."

He'd landed in a sheltered clearing on the far side of the grove, which meant we were at least a half hour walk away from his paddock. I'd be pushing it to get back before I was missed. I made it a dozen strides before it became apparent he wasn't following. I looked back to see him scraping the ground with one front talon and tossing his head as he eyed the treeline.

"What? Relax, would you? We're not going in there. We're going round."

I reached my hand up to take hold of his headcollar before remembering he wasn't wearing one, and his head whipped round, his sharp beak snapping at me. I snatched my hand back, narrowly avoiding losing a finger.

"Hey! I already told you we don't have to go in there. And if you didn't want to be near the grove, maybe you shouldn't have landed here."

I glared at him and he glared right back, scraping up the grass under his feet. I sighed and rolled out my shoulders. Arguing with a creature who couldn't talk and probably didn't understand a word I was saying – I was officially losing it. I reached up towards his shoulder. He backed off, snorting loudly.

I cursed under my breath.

"You know what? I'm going. Follow if you want."

I set off towards the edge of the grove and made it halfway to the treeline when I heard it. The rustle of foliage being disturbed. Not coming from Stormclaw's direction, and not coming from the grove.

"H… Hello?"

I peered round, straining my ears to pick out any sound above my pounding heart, and then laughed at myself. It was probably just a bird. A *big* bird, maybe, but nothing to worry about. I was safe as long as I didn't go into the grove.

Still my eyes searched the branches of the flower-covered trees, and the spaces between the trunks. Just as I was about to turn away, the setting sun glinted on something about five foot above the ground. An eye.

I gasped and backed away. That wasn't a bird, and it wasn't small, and whatever it was, it definitely shouldn't have been able to get out of the Unhallowed Grove. I watched, horror-struck, as a dark shape pushed through the long grasses between two trees. The setting sun silhouetted a massive bulk, a furry muzzle, and very big paws.

I knew instantly what I was looking at. I'd seen one before.

It was a werewolf.

Chapter Seven

N ever run from a predator.

That was what they said, right? Don't run from a rabid dog, or an angry bull. Or a feral werewolf who'd been illegally creating other werewolves. And it had to be the one doing it – what other shifter would dare trespass here? I took another slow step backwards, not taking my eyes from the monster in front of me. It wasn't a full moon, which meant this shifter had chosen to assume its wolf form. I could think of only one reason it'd be here in the academy, lurking near the Unhallowed Grove, in its wolf form. It was looking for victims.

I risked another step back, and it stepped forward in time with my retreat. As it emerged from the treeline, never taking its yellow eyes from mine, the setting sun rippled across its fur, and the slabs of muscle it didn't quite conceal. My legs trembled under me and I knew running wasn't an option even if I wanted to.

The wolf took another step, and then paused, cocking its head at me. I couldn't quite make it out, but there was something off about its gait. Uneven. Was it limping? Maybe something in the grove had kicked its ass, and that was why it was skulking about out here. Good. Served it right for trespassing at the academy. Only, not good. I didn't like the idea of there being something even tougher than a werewolf lurking in the grove that was right behind me. I tore my eyes from the beast long enough to toss a worried look at the trees behind me, then wrenched them back again. Whatever might be in there, it was staying there. Unlike the shifter.

Off to my right there was a rustle of feathers and a snort, but I daren't risk taking my eyes from the shifter again. I just hoped Stormclaw wasn't planning to take off and leave me here. At least together we had half a chance against the wolf. Alone, I was puppy chow.

But I wasn't defenceless. I raised my hand, letting it pulse red.

"Stay back," I warned the shifter. It might be in its wolf form, but unlike Stormclaw, it could understand every word I said. And if it could shift into its wolf form at will, then there was a pretty good chance it could control itself in this form, too. Not all shifters had the same disadvantages as Kelsey.

The wolf started to shake and blur around the edges, and I risked a glance at Stormclaw. If I ran now, could I get to him before the wolf finished changing forms? If I did, would Stormclaw even let me back on?

I twisted my head back round, and already the shifter had finished its transformation and was standing in front of me, stark naked, weight on one leg as he watched me warily. My mouth popped open in surprise.

"What the hell are *you* doing here?"

"Easy, druid girl."

My eyes flicked to the heavy burn on Leo's leg. It hadn't healed up much. It wouldn't have been surprising in a human, after all, it had only been a few days, but I'd always thought shifters healed faster than that.

"My eyes are up here."

I could hear the grin in his voice, and I averted my eyes even further as I reached for the clasp on my cloak. I yanked it loose and tossed it in his direction. He sighed.

"Really? What are you, twelve?"

I said nothing, staring at the ground, because if I took another glance at the handsome – but downright annoying – shifter in his total nudity, there was no way I was going to be able to look him in the face and tell him what an ass he was. I waited until I heard the rustle of clothing before I looked up again, and saw my cloak tied loosely around his waist, covering his lower body, if not his ridiculously well-toned abs. I mean, how much did a guy have to work out to look like *that*? I was pretty sure none of the guys in my year had a body like that.

Dammit! So much for not looking.

"I asked you what you were doing here," I snapped.

He shrugged.

"I needed a place to crash for a while. This seemed as good a place as any."

"Yeah, right. The academy grounds are warded six ways to Sunday. How did you even get in here?"

I eyed him suspiciously. I wasn't sure if shifters could portal or not, but no-one other than a student or a professor could open a portal in or out of the grounds. One of the new protective measures after the academy's mascot wampus cat turned out to be a fugitive druid in disguise, bent on bringing about the zombie apocalypse – or just upsetting the status quo, I hadn't been exactly clear on which. Either way, I did know that since Raphael had been outed, Talendale had stepped up all the academy's wards.

"I followed you through your portal."

"Excuse me?"

"I stayed hidden in your grove – though I'm not going to lie, it was a little tricky given how... quaint it is. Then when they sent your portal, I snuck through behind you."

I raised a hand, watching the smirk play across his face, and tried to decide where to start. It wasn't a tough decision.

"I told you, there's nothing wrong with the size of my grove!"

He laughed, and the sound bounced back at us from the trees surrounding the meadow, picking up a more sinister tone on the way. I glanced back at the Unhallowed Grove and reminded myself there were more important things at stake than the honour of my grove.

"Why? And don't give me any more of that needing a place to stay crap. There are dozens of places you could have stayed – like with your own pack, for a start. Or have they chased you out? In fact, shouldn't you be off at shifter school somewhere? Why did you come here? And why has your leg still not healed?"

"Easy, druid girl," he said, raising his hands in mock surrender under my barrage of questions. I stared at him, unimpressed. "Okay, yes, you're right. I should be at Fur 'n' Fang. I'm taking a little time out."

"Why?"

He shook his head, shifted his weight onto his injured leg, winced, and shifted it back again.

"If you keep asking questions every time I say something, we're going to be here all day."

"Then stop giving me answers that raise more questions. And *you* shouldn't be here at all. Shifters aren't allowed inside the academy, not without Talendale's permission."

"Well," he said, his voice abruptly bitter, "There aren't exactly many places I'm welcome right now."

I swallowed the question before it made it out of my mouth and waited for him to continue. He didn't. The silence stretched on until I couldn't help myself.

"It's you, isn't it? The one who's been creating other werewolves."

He snorted, and scowled in disgust.

"Yeah, you *would* think that, wouldn't you?"

"Well, what else am I supposed to think, Leo? You turn up in my grove, injured, and you say you can't go back to your pack, or your own school. You risked being arrested to jump my portal into Dragondale – where there are hundreds of untrained druids you could kill or turn. Did you get bored of going after mundanes? Aren't they enough of a challenge for you?"

"How do you even know about the attacks?"

"No. I'm not answering any of your questions. In fact, I'm going to Talendale right now to report you. I'm not going to let you hurt anyone else."

I turned and started towards Stormclaw, who was watching the exchange in silence. He didn't take his eyes from Leo as I reached him. He was smart enough to recognise a threat when he saw one. I had one hand on his shoulder when Leo's voice cut through the air.

"Wait. Please."

I turned, keeping my hand on the gryff.

"For what?"

He hobbled closer and I backed up, forgetting I was already right next to Stormclaw. He snorted softly as I thumped into him. Leo stopped moving and raised his hands again – a gesture that meant nothing, because I'd seen how fast he could shift.

"It wasn't me. I didn't bite anyone, I swear."

"Yeah, well, you would say that, wouldn't you?"

"It's the truth. Please. No-one else believes me, but do I look feral to you?"

I searched his face carefully, and though there was a certain intensity in his eyes, they weren't the eyes of a criminal. I couldn't believe, looking at his face, that he would hunt and infect mundanes, just for the hell of it. But I'd been wrong about people before.

"I'm not here to hurt anyone. I promise. I just need somewhere to hide, until I can prove it wasn't me."

"And how do you plan on doing that?" The words slipped out of my mouth of their own accord. He gave me a grim smile.

"Well, I'm not the one doing it, but someone is, and they're not going to stop. I'm trapped in your academy. When someone else gets attacked, you'll know it wasn't me."

"Oh, so it's okay if mundanes get attacked, as long as it's not by you?" I stalked towards him, my hands trembling. God damned shifter, thinking that only supernatural lives counted. "Mundanes like my parents?"

"No, it's not okay," he shot back, his voice tight with frustration. "But what do you want me to do? I'm injured, in case you hadn't noticed. And half the shifter community thinks I'm guilty, they'll kill me on sight. Do you really think a dog did this?"

He gestured to his leg and I immediately recalled my earlier cynicism.

"Do you honestly think there's any dog I couldn't outrun, or scare away with a single snarl? They didn't even stop to ask questions. They just attacked. I was lucky to get away."

"Okay, you're right. I'm sorry. But you have to tell Talendale the truth. He'll listen, I know he will. And he can help you."

"No!" His eyes widened with panic. "I can't risk it, not until I can prove I'm innocent."

"But your leg–"

"–Will be fine. I'm a shifter. We can handle pain. But if you tell your alpha–"

"–Headmaster–"

"–that I'm here, he'll have to tell the alpha pack. Or risk war."

I hesitated. He was right. Relations between shifters and druids were strained. Talendale couldn't risk them deteriorating even further, not when the safety of the entire druid community was at stake. He was duty bound.

Leo saw the indecision play out on my face and nodded.

"Just let me hide out here a while. If I really was what you think I am, wouldn't I have attacked you in your grove, when you had no-one to protect you?"

"You needed me to heal you," I said uncertainly.

"Bang up job you did of that, by the way." He gestured to his burned limb with a grin. I slapped his chest, then suddenly registered how close I was standing to the semi-naked shifter and his ridiculous abs. His earthy scent filled my nostrils, and I could feel the heat pouring from his body. I backed up a hasty couple of steps and the grin slipped from Leo's face.

"I could have hurt you any time after you finished. But I didn't. I wouldn't. That's not who I am, Lyssa. Give me a chance to prove it. Please."

"Fine. But if a single student comes to harm, I'm going to come looking for you, and the packs will seem like kittens by comparison."

"Heard and understood." He fired off a mock salute. "Want your cloak back?"

I glanced down at the red fabric wrapped around his waist.

"Keep it."

I walked back to Stormclaw, and he lowered his front end, tucking one claw behind him to make a mounting platform. I climbed up onto his back, then looked down at the shifter.

"I'll be watching you, Leo."

Chapter Eight

The sun had set by the time I made it back to the academy's main door, but I managed to slip back inside without anyone spotting me. I headed straight for the Fire common room, and searched through the hundred or so students, looking for my two friends. They found me first.

"Lyssa!"

Kelsey came hurrying over, with Sam in her wake.

"Where were you? We were getting worried. You know Talendale's new 'after-dark' policy."

I glanced around the crowded room.

"Not here," I said. They frowned, but followed me out of the common room and into the corridor.

"What's going on?" Sam asked, as soon as the door shut behind us, but I shook my head. It still wasn't secluded enough. There was an old storage room a short walk from here, which my friends had used to tutor me last year without us risking being caught and expelled. That was where I led them, not saying a word until we were safely ensconced inside.

"I met someone right before I came back to Dragondale," I said. With the chaos of the new semester, and my single-minded commitment to save Stormclaw from Talendale's death sentence, I hadn't really had any time to fill them in on my visitor.

"Like a guy?" Kelsey probed with a slight flush to her cheeks, but I shook my head.

"Like a werewolf. He turned up in my grove."

Kelsey gasped, and Sam looked uneasy. A druid's grove was sacred. Entering one uninvited was akin to breaking into someone's house, and taking a shit on their bed.

"Have you reported it?"

I shook my head.

"He was injured, he said he needed help."

"But… you're not a healer," Sam ventured, giving me a puzzled look. "I mean, I know you've got some unexpected powers, but that's not one of them, right?"

"Right. But he was pretty insistent, so I used my pulse to burn off the infection. Badly."

"I don't understand," Kelsey said. "Why couldn't he heal himself?"

"I don't know – he wouldn't say. But that's not the weird part."

"Seems pretty weird to me," Kelsey said. "I've never met a shifter who couldn't heal themselves, not after they've come of age, anyway. Are you sure that's what he was?"

I nodded, recalling the massive wolf in the meadow.

"Yup. Pretty sure. I just saw him again."

The pair of them exchanged a look in utter silence. Eventually Kelsey broke it.

"Here?"

"Yeah. Out on the grounds."

"There's a shifter here in the academy?" Sam clarified. "Does Talendale know?"

"Yes, there is, and no, he doesn't."

Kelsey's face had gone sheet white.

"Lyssa, do you have any idea how big a deal this is? You've got to tell him, right now."

"I can't. I promised. But I had to tell you. I know there's a full moon coming soon, and you're going to be out there. I didn't want you running in to each other while you're…"

I broke off, trying to think of the diplomatic term for 'a temporarily feral psychopath' but it turned out there wasn't one.

"It's not just that." Kelsey's hands were trembling as she spoke. Not in the way Leo's did when he was struggling not to shift, but trembling with fury. "It's got to be him. The one who's been biting mundanes."

"It's not." She opened her mouth but I pressed on before she could interrupt. "He swore, and I believe him. You can't tell Talendale."

"Lyssa," Sam said, and his voice took on a soft edge that could have been pity. "We have to. You must see that."

"No, I don't. He's not a threat to anyone. If Talendale sends him back, they'll kill him. Just give me a chance to prove he's innocent."

"And if you're wrong?" Kelsey snapped. "The rogue wolf has been terrorising the mundanes. Do you know how close we all came to being exposed this summer? Have you got any idea what that would have meant for the entire magic community?"

I paused, because I didn't, not really.

"Our survival relies on our ability to hide our true nature," Sam said, his tone still gentle. "If the mundanes found out we existed, they'd fear us, and they'd hunt us down. Our secrecy keeps everyone safe."

"Fine. I get it. But he's hardly an exposure risk inside a magical academy, is he? And he's not a danger to anyone, either."

"How can you be sure?"

"Because he's hiding out by the Unhallowed Grove. No-one goes out that way."

Sam narrowed his eyes at me.

"What were *you* doing out there?"

"Uh. Well, Stormclaw kinda bolted that way… after we had a little run-in with a dragon."

I braced myself for a lecture, but he just shook his head in mock disappointment.

"Werewolves, dragons, and run-away hippogryffs – and it's not even the end of our first week yet. Why do I get the feeling we're not going to have a quiet year?"

I grinned. At least he wasn't pissed at me.

"Oh, please. You'd be bored out of your mind if I wasn't around to shake things up."

"That much is true. What else am I going to think about when Godwin's droning on about the harpy insurrection of 1109? Do you think you can find some more zombies this year?"

"I want to meet him." Kelsey's voice cut across our banter and I snapped my head round to her.

"I'm... not sure that's a good idea," I hedged. It wasn't like I'd told Leo I was going straight to my friends to fill them in right after promising to keep my mouth shut.

"Why not? I thought you said he wasn't dangerous."

"I did. He's not. But..." I recalled the look on his face, the panic in his voice when I suggested telling Talendale. "Look, he's pretty freaked out right now. There's no telling what he might do."

"Like bite us?" She put a hand on her hip and glared at me like she'd made her point.

"No," I snapped back. "Like try to run from us and get seen by Talendale."

"Well, maybe that's not such a bad thing."

"Why are you being so unreasonable about this?" I could hear the anger in my raised voice, but I didn't care. What the hell was Kelsey's problem? It wasn't *her* grove he'd stumbled into. It wasn't *her* who'd been face to face with him in his wolf form. It wasn't *her* who was putting herself at risk of expulsion to protect him.

"He ran straight through my pack's territory! He attacked one of the mundanes in my town. Turned her. Maimed her for life!" She was shouting now, and glaring at me with a ferocity I'd never seen in her, and I didn't care. She was wrong. She didn't know what she was talking about. "Do you have any idea what a werewolf attack looks like? No. No, you don't, because you've never had to clean up after one. *You've* never told someone they can't go home to their family. Because of one rogue wolf. He crossed a line, and you can't even see it!"

"It wasn't him!"

"Hey!" Sam's voice interrupted our shouting match and he stepped in between us. It was only then that I noticed my palms were pulsing bright red, and hers were trembling, blurring around the edges. I looked down at them in horror.

"What's happening, Kels?" I asked. "Are you shifting?"

"I... I don't know." She sounded terrified, backing away from us and raising her hands. "I can't stop it. I think I'm going to change! You need to get out of here, I can't control it!"

"Get Underwood," Sam said, yanking open the door and shoving me out of it and following behind. "I'll make sure no-one goes inside. Hang in there, Kels."

I nodded as he closed the door, shutting Kelsey inside the room by herself, then I turned and sprinted down the corridor. I'd covered the entire length before I even stopped to think where I was going. Where would Underwood be this time of night? The staff room? His quarters? The grounds? I had literally no idea. I rounded the corner at full pelt, and bounced right off something, sending me sprawling to the floor.

"Ms Eldridge, what on earth do you think you are doing?"

I looked up into the scowling face above me.

"Professor Alden," I gasped in relief. "It's Kelsey. We need Professor Underwood."

She took one look at the panic on my face, and didn't ask questions.

"Up. Quickly."

She hauled me to my feet then raised her hand in front of her, and mumbled a few words. A portal sprang into life, though the destination was barely discernible from the corridor we were standing in. Another corridor in the castle. She narrowed her eyes at me, then apparently reached a decision.

"You'd best come with me."

She stepped through the portal and I followed on her heels, worried that if I didn't move quickly enough, it would close when I was only half-way through. Portals were tricky magic. Druids didn't even start to learn them until their third year in the academy.

As I stepped out of the portal, Professor Alden was already swinging open a door I didn't recognise, which I supposed led to Underwood's private quarters.

"Tom, could I see you a moment?"

He stepped out into the corridor and then frowned when he saw me waiting there. Alden swung the door shut.

"What's wrong?" he asked curtly.

"It's Kelsey. I think she's shifting."

His eyes widened a fraction, but he gave no other sign of being concerned that Kelsey was about to shift into her wolf form without the influence of the full moon for the first time, or that she was trapped in the castle surrounded by hundreds of students and that only a single door was keeping her from them.

"Lead the way, please, Ms Eldridge. Janice, please ensure all students are in their common rooms whilst I take care of this."

Maybe he did get it. Alden nodded, then turned in the direction of Talendale's office. I didn't waste time watching her go, instead stepping back through the portal and praying it didn't close before Underwood made it through, but Professor Alden knew her portal magic and it stayed stable long enough for us both to make it. I wasted no time dwelling on it, instead hurrying back to the storage room at a pace that was only a little less than a headlong sprint.

I raced round the last corner and relief flooded me as I saw the door intact, and Sam still sitting guard from the outside.

"She's inside?" Underwood asked, not even out of breath. I nodded, gasping in a lungful of air, and Sam spoke as he got to his feet.

"Yeah. I think… I think she's changed. I heard furniture smashing."

"Very well. Back to your common room, both of you."

I shared a frantic look with Sam, my jaw popping open. I couldn't just leave her. This was my fault.

"Professor, we want to help."

He shook his head and moved right up to the door.

"You can help by going to your common room. Go. Now. Kelsey, it's Professor Underwood. Can you hear me?"

"No," Sam said. There was so much defiance in his voice that even Underwood turned to look at him for a moment. "Kelsey's our friend. You need us."

"It's too dangerous."

"Sam's right," I said, then for good measure added, "Sir."

"Mr Devlin is apparently trying to get the pair of you killed."

"We've been around her in her shifted form. She responds to us. You've seen her."

"This is different."

A snarl erupted from the other side of the door, as if to underscore his point.

"We're not leaving her, Professor."

He looked us up and down for a long moment and I got the sense he was weighing us up.

"Fine. But you do what I say, when I say, is that clear?"

"Yes, sir," we both agreed before he could change his mind.

"Good. I'm going to open a portal inside the room. You will stay behind me and if I tell you to get out, you go."

He waved his hand and murmured under his breath in the same way Professor Alden had, and a portal sprung into existence just in front of the door. Through it I could see the inside of our dank storage room, with boxes and cleaning products strewn everywhere, and shredded book pages floating through the air. I caught a flash of reddish-brown fur as Kelsey streaked across the room, her razor-sharp claws tearing everything in their path.

Underwood stepped through the portal. I shared a worried look with Sam, guilt cramping my stomach at the sight of what I had done to her, and then we stepped through behind him.

Kelsey immediately fixed her yellow eyes on us, and curled her lip back in a snarl.

"Kelsey, it's Professor Underwood," Underwood said calmly, standing in front of the pair of us. My heart thudded in my chest as her eyes slid from him to me, and the hackles raised along her back. She was still pissed at me, and in this form, she was deadly. But... if she remembered enough to be angry with me, then couldn't she remember who she was, too?

"Kelsey?" I took a tentative step forward, past the professor. Underwood grabbed my cloak and hauled me back. I tried to shake off his hand, but his grip was too strong.

"Please," I said, looking back over my shoulder at him. "She'll listen to me."

As I turned back to Kelsey, she sank onto her haunches. Everything happened so quickly it was a blur. Suddenly Kelsey was lunging through the air at me, and the hand on my shoulder was gone. There was a whoosh of air from behind me, and fur brushed my shoulder as something leapt over me. A black-furred figure collided with the red one mid-air, with an audible crash and then both figures hit the floor with a thud that reverberated through the ground and up my legs. Jaws snapped and teeth flashed as the two wolves fought, tearing at each other. Tuffs of fur joined the shredded paper floating through the air, and then they broke apart, circling each other.

Kelsey snapped her teeth again at the other wolf, but he didn't so much as flinch.

"What the hell?" Sam breathed behind me. "Underwood's a..."

I didn't reply, I couldn't spare one ounce of energy from watching the battling pair, and my own shock at Underwood's transformation barely registered.

Kelsey snapped her teeth at the black wolf, but Underwood didn't falter in his stride. She was all feral aggression, he was calmed and controlled. She was proactive, he only reactive. Yet of the two, he was the one who exuded confidence. I watched on, a helpless observer, as she snapped at him, and again, and each time he barely seemed to move, but each time her teeth closed on empty air.

"What do we do?"

At my words, the black wolf sent a withering glare in my direction.

"Uh, I don't speak wolf," Sam said, "but I'm pretty sure Professor Underwood just told you to stay the hell out of the way."

The wolf dipped his head in what was unmistakably a nod – and that's when Kelsey plunged. Not at him. At me.

I flung up my hand in panic – to do what, I had no idea. I trembled in panic for a quarter second, but somehow, the wolf didn't plough into me. One moment she was coming at me, then next she was flying back, propelled by some invisible force. She thudded into the wall, then fell to the ground.

Underwood's head cocked to one side, and Sam stared at me, eyes wide. My mouth popped open.

"Did… Did I do that?"

I turned my hand over and looked at it like I'd never seen it before. Between my fingers, I saw movement:

Kelsey was starting to blur around the edges. Underwood rose from his crouch in human form, snatched up his discarded and partially torn cloak from behind us and draped it over her. Sam pulled off his own cloak and held it out to the professor, who accepted it with a nod of thanks and wrapped it round his waist. I was starting to see some serious inconveniences to being a shifter. Beneath Underwood's ripped cloak there was movement, and Kelsey's wolf-form shrunk back to her human one. She sat up slowly and wrapped the cloak around herself. Sam coughed awkwardly and looked away. His eyes fixed on my hand.

"So, two elements weren't enough for you, super-druid?" he asked. I turned his words over in my mind, floored by a horrific realisation.

"Shit. Does this mean I'm an airhead now?"

Chapter Nine

We didn't speak about what happened in the storage room the next day, nor in the days that followed, but the following week, I received a summons from Talendale to appear in his office before dinner. I traipsed up the dozens of steps, my guts a churning mess as I wondered which of the many academy rules that I'd broken since the semester started I was about to be punished for.

I knocked once on the massive door that was nearly twice my height, and wide enough for four people to enter abreast. It swung inwards on hinges that were as wide as my hand, and I took a hesitant step inside.

"Ah, Ms Eldridge, thank you for coming. Please, take a seat."

He rose from behind his huge wooden desk and gestured to one of the chairs in front of it. I knew that both the desk and the chair were made of wood harvested from the Tilimeuse Tree – the sentient tree at the heart of the academy's grounds, which, amongst other things, was responsible for tracking the lineage of druids, and determining which belonged here at Dragondale. Though the wood for the furniture had been harvested centuries ago, they still maintained some sort of connection to the tree – as I'd discovered last year, when Talendale's desk had started engraving itself with information about me from the moment I'd been seated. Yet when Talendale had finished with them, the engravings had vanished as if they were never there.

Warily, I perched on the edge of the chair and looked at the headmaster. If he was telling me to sit, that had to be a good sign, right? I mean, if he was just going to yell at me, surely he'd leave me standing in front of him. Right?

He regarded me in silence for a long moment before he resumed his seat, and spoke.

"I'm sure you recall, Ms Eldridge, the first time you entered my office, and the reason you were summoned."

"Yes, sir," I said, trying and failing to keep the confusion out of my voice. He'd called me because the Tilimeuse Tree had said my elemental power was both fire and water. Druids could possess more than one elemental power, Talendale had explained to me, but rarely before their second or third years, and never two opposing elements. Ever. So a druid who had control of earth couldn't also have air. And a druid who controlled fire couldn't also control water. According to the tree, I was the exception to that rule, though nobody had any idea why. And we'd all assumed for the first time in history, the tree had been wrong. Guess it showed us.

"I heard what happened last week, in the storage room on the east corridor."

Shit. Was that why he'd called me up here, to expel me? I thought back frantically, trying to work out exactly what rule we'd broken that day. I mean, I disobeyed Underwood, sure, but…

"You manifested a third element. Do you know how many druids in our history have been able to do that?"

Well, given that to have three elements, you had to have two opposing ones and that had never happened before I'd come here, I'd have to have said none. But Talendale's moods were mercurial at best. If he wasn't mentioning expulsion, then I was keeping my mouth firmly shut until I was told otherwise.

"Only one, besides yourself."

"But, sir—" I clamped my mouth shut again before I could blurt something I shouldn't. Talendale rose from his seat again and turned his back on me, staring out of the window set into the brick and vine wall.

"Despite what you may believe, you are not the first. Nor were you the first druid to manifest two opposing elements – though by decree of the circle, it has never been spoken of outside of the circle's chambers."

"Who?" The word slipped from my mouth before I could stop it, and I bit down on my lip to stop the rest of my questions tumbling out with it. Why was it such a big secret? Why hadn't he told me about it last year, instead of leaving me to believe I was some sort of freak? Wasn't it enough that my entire life had been turned upside down when I came here, discovering that magic was real? Finding out my family weren't who I thought they were, my real mother was some woman who'd abandoned me at birth and not even the Tilimeuse Tree knew who my real father was? Wasn't it enough that I'd been an outcast, struggling in nearly every single class I'd attended? Did he really think that I needed to believe that even in the magic community I was a freak, an aberration who shouldn't even be possible? What wouldn't I have given to have heard about this last year?

"You have already met him." Talendale turned to regard me again, and this time I caught myself before I spoke. I was pretty damned sure I never had... Unless...

"You?"

He laughed, a mirthless sound.

"No, Ms Eldridge, it is not I. You knew him for some time as Toby."

Toby. The wampus. Only, he wasn't. His real name was Raphael, and he was a skinwalker – a druid who could assume the form of other creatures. Not like a shapeshifter, like Kelsey; a skinwalker never took on the nature of the creature whose form they assumed. It was a purely physical transformation. They didn't have greater strength, or heightened senses, or experience the feral nature of the animal. They just borrowed its appearance. And if you were skilled enough at it, apparently, you could fool an entire academy, and then try to raise the dead.

"He didn't manifest his third element during his studies here at the academy, but rather after he left. That, in itself, is highly unusual. Few druids gain control of a further element beyond their three years of study, though it is not unheard of. To gain a third element, though; that earned him the attention of the circle. Attention that became concern as his darker leanings came to the fore. For many years, there has been a cell awaiting Raphael at Daoradh, though none have been able to apprehend him."

He leaned on his desk, staring down at me.

"Perhaps you are wondering why I am telling you this?"

I was still wondering why he hadn't told me *sooner*, but I kept my mouth shut.

"In light of what happened last week, and your newly acquired element, it would seem you have something in common with Raphael."

I shuddered. The guy was a criminal. He tried to kill dozens of people last year. I didn't want to have any damned thing in common with him.

"I'm not a killer," I blurted.

"No, you're not." He frowned. "Though you have the same impulsive streak I knew him to possess."

I lowered my eyes, and Talendale's tone softened.

"We strive to instil our students with certain qualities, Ms Eldridge, not least patience and temperance. But a lapse in manners is not what concerns me. No. Of far more concern is that it seems reasonable to assume Raphael had some knowledge of your third element before even the Tilimeuse Tree."

It was my turn to frown, but before I could find the words to ask the question, or decide whether doing so was a good idea, Talendale said simply,

"Why else would he have sought you out last year, and showed restraint when he could so easily have killed you?"

I slumped back in my chair. I'd wondered the same thing myself all summer. Could it be true – was I alive right now because somehow Raphael had suspected I was like him?

"Understand, Ms Eldridge," Talendale said, sitting back in his own chair, his voice unusually soft for the gruff man, "that you are not in any trouble. I do not hold you accountable for your manifestation of a third element, or for the sympathies of a criminal. Nor would anyone. Whatever connection Raphael believes might exist between you because of your shared abilities, I do not see the same things in you that I saw in him. When I look at you, I see goodness."

I dared raise my eyes to meet his. Despite everything I'd done, all the rules I'd broken, the werewolf I was helping to hide right now, he believed in me. He didn't think my similarities to the rogue druid made me evil. I hoped he was right.

"Still, to best protect you from whatever Raphael's intentions towards you might be, we must learn as much as we are able. I need you to recount to me everything he told you last summer."

When I'd broken yet more of the academy's rules to sneak around the grounds after dark, because I wanted to check on Stormclaw, and worse, had allowed Kelsey to come with me. When I'd fought with Felicity because she threatened to have us expelled, and then together the three of us had defeated the undead creature Raphael had raised. When he'd cornered me, alone, in the greenhouse, trying to protect the one Beathanian plant that was our last chance to save the students and professor he'd sic'd his abomination on. And he'd said some weird shit.

"He said he didn't want to hurt me. He used his disguise – as Toby – to lure me away every time I got close to that… creature he raised."

I shuddered. Even now, I had a hard time thinking of the savage walking corpse as the innocent body of someone's loved one. I'd been so close to it, so many times. And Raphael had saved me.

Talendale nodded, as though none of this was new to him, but I noticed his palms were pressed to his desk, and etchings were racing across the wooden surface. I looked down at my hands, picking at the dirt and hippogryff grease beneath my nails. I'd never told anyone what I was about to tell him, not fully. Guilt rose like bile at the back of my throat, but I forced the words out anyway.

"He said he attacked them because of me. Keira, because she rode my position on the Itealta team. Ethan because he was… inappropriate with me. Felicity to stop me being expelled."

"Interesting," Talendale said, without a trace of accusation in his voice. "He seems to have known rather a lot about you."

"I asked him why he cared, and he said that I'd understand one day. I think there was more he wanted to tell me."

I recalled how we were interrupted, right before he could destroy the last plant, and wondered not for the first time since that night, what would he have told me if they hadn't come when they did? What was it he'd wanted to say?

"Anything else?"

"No, sir, I think that's everything."

"Very well. That will be all, Ms Eldridge."

I jerked my head round at the abruptness of my dismissal.

"That's it? But, what does it mean, Professor?"

"Hm? Oh, I'm sure that will come to light in due course. Meanwhile, I have arranged for you to have additional study sessions with Professor Swann to help you harness the power of your new element. Hurry along now, or you will miss dinner."

"Yes, sir," I said, scraping my chair back loudly and heading for the door without a backward glance. It opened as I approached, and I slipped out into the corridor, my appetite wholly gone. How could I possibly have any interest in food after what he'd told me? I wasn't the first druid to possess three elemental powers, and the other one was evil, bent on causing chaos and destruction. I had even more questions than before I'd gone into his office. But I knew one thing for sure: Talendale knew more than he was letting on.

Chapter Ten

My lessons with Swann were on a Monday evening, but I was able to convince her to move them to after dinner, so they didn't interfere with my plans for Stormclaw's training. It turned out that controlling my third element came as naturally to me as the first two – which is to say, it was an absolute nightmare, and I didn't even manage so much as a yellow glow in our first lesson, never mind a replication of a gust strong enough to send a werewolf flying across the room.

Between lessons, homework, tuition with Swann, working for Alden and training Stormclaw, it was starting to feel like I had too many plates spinning, even with Kelsey's help on my assignments. My days were scheduled down to the minute, and it was exhausting. Sam and Kelsey had kept Leo's presence secret, but we didn't speak about it again. After what happened in the storage room, it had seemed best to let it slide, and try to move on from the whole thing. I knew neither of them were thrilled about it, and I felt sure that Kelsey's opinion hadn't changed, but none of us was willing to risk falling out. Hell, those two and Stormclaw were what made Dragondale home for me. There was already a huge question mark over the gryff's future; I wasn't about to jeopardise my friendship with the other two.

It was Friday a couple of weeks later when, released early from lessons for a 'study period', I took advantage of the last few hours of daylight to slip down to the gryff barn. I spotted Alden's outline bent over a bucket – though I'd seen what she put in those buckets, and frankly in her position I'd have been keeping my nose as far away from their contents as possible. I guess thirty-odd years working with the gryffs had killed her sense of smell. I frowned. I hoped I wasn't looking at my future. Cool as it would be to hang out with gryffs all day, I couldn't see myself sticking around here longer than I had to. Education was never really my thing. It was more… well, truth be told, I hadn't really spent that much time thinking about my future since I got here. The present had kept me busy enough.

Professor Alden straightened and turned to greet me, and the thought was driven from my mind.

"Professor Alden," I said with a gasp. "What happened to your arm?"

"Hm?" Alden glanced down at her arm like she hadn't noticed that the sleeve was hanging in shreds, or that those shreds seemed to have soaked up a whole lot of blood. "Oh, that's nothing, dear. I'm afraid someone wasn't feeling very cooperative this afternoon."

My heart sank, but I forced myself to say it anyway.

"Stormclaw."

It wasn't nothing. He'd attacked her. I mean, I'd always known Stormclaw was a bit sharp, and sure he'd been going through a rough time, but I thought he'd been coming around. I thought he'd been getting better. But he wasn't. He'd bitten her.

So why did she look so cheerful about it? I frowned as I searched her ruddy cheeks and hazel eyes beneath bushy brows. She wasn't faking. She was happy.

"Shouldn't you go to the hospital wing, Professor?" I ventured.

"Oh, no, dear, I'm much too busy for that. It's only a scratch."

But as I got closer, I could see it was a lot more than a scratch. The bleeding had stopped, but the wound was wide, and it looked deep. And it sure as hell had to be hurting. I wanted to insist, but no matter how well we got on, she was still a professor, and I was still just a student. If she didn't want to go, there wasn't much I could do to make her. Still, I had to try.

"Why don't you let me do that? I can deal with all the feedings while you see Old Le– I mean, Madam Leechington."

"Nonsense. I can't be away from the herd at a time like this. But it was very naughty of you to keep it from me."

She shot me a conspiratorial wink and a grin, but whatever the conspiracy was, I sure wasn't in on it. I didn't bother to hide the confusion in my voice.

"A time like what? Keep what from you, Professor?"

"Why, that Stormclaw is courting, of course. A little nip or two is to be expected."

"Courting? What do you mean?"

"Well, unless I'm very much mistaken, there is going to be a foal in the not-too-distant future. As if you didn't know."

A foal! Then I remembered that first day I brought him back in from the herd, when he'd been fishing…

"With Redwing!"

My grin was so wide it felt like it was going to split my face in two. What could be more amazing than a foal – a tiny Stormclaw running around the academy?

"That's right. But we must be extremely careful. Breedings are exceptionally rare, and the conditions must be exactly right. We mustn't do anything to disrupt the courting process."

"So… no riding today?"

Alden set her bucket aside and considered.

"He does seem to be enjoying his rehabilitation, and there can be no question that it is doing wonders for his condition… I think it must be his choice. We will give him the option each day and let him decide if he wishes to be separated from his mate. Now, I must warn you Lyssa, it's not uncommon for gryffs to become aggressive even towards their riders during this time." She frowned. "He hasn't attempted to bite you at all over the last week?"

I shook my head. If anything, Stormclaw had been becoming more docile by the day. And true, whenever I ventured out to the paddock, he could invariably be found side by side with Redwing, but he always came when I called, and greeted me with the usual headbutt that passed for a nuzzle in his eyes.

"Well, that's promising. With any luck that will continue. And if you can get him to introduce you to his mate, then it will certainly help with the foaling when the time comes."

"Introduce me? But Professor, I've met Redwing before. I handled her a dozen times last year."

This conversation was growing weirder by the moment, and I was starting to realise just how little I really knew about the majestic creatures – and the inner workings of their keeper's mind.

"No, no," Alden said, picking up two of the buckets and thrusting one in my direction. "Formally introduce you – bring her over to you as his mate. Very rare. Very, very rare, and yet, your bond is most impressive."

I took the bucket, looking away quickly from its contents, but not before I caught a glimpse of piles of guts and something I couldn't identify sitting on top of the usual fish.

"I probably don't want to know this, but… What's in the buckets?"

"My special courting mix. This should give just a little extra sheen to his coat, and boost his scent. Just to help the process along."

If Stormclaw was going to smell like the contents of this bucket, I was pretty sure that any romance would be halted in its tracks, but I didn't say anything – because that would have meant opening my mouth again, and I wasn't willing to take another lungful of the odours leaking from the dead stuff.

"Quickly now, let's head down to the paddock. I need to be back in time to prepare the Air team's gryffs for their training sessions, and I gather I'm not going to have your assistance tonight?"

"Sorry, Professor," I said, and immediately regretted it as the stench made my eyes water. I waited until we'd stepped outside the barn and into the open air before I added, "With my schedule at the moment, and Stormclaw's rehabilitation, I don't think I can manage any more than two nights a week helping you out."

Just enough to pay my way through the year, with a little careful budgeting.

"Not a problem," she assured me, marching out towards the back paddock. I hurried along beside her, stretching my legs to keep up. "Stormclaw is the priority. I'll manage the others. I may have to take on a second assistant, though volunteers are a little thin on the ground."

Not least because of the rumours circulating that the last volunteer ended up *in* the ground, I suspected. I was pretty sure it wasn't true though. I mean, the gryffs were way less dangerous than the dragons, and *they* hadn't killed anyone in decades. And everyone was less dangerous than Ares, the gryphon who even Alden didn't handle unless she had to. The gryffs were pussy cats compared to him.

"Maybe someone from one of the Itealta teams?" I suggested, swapping the heavy bucket from one hand to the other and trying not to inhale as I did. "I mean, they know how to handle the gryffs, right?"

"What you need to understand, Lyssa, is that not every rider is like you are." She glanced back over her shoulder at me and slowed her brisk pace a little. "Every rider has a decent bond with their own gryff, of course, but it's rare to find someone who understands enough to handle all of them."

I grinned at the implied compliment, and felt my cheeks glowing. I'd never excelled at anything before, unless you counted being late as a skill. The professor smiled back at me, and then I saw a flash of movement in her path.

"Professor, look out!"

She pivoted her head to look in front of her again just in time to avoid walking right into it. A portal had appeared just feet in front of us, right where she'd been about to step. Her face flushed red with anger, then she exhaled heavily through pursed lips and shook her head.

"They must have started portalling lessons for the third years. I do wish Professor Kaversal would keep a closer eye on where her students open portals. You'll want to watch your step for the next few weeks, until they get some control."

She glanced at a watch around her wrist, as if waiting for something, and then a face and hand appeared through the portal. I waited for the rest of the third year to emerge, but it looked like he wasn't going to. He seemed to realise at the same moment I did, and then his face blanched with panic.

"I… I'm stuck!"

Alden sighed.

"I'm sure Professor Kaversal will disembark you shortly, do try not to panic."

The disembodied head shook from side to side.

"She doesn't know. I, uh, I was trying to get some extra practice in."

"And that is precisely why this sort of thing is not allowed! The rules are in place for a reason, young man. What do you think would have happened if Lyssa and I weren't passing?"

"I'm sorry, Professor."

I'm sure his head would have hung if enough of his neck had come through the portal to allow it.

"Well, don't look at me," she huffed. "I certainly can't get you out of a malformed portal. It'll have to be Professor Kaversal. Lyssa, be a dear, pop up to the castle and inform Professor Kaversal that one of her students is stuck."

She gave me a long-suffering look that I suspected had as much to do with our trip to visit the gryffs being delayed as dealing with wayward students. I abandoned my bucket and hurried back towards the castle. Stormclaw would have to wait.

Chapter Eleven

It took nearly half an hour to get back to the castle and track down Kaversal, who immediately portaled to Professor Alden, having told me I was to stay well clear of the entire area until the situation was resolved. So much for seeing Stormclaw today and finding out if he really was courting. I was feeling thoroughly cheated as I scuffed my way through the corridors with poor grace. I hadn't planned to spend my study period cooped up – or, heaven forbid, actually studying – but it looked like I wasn't going to get much choice.

I was so busy feeling sorry for myself that I almost walked straight into Kelsey before I saw her.

"Lyssa, I've been looking for you."

"You've found me," I grunted, then saw the hurt look flash across her eyes. I raised a hand before she could reply. "Sorry, sorry. Ignore me, I'm having a bad day."

She hesitated for a moment.

"I don't want to make it worse, but…" She trailed off, chewing her lip. I rolled my eyes.

"Come on, out with it." When she didn't speak, I added, "*I'm* not the one who bites round here."

A small smile caught at the corner of her mouth until it spread into a full grin, which faltered again as she met my eye.

"I need to talk to you... about Leo."

Her voice twisted around the name, and my grin faded, too, but I nodded and resolved to keep hold of my temper, no matter what she said. I didn't want him to come between us. But then, it wasn't me who'd lost my temper and transformed into a murderous wolf last time we spoke about him.

"Okay."

"It's the full moon tonight."

"Shit, is it? I'm sorry, I've been so caught up with Stormclaw..." I normally tracked the moon's cycles religiously. Kelsey still couldn't stop herself shifting under a full moon, which was fine when she was at home, but not when she was in a castle full of vaguely xenophobic druids who had no idea that she was a hybrid. As her best friend, the least I could do was help her sneak out of the castle without being seen, and cover for her while she was gone.

"It's fine," she waved me off. "I know you've been busy. It's just," she glanced around to make sure we were alone. "You said Leo was hiding out by the Unhallowed Grove. If I run into him in my shifted form... Well, my wolf side is really territorial about the grove, and you know I can't fully control it yet. There could be a fight."

"I could ask him to move," I suggested.

"No!" Panic fluttered in her voice, and I waited until she continued. "That'd be even worse. If I caught his scent, I might leave the grove to track him down. I think… I think if I met him beforehand, I might be able to control myself better when I shift."

I was silent for a long moment.

"You want to *meet* him?"

She nodded, looking at her shoes, while I processed the turn around. It had to be hard for her, I acknowledged. Having him here when she was convinced he was guilty – well, I knew how I'd have felt if there was a killer living at the academy and one of my friends had asked me to cover it up. *I* knew he was innocent, but she didn't. And that was without even taking into account her shifted form's territorial instincts. It hadn't even crossed my mind. I cussed myself silently. There was so much I didn't know about shifters. Like how they'd react if they came face to face with another of their species when they were still learning control. How could I have put that on her? And she couldn't even talk to Underwood about it, because I'd made her promise she wouldn't tell.

"I'm a shit friend, aren't I?" I said eventually.

"No, you're a good friend. And a good person. I'm glad you're looking out for Leo." She met my eye. "I still think you're wrong about him, but there aren't many druids who'd put their neck on the line for a shifter. I'm proud to call you my friend."

I turned pink for the second time in the last hour, and squeezed her hand.

"Alright, let's get over to the grove before this gets any slushier."

We made our way out into the grounds, and started along the path that would eventually lead us to the Unhallowed Grove.

"Where do you two think you're going?"

The voice boomed out from behind us and we both jumped, then spun around.

"Dammit, Sam, don't do that!" I snapped, with a distinctly unflattering quiver in my voice.

He shrugged.

"Don't make it so easy, then. Seriously, where are you headed?"

"To the grove," Kelsey said, her voice much calmer than mine. "You know, *the* grove. To meet *him*."

Sam stared at her blankly and I could almost see her emphasis rolling around inside his head until his eyes suddenly widened.

"Oh! Cool. I'll come with you."

I'm sure he meant it to sound casual, but there was no missing the protective note in his voice. I didn't argue, because it was kind of sweet, even if Kelsey did have shifter-strength and I was some sort of super-druid.

We glanced around to check no-one else was about, then hurried off down the track, not relaxing for a moment until we were round the bend and hidden behind a copse. The walk to the Unhallowed Grove took about twenty minutes – longer still when we had to go to the meadow on the far side of it. None of us were going to be eating dinner today. That was a pretty big deal for a shifter; Kelsey was meticulous about mealtimes. But I guessed she'd eat as much as she needed in the grove once she'd shifted tonight. I tried not to dwell on the thought.

We skirted round the edge of the grove, not getting too close – I mean, if we didn't actually step inside, then technically we weren't breaking any academy rules. Aside from harbouring a wanted fugitive. I knew we were getting near when Kelsey stiffened, her nostrils flaring as the light breeze blew in our direction. I couldn't smell anything, but I wasn't the one with werewolf senses. I watched her closely, but she forced the tension from her shoulders and gave me a curt nod that I translated to mean 'I'm fine.' It took only another moment for us to reach the meadow, but when we did, it was completely deserted.

"Leo?" I called softly. "It's me."

The wind rustling the leaves was my only answer. I opened my mouth to call again, but Kelsey touched my arm lightly, and shook her head. He was close, then. He knew I was here. And he didn't want to show himself. Charming. I glanced over at my two friends, and figured I knew why.

"They're my friends, Leo, you can trust them."

Still nothing. I ground my teeth together and sighed with impatience.

"They've known about you for weeks, and they haven't told anyone. So get your arse out here before I decide to stop protecting it."

The bushes parted and the six foot mound of man-muscle walked through, wearing nothing but a pair of blue jeans. I wasn't sure where he'd got them from, but it was a big improvement on his nudity. Or at least, that's what I told myself.

"Alright, druid girl, don't set yourself on fire."

His face wasn't quite as cocky as usual, and his voice had a hardness to it that hadn't been there before. Guess he really was pissed I'd told his secret to my friends. Only, it wasn't both of them he was staring at. Just Kelsey.

"Want to tell me why you've brought a shifter out here? I didn't think they were allowed in your precious academy."

"She's a druid," I said. "And a shifter."

His eyes widened a fraction, and then narrowed. His lips parted in a silent snarl.

"A half-breed."

Kelsey flushed under his criticism, but she didn't respond. She must have been used to it by now. But I wasn't. It was so unfair; it wasn't her fault she was a hybrid, and it didn't make her any less of a person. Or a friend.

"Put your prejudice back in its box," I snapped. "She's my friend, and she's kept quiet about you, so you owe her."

"Owe a half-breed?" He barked a harsh laugh. "You've got to be joking."

"What the hell is your problem?"

"Lyssa, leave it," Kelsey said in a quiet, defeated voice that only made me angrier.

"No, I won't leave it. There's nothing wrong with what you are, Kels."

"Nothing wrong?" Leo said, looking at me like I was a naïve child. "It's unnatural."

I snorted, and he cocked his head at me.

"I'm a freaking druid who can throw fire. You turn into something off National Geographic. Neither of us is natural."

He flicked his eyes to Kelsey and then back to me again, but didn't say anything.

"So her father is a druid," I said. "So what? Are you telling me shifters only hook up with other shifters? None of them ever have families with mundanes?"

"That's different," he grunted.

"Different, how?" I pressed.

"I don't know, just… different."

I cocked an eyebrow at him, and he carried on defensively.

"Druid magic and shifter magic aren't compatible."

"Listen, jackass," Sam said, stepping in front of me and Kelsey. Leo shifted his attention to him, and squared his jaw. Sam pressed on, apparently unintimidated. "I don't know you, but I know Kelsey, and she is a damned good druid. One of the best in our year."

Leo frowned, and for the first time I thought I saw a flash of uncertainty in his hard eyes. He looked at me over Sam's shoulder.

"That true, druid girl?"

"Top quarter of every class," I said.

"But all the stories say–"

"The stories are wrong," I told him flatly, crossing my arms over my chest. "And it's lucky for you I believe in getting to know people before I judge them."

"Alright, alright," he said, holding his hands up in mock surrender. A ghost of a smile flickered over his lips. "I take your point. What's it got to do with me? You might not have noticed, but I don't exactly have much sway with the packs right now."

I groped for the right words, but Kelsey spoke up from beside me.

"It's the full moon tonight."

He stared at her in silence for a long moment.

"You don't have control yet."

Her cheeks reddened again as she shook her head, and stared down at her feet.

"Are you still learning to walk on four legs, too?"

Sam moved quickly, placing both palms on the shifter's chest and shoving him hard. Leo stumbled backwards, then his face twisted in fury and he threw himself forward, hand balled into a fist.

"Stop it!" I shouted, throwing up my hands. My palm flared yellow and a gust of wind thudded into the shifter, tossing him back into the dirt hard enough that I felt the thud from where I was. I jumped in between the two of them, doing my best to keep my surprise from showing on my face: I definitely had *not* been trying to do that. I cut Sam an angry look and then glared down at Leo where he was half-laid, dust staining his short hair, and his jeans blown almost back to his knees. One hell of a gust. My powers were growing. Rapidly.

"That's enough. Grow the hell up."

He stared up at me, then then nodded stiffly to Sam.

"Yeah, alright, that might have been out of order."

"It's not me you need to apologise to," Sam grunted.

Leo rolled his eyes, but looked past Sam to where Kelsey was standing, arms wrapped around herself.

"Sorry, half-breed. That was a low blow." He jerked his eyes back to me. "Better?"

I heard Kelsey sigh behind me.

"It's fine," she said – to me, not him. "Really. People say worse."

"Great," Leo said, yanking his trouser legs back down, but not before I caught a glimpse of his wound. The burn was healing but there was still a grey tinge on his skin. "Do you mind if I get my butt out of the mud now?"

"Sam's right. You *are* a jackass."

I turned my back on him and crossed to Kelsey, squeezing her hand. Behind me, the whisper of fabric on fabric signalled the wolf getting back to his feet. I glanced over my shoulder and saw him dusting down his jeans.

"What? I apologised to the half-breed."

"You don't get it, do you? You're standing in front of probably the only three people in the entire country who believe you're innocent—"

"That's a stretch," Sam muttered.

"—and you want to insult one and hit another? What sort of an idiot are you?"

"A gorgeous, charming one?"

"Listen, Kelsey's going to be out here tonight, and I swear, if she comes back with so much as one hair on her head harmed, I will end you. Are we clear?"

"Yes, ma'am," he drawled in a Southern accent, tipping an imaginary hat in my direction. I just glared at him.

"Scouts' honour. I'll stay out of her way. I'll keep well away from the Grove tonight."

"Good. Make sure you do, or this little truce of ours is over. Come on," I added to Sam and Kelsey. "Let's get out of here."

The three of us turned and started for the edge of the meadow.

"Hey, druid girl."

I glanced back at the shifter.

"Uh, thanks. For the heads up. I appreciate it."

Chapter Twelve

When the sun started to set, Kelsey grabbed her heaviest cloak and tossed it over the top of the work out clothing she'd put on. It was a cover story we'd worked on last year – if anyone saw her heading out this evening, or coming back the following morning, she'd just tell them she'd been going for a run. Of course, none of the professors would stop her, they all knew her secret, but our ruse would stop most of the students from paying her too much attention.

"Well, I'm ready," she said, sounding anything but.

"You'll be fine, Kels," I said. I knew what was bothering her. "He'll stay away from you. You won't hurt anyone."

"I wish I had your optimism."

"It's not optimism, silly. I know you. You remember last year when I came stumbling round in the grove? You recognised me. And you made a choice not to hurt me."

I gave her a hug, then turned her around and pointed her at the door.

"Go on, get out of here."

I was just about to shove her through the door when it opened. A blonde stood in the doorway, dressed in mundane clothing, looking uncertainly at us.

"Hey. I'm Ava." There was an American twang to her voice and I did a double take. I'd only ever seen Brits at Talendale before. You know, because of the paternal link that decided which academy you belonged to. "Professor Talendale said I was to bunk with you."

I glanced across at the made-up bed that had sat empty since the start of the semester. I guess they'd been expecting her. But seriously, was there no other room in the entire academy they could have put her in? I caught Kelsey's panicked look. It was hard enough keeping her secret when there *wasn't* a total stranger sharing our dorm room. The working out story wasn't going to hold out for long, not when she noticed that Kels didn't come back by bedtime – long after darkness had fallen. I gave my friend a gentle shove towards the door, before Ava could notice anything.

"Go on, or you'll be late for your... astronomy lesson. Hi, Ava, I'm Lyssa. This is Kelsey. She's got to go."

Kelsey shot me a grateful smile then ducked out past Ava, who still stood in the doorway, a small bag slung over her shoulder, and an expression of shellshock on her face. I recognised that expression. I'd worn the same one when I first found out about the academy.

"So," I ventured, "You didn't know about magic before today?"

She shook her head.

"No. I mean, some weird stuff happened a few weeks back, but – well, it was just weird stuff. I didn't think it meant anything."

"You're adopted?" I guessed. She shook her head again, sending her blonde locks tumbling around her face.

"Foster kid, until I aged out."

Well, I guess that explained why Talendale had put her in my room. He figured to put the 'raised by mundanes' kids together. Probably would have made more sense to put her with someone from her own year so they could show her the ropes, but whatever. If Talendale had made up his mind, he was hardly going to change it on my say-so.

"Okay, so here's what you need to know. Magic's real. They'll teach you how to use it here, but if you mess up, you get expelled, and then they bind your magic – take it away. So don't break the rules. And if you do, don't get caught. Most people are pretty friendly, but watch your back, some people will think you're easy prey because you're new to our world."

"Um... thanks?"

She was still standing in the doorway, looking like her world had just collapsed around her. I sighed.

"Come on, that's your bed over there. It's not so bad here. It's a little strange, but you'll get used to it soon enough."

She ventured tentatively into the room, and set her bag down on the bed I'd indicated.

"What are these uniforms I keep seeing everyone in?"

Ah, right. American. Not used to school uniforms. To be fair, given that I'd been planning to go to university before I wound up here, I hadn't really been expecting it, either.

"You can get them from Fantail Market. You're not really allowed to go in your first year, but I'm sure they'll make an exception for you. The academy gives you a small stipend to buy what you need." I grimaced, remembering the hard time Felicity and her bitchy besties had given me about relying on the stipend when I first got here. Ava must have caught the look in between staring at her hands, because she said,

"Is there, like, somewhere I can get a job round here?"

I looked her up and down, appraising her.

"How do you feel about animals?"

"One of my foster homes kept dogs," she said with a shrug. I grinned.

"I might know just the thing for you."

*

With Ava busy learning the ropes under Alden's careful supervision the following morning – and hopefully not losing too much blood in the process – me and Kelsey were free to talk in private. Having someone sharing our dorm was definitely going to complicate Kelsey's secret, but I had more immediate worries.

"Did Leo keep his word?" I asked her, as she tugged a brush through her red locks in front of the mirror. "You didn't see him last night?"

Her reflection grimaced.

"I don't remember much – it's getting better, but I'm still only getting flashes when I change back. Underwood has me doing trance work every day, and I meditate every time I get an hour to myself, but I'm still not having much luck."

I frowned as a thought occurred to me.

"What about Underwood?" I asked. I was still struggling to get my head around him being a shifter. Even though I'd known for half of last year that he was mentoring Kelsey, I'd had no idea he was a hybrid. Kinda obvious, in hindsight, I supposed. "Does he have memory loss, too?"

"He used to," she said, twisting her hair back into a ponytail. "He thinks it's something to do with the fact we're hybrids. The druid magic clashing with the shifter magic."

She tossed the brush back onto her dresser, and her voice took on a bitter tone.

"No-one knows for sure, because no-one ever took the time to document it. You know, what with us being such a disgrace to both communities."

"It won't always be that way," I said softly, knowing even as I said it that the chances of the bigoted communities ever changing their ways were slim. Kelsey's eyes met mine in the mirror, and caught me in the lie. Her lips curved up in a sad smile.

"Thanks, anyway. One person caring is more than I'd hoped when I came here. Leo's reaction to me yesterday… Well, it's not exactly unusual."

"Well, it's wrong," I snapped, and then shook my head and exhaled slowly. "The world sucks, huh?"

"Not all of it," she disagreed.

How the hell did she do it? She was an outcast just because of how she'd been born – not who she was, or what she did, literally just an accident of birth – and she'd been treated like shit by pretty much everyone except her parents her whole life. In her shoes, I'd hate everyone and everything around me.

"You're amazing," I told her.

"It's all about the breeding – some people are just better than others," she said, in a passable impression of Felicity's voice. I tossed her cloak at her on principle. She caught it and then her face turned serious again. "I don't know what Leo was up to last night, or if he stayed away from me after I shifted. But when I woke up, after I shifted back, there were a set of pawprints all around my body. They weren't my pawprints."

"He came back."

She nodded.

"What did he want?"

"No idea. He was gone by the time I woke." She turned away quickly, but not before I noticed her cheeks flush a little under the dull light leaking in through the windows.

"If I didn't know better," I teased, "I'd say you liked the idea of him watching over you."

"Oh, please. He was probably trying to decide if he could get away with killing the half-breed."

"Just keep telling yourself that." I grabbed my own cloak and wrapped it around myself – it was draughty in the hallways. I didn't think Leo was a good match for her – the guy was an arse, and too full of himself by half – but knowing someone was sweet on her never hurt any girl's ego. And Kelsey needed an ego boost like no-one I'd ever met.

I was about to open the door when she spoke again.

"Do you really think he's innocent?" she asked, ducking her head and tucking a stray strand of hair behind one ear. "Of those mundane attacks, I mean. You believe him?"

"I do. Really, Kels, the guy's a prat but he's not a killer. Or maimer… infecter…?" I shot her a quizzical look. "Not really sure what the right word is."

She shook her head.

"There isn't one. Such a heinous crime hasn't been heard of for centuries. Can you imagine those poor people, their whole lives ruined?" She shuddered, and then sighed. "I want to agree with you, I want to believe he's innocent, but… Well, there haven't been any more attacks since he's been here, have there?"

I couldn't answer. I hadn't heard of any, and if someone had been attacked, she was the one who would know, what with her family connections. I had to admit, it didn't look good.

"I think we have to tell someone," she said. I shook my head.

"Talendale would have to report him to the packs. While he's headmaster, he has a seat on the council, and the council couldn't risk keeping something like that secret. It'd mean war."

"Not Talendale," she said, reaching for the door handle. "Underwood."

Chapter Thirteen

We talked about little else for the rest of the day, aside from when we took Ava to Fantail market. Sam agreed with Kelsey, at least partially – except he was in favour of telling Talendale, and letting the packs take Leo if that was what they wanted. It was clear he didn't trust the cocky werewolf.

The debate wore on for over a week, during which time there were no attacks, either on campus or off. Not, as Sam was keen to point out, that even Leo would be foolish enough to risk attacking a student. It would be tantamount to a signed confession, given that no other shifters could get on site. We talked about it every spare moment we got, whenever there was no-one around to overhear us, but we couldn't reach a decision we could all agree on, and the one thing we *could* agree on was that none of us would do anything until we were all in agreement. It wasn't that they didn't have a point. If something did happen, if someone got hurt because of Leo being here, that would be our fault. But there was no way Leo would hurt anyone, not on purpose. For all his faults – and honestly, there were a lot – I just didn't think that was in him. Still, we didn't go out and see him again.

It was a week before the following full moon that I caught up with the rest of our class, clustered out by the barn in the grey pre-dawn, their breath hanging around them in white clouds as they waited for Professor Alden to start our Supernatural Zoology lesson. The good news for me, as I hurried to join them, clapping my gloved hands in a futile effort to warm them, was that Alden hadn't come out of the barn yet, which meant I wasn't officially late.

Sam was near the back of the group, looking round anxiously. His face relaxed a little as he saw me emerging from the fog. I scowled and scanned the rest of the faces for Kelsey. I couldn't believe she'd left without even waking me. We never went to first class without each other. And if she'd been running late, would it have killed her to at least given me a nudge before she'd darted out of our dorm? I'd have waited for her. Only, as I caught up to Sam, I couldn't see her in the group.

"Where's Kelsey?" Sam asked, before I could get in the exact same question. He peered into the fog I'd just emerged from. I shook my head, snapping my eyes from the group to him.

"I thought she was already out here. She wasn't in the dorm when I woke."

"No, she's not here. I waited for both of you in the common room, but you didn't show."

"Quiet, thank you, everyone," Alden's voiced boomed across the damp field as she stepped out from the barn. Shit. Kelsey was late. Kelsey was never late.

"Do you think she's okay?" Sam said, earning himself a glare from the normally jovial professor. I didn't dare answer while her eyes were still on us, and I didn't want to consider what that answer was. Why wouldn't she show up for Zoology, and where had she gone this morning before I woke?

"This morning we will not be cleaning and feeding the hippogryffs," Alden informed us.

"About time," I heard someone mutter from nearby – probably Felicity or one of her ilk. She'd been pretty vocal about it, calling it servants' work and insisting that she'd never been made to clean the gryffs her family kept at home. Of course, no surprise that the airhead wasn't keen on physical work. Too much danger of breaking a nail, probably. Not that it was all we did in class, we had loads of theory lessons on the various types of supernatural creatures. Most of us agreed that the hands on stuff was better, though.

"We will instead be going into the Unhallowed Grove."

"What?" The horrified voice definitely belonged to Felicity this time.

"But, Professor," Paisley ventured, "Students aren't allowed in the Unhallowed Grove."

"Hm? Oh, don't worry about that," Alden said, already moving away from the barn. "Professor Talendale has given us his blessing. This morning we will be harvesting Rothaich plants, which grow inside the grove. They're essential for the nourishment of pregnant hippogryffs."

She shot me a knowing look, but I was too panic-stricken to return it. Going into the grove meant we'd be near the Lost Meadow. Where Leo was hiding out. I shot a panicked look at Sam, but he was still peering out into the fog back in the direction of the academy. I followed his gaze and caught sight of the dark shape in the distance, moving at slightly faster than human speed. I blew out a sigh of relief. Kelsey. One less thing to worry about, at least. And hopefully she'd be able to track Leo if he was hiding up near where the group were headed. Because somehow I didn't think we could rely on Felicity to keep our secret.

"Where've you been?" I hissed at Kelsey, as we fell in behind the rest of the group heading towards the grove. I looked her up and down, taking in her slightly damp and dishevelled appearance – probably a result of running through the fog. Good job her sight and balance were better than most people's or she'd probably have turned an ankle running through the dark, wet grounds.

"Trance," she panted. "Must've gone deeper than I realised. Did Alden notice?"

I shook my head.

"I don't think so. But we've got a bigger problem. She's taking the class into the grove."

"The Unhallowed Grove?"

"No, the grove of sunshine and unicorns. Yes, the Unhallowed Grove!"

"Unicorns aren't something to joke about," she said reproachfully. "Why are we going into the Unhallowed Grove?"

"To find some plant or other," Sam said. He shot a glance at the rest of the group just in front of us. "I just hope that's all we find."

"You mean Le–"

I elbowed her in the ribs and she cut off abruptly, clamping her hand over her mouth and looking at Felicity, whose back was turned to us but who had stiffened noticeably. There was no way the nosey little airhead didn't have one ear on our conversation.

"Yeah," Sam put in quickly. "I'm really hoping we don't find any leopards in there."

Felicity turned and glared at us over her shoulder – although whether because she thought Sam was an idiot

136

or she knew we'd rumbled her, I had no idea. Probably both. We walked in silence the rest of the way to the grove, not daring to voice our concerns with Felicity, Paisley, and Cecelia so close by. Them suspecting we were up to something I could live with. They always thought we were up to something. Them finding out we were covering for a fugitive werewolf who may or may not have been preying on mundanes was another matter entirely. She'd wanted me expelled from the moment she'd first met me. For someone who'd vowed not to give her any excuse to get her way, I was doing a pretty poor job of keeping to the rules.

"Alright, everyone," Alden said, turning to face us as we reached the towering, twisted oaks that marked the edge of the Unhallowed Grove. "Most of the creatures living in the grove will fear your magic. Should you find yourselves in trouble, you are to give off energy pulses from your palm. Nothing more. We are not here to damage the grove's fragile ecosystem. Is that understood?"

I didn't think the ecosystem could be all that fragile if it coped with Kelsey running around it every full moon, and honestly I was more concerned about it damaging us, but I kept that thought to myself. I shot the hybrid a look while everyone was busy listening to Alden, and raised an eyebrow at her, nodding in the direction of the meadow.

She shook her head. Leo obviously wasn't nearby – good news for us. With any luck, Alden would mistake any tracks he might have left for Kelsey's. So long as we didn't actually stumble across him, we should be fine.

"The plant you're looking for grows low to the ground. It has broad, flat leaves, with a reddish vein growing through the centre. It's very distinctive, but what will really give it away is the smell."

"What does it smell like?" one of the students ventured. Alden grimaced.

"You'll know it."

"Puke, then," Sam said from the corner of his mouth. "Or rotting guts."

I'd have to go with the guts, given that it was for a gryff, and their taste in food was pretty singular.

"The first one to find it will be excused from this week's homework. And while we're in the grove, I want each of you to identify and note down at least three different species that aren't found anywhere else in this country. Any questions?"

There were none, probably because half of the students were too busy eyeing the shadows between the trees that seemed to flicker out of time with the sunlight.

"In we go, then. Stay in groups – don't wander off alone, and keep close to the path."

I allowed a little space to open up between us and the rest of the group, who were staring around and chattering nervously in hushed whispers.

"What are we going to do about Leo?" I asked.

"Let him get caught," Sam said, with a shrug of his shoulders.

"Great plan," I snapped. "And I'm sure he'll keep our names right out of it when they drag him in front of Talendale."

"I could go looking for him," Kelsey said, glancing off into the trees lining the track. "I know my way around here."

I shook my head.

"Too dangerous. You can't shift at will yet. You could run into trouble."

"She's right," Sam said. "And someone's bound to notice you're missing."

"Keep up, you three," Alden's voice boomed from the front, as if to underscore Sam's point. There was nothing for it. We were just going to have to hope Leo wasn't lying up anywhere near here.

"Let's just find this damned plant so we can get everyone out of here."

That proved easier said than done. The Rothaich plant was nothing if not elusive. Twenty minutes into our search I was starting to question whether it actually existed anywhere outside of Alden's imagination, and though I had my notepad out, I hadn't managed to identify any of the creatures peering at us through the dense leaves, much less work out which weren't native to this country. No matter. Kelsey knew every type of creature inside the grove; she could tell me a couple. I looked up from the trail and frowned at the clusters of bodies in front of us. None of them had red hair.

"Sam," I hissed. "Where's Kelsey?"

"What?" He jerked his eyes up from an impressive doodle in his notepad of a dragon eating what might have been a werewolf, and scanned the fragmented groups in front of us. "Shit. Do you think she decided to go looking for Leo?"

That was exactly what I thought she'd done. What stung was that she'd done it without even telling us. We were supposed to be friends.

"So much for someone will notice," I grumbled. "We didn't even see her slip off."

"We can't just leave her out there alone." Sam cast a worried look into the dark shadows, and several pairs of eyes blinked back at us from them.

"Well, we can't go blundering around the grove, either. She knows this place like the back of her hand. She could be anywhere by now."

"Then what?" Sam said, and there was no mistaking the worry in his voice. Badass werewolf she might be, but right now she was just as vulnerable as any human. Nearly as vulnerable, I amended: she was stronger, faster, and her senses were a hundred times better.

"Trust her," I said. "And make sure no-one else notices she's gone."

We drifted a little way further from the other groups. Alden would assume the three of us were together, looking for the Rothaich plant. She wouldn't say anything, because unlike the students, she knew Kelsey was a shifter, and she'd assume that we were following her nose. If she saw just the two of us, she would know something was amiss.

Another twenty minutes passed, with no sign of her coming back. Anxiety was beginning to gnaw at the pit of my stomach. What if she *had* run into something she couldn't handle? I closed the gap between me and Sam, who'd long since stopped doodling or looking for the plant – instead, he'd spent most of the time peering into the gloom that we'd drifted deeper into as we parted company from the trail.

"She should have been back by now," I said, keeping my voice low, even though we were far enough from the other groups that no-one could possibly have overheard us. I could only just about make out their forms up ahead.

"Do you think we should tell Alden?" He sounded uncertain, probably because voluntarily talking to a professor was not something that came naturally to him, and neither of us wanted to get Kelsey into trouble. If she wasn't in trouble already. I chewed my lip, and then nodded.

"I don't think we have a choice. She could be hurt."

"Who could be hurt?" The voice came from behind us, and I jumped out of my skin before rounding on the newcomer.

"Kelsey! Where the hell have you been?"

I grabbed her and wrapped her in a hug before she could answer, then shoved her back at arm's length and looked her up and down. She didn't seem any the worse for wear.

"Relax, mother," she said with a grin. "I was just looking for… leopards."

I rolled my eyes and resisted the urge to shake her, instead stooping to grab the notepad I'd dropped when she'd scared me half to death.

"Did you find him?" Sam asked. Kelsey shook her head.

"I did a half-loop from here to his meadow. I didn't cross his trail."

"And he wasn't in the meadow?" That was odd.

She shook her head again. Dammit. Let's just hope he wasn't lurking somewhere in the area we were headed. And come to that, how had no-one found that blasted plant yet?

"Come on, let's catch up to the rest of the group before someone notices we're gone."

We beat our way through the trees back to the trail and had just reached it when a loud scream rang out from somewhere ahead. I tossed a quick look at Sam and Kelsey, and I could tell we were all thinking the same thing: had someone seen the missing werewolf?

I raced along the track, leaping off it and into the foliage somewhere near where the scream had come from. Professor Alden was already out in front, and I could see her standing over a figure.

"Back, everyone, stay back," she called, but most of the students ignored her and pressed closer, me among them. As I got closer, I could make out the faded yellow, dirt stained cloak. Felicity and Cecelia were standing nearby, but for once they weren't gloating. They were staring down at the savaged form of Paisley.

Chapter Fourteen

I just can't believe it," Kelsey said, as we sat alone in our common room. None of us had much felt like going for breakfast after Paisley had been attacked. I shook my head mutely. I'd honestly thought Leo was innocent.

"It's my fault," I said numbly. "I should have known."

"Lyssa, no!" Kelsey said, gaping at me in horror. "How could you have? You're not to blame. Leo did this, not you."

"And we let him," Sam said grimly.

None of us answered. He was right. If we'd just told Talendale as soon as Leo had shown up, this could have been prevented. Now Paisley was in the hospital wing, bitten, and her whole future was changed, forever. If she survived.

"We need to find him," I said, reaching a decision and getting to my feet.

"No!" Kelsey grabbed my arm. "He could do the same to you. He's dangerous."

"Yeah, he is," Sam agreed. "We're going to see him, but we're taking Talendale with us. It's gone far enough."

Kelsey shook her head, but before either me or Sam could speak, she said,

"Not Talendale. We can't risk him being attacked. Underwood."

It made sense. Underwood was stronger, faster, and the rogue shifter's bite couldn't hurt him. Or at least, it couldn't curse him.

"Alright, let's go."

Underwood seemed surprised when we tracked him down in his office – probably not least because our Spellcraft lesson was just getting started, and being here right now was likely to earn all of us a black mark.

"What can I do for the three of you?" he said, but his eyes were on Kelsey. Kindred spirits, I guessed – outcasts sticking together. I glanced at the thick cloak he had draped over his arm, like he'd been about to pull it on when he opened the door to us.

"Where are you going?" I blurted, because apparently I still hadn't mastered the art of thinking without speaking. He gave me a look that said it was none of my business, and that I was overstepping a whole lot of boundaries by asking. Oh well, it was hardly my biggest crime.

"Please, Professor," I added, trying for a more respectful tone. "Is it to do with the attack?"

He looked momentarily taken aback, and then his face softened with understanding.

"Ah. I take it that it was your zoology class who were in the grove this morning?"

"Yes, Professor," Kelsey said. "We think… we think we know something."

"Oh?" He somehow managed to cram cynicism, expectancy, wariness and suspicion all into that one word. I couldn't quite meet his eye, but I answered anyway, because this wasn't Kelsey's mess to clean up.

"There's been a werewolf on the grounds since the start of the semester." An image of Underwood in his shifter form, flying through the air at Kelsey, flashed through my mind. "Uh, another werewolf, I mean."

I flicked my eyes up to meet his, just for a split second, and I could have sworn I saw relief flash through them. And then I realised. When he heard about a werewolf attack, he'd thought it was Kelsey. My lips curled in disgust. How could he have even thought that? He knows Kelsey. He'd spent all last year tutoring her. He must have known how horrified she'd been by the attacks. How could he have imagined, for even one moment, that she would ever hurt someone?

I shook off the feeling. Now wasn't the time for outrage. We needed Underwood's help.

"Where is this shifter now?" he asked, tossing his cloak on his desk. I'd been wrong. He hadn't been about to put it on. He'd been taking it off. He was planning to go wolf to hunt down the perpetrator. Even if it had been Kelsey. I was starting to get an idea of how strongly ingrained the shifter code of not harming mundanes truly was. Leo had been right – they'd have killed him if they'd caught him last summer. Now I just wished they had.

"We know where he hides out," I said. "We'll take you to him."

For a moment I thought he was going to refuse our help, but he simply stepped out of the office and shut the door behind us.

"You will do exactly as you're told on this little field trip," he said, enunciating each word carefully. "If I tell you to run, you run. Do you understand?"

I physically couldn't raise my eyes to meet his, and Kelsey seemed incapable of raising her eyes from her shoes. Sam was the only one who kept his head up.

"We understand," he said calmly.

Without another word, Underwood led us out into the grounds. Following behind, I could see the tension in his shoulders, but whether he was angry with us, Leo, or both, I couldn't be sure. Until he spoke.

"You've kept this rogue shifter's presence a secret since the start of the year?"

"Yes, Professor. But Kelsey and Sam didn't know right away, and then I convinced them to keep it quiet."

"Why?"

I was glad he was still striding out in front of us, towards the grove, so I didn't have to see his face, which I was certain was as accusatory as his voice.

"I thought he was innocent," I managed eventually.

"We all did, Professor," Kelsey put in. "It wasn't Lyssa's fault."

"You're lucky you're not all being expelled," Underwood snapped.

"We're... we're not?" It was more than I dared to hope. More than I deserved, in fact. Paisley was in a hospital bed because of my bad judgement.

Underwood rounded on us so quickly I almost walked right into him.

"If you lead me to this rogue shifter, and *if* you convince me that you were truly fooled by him, then no. I'll ask Talendale for leniency. After last year, I have no doubt he'll grant it. Though do not think for one moment, Ms Eldridge, that your tendency to break the rules is lost on me – and worse, your habit of leading others into doing the same."

I hung my head.

"I'm sorry, Professor. I didn't mean any harm, honestly. He showed up in my grove in the summer, hurt, and I trusted him. I know I should have told you right away when he turned up here, but–"

"In your grove?" he cut across me sharply.

"Yes, Professor."

"And you didn't wonder how he'd been injured?"

"He told me it was a dog."

Underwood stared at me like I might have been the most naïve person to ever cross his path, which wasn't entirely unfair, and then he shook his head.

"You and I will have a serious talk when this is through."

I swallowed. That didn't sound like fun.

"Yes, Professor."

"Which way from here?"

I glanced up at the Unhallowed Grove looming in the near-distance and jerked my chin off to one side.

"In the Lost Meadow. At least, that's where he was before."

Underwood grunted.

"Let's see if he's stupid enough to go back there. Tell me everything you know about him."

I filled Underwood in on everything I'd seen and heard from Leo, which was surprisingly little. I couldn't believe I'd decided to trust him, barely knowing a thing about him. And those things I did know – his injury, his cockiness, his fear of discovery and casual disdain of non-shifters – none of it pointed to his innocence. Only his word. What the hell had I been thinking?

"Professor?" I ventured as we drew close. "What are you going to do?"

"Stop him," the professor answered simply.

I wanted to ask what that meant. If he would capture Leo, or kill him. If he would send him to Daoradh or back to the packs. I wanted to ask how he was going to do it. But I didn't. The time for asking questions was over.

He raised a hand, and we all came to a halt. I gave him a curious glance, but he wasn't looking at me.

"We've just crossed his scent," Kelsey said to me, under her breath. "He's been here recently."

"Wait here, all of you," Underwood said, without looking back at us, and started forward into the meadow. To hell with that. Leo lied to me. Lied to all of us. I wasn't about to hang back here and let Underwood confront him alone. I followed behind him. Kelsey grabbed at my arm but I shook her off.

"Lyssa!" she hissed.

"You want to let Underwood deal with him alone?" I asked, fighting to keep my voice calm despite the adrenaline pumping through me. I didn't give them a chance to answer. Underwood was moving quickly, already in the centre of the meadow. He slitted his eyes at me as I caught up with him, and I just shrugged. Behind us, I could hear the rustle of clothing as Kelsey and Sam moved through the damp grass.

Then there was another rustle; this time from in front of us. My eyes scanned the treeline, but I heard him before I saw him.

"Thought you said you wouldn't tell, druid girl."

He stepped from between the trees, still wearing the same pair of jeans, now discoloured with ingrained dirt. He moved with a slight limp, and beneath the cockiness in his eyes, there was a wariness that hadn't been there before.

"Thought you said you were innocent," I returned.

"I am. You know that."

"You're a liar, Leo."

I stalked forwards, my eyes locked on his. How could he just stand there, still lying to me, right to my face? How *dare* he? An armed barred my path; Underwood's. I raised my hand to push it aside, then thought better of it.

"I've got no idea what you're talking about," Leo said, and his eyes flicked from me to Underwood and back again.

"Really? You don't know anything about the girl back there in the hospital wing?" I flung an arm in the direction of the academy. Abruptly, the werewolf's cocky façade disappeared.

"What... what girl?"

151

"The one you *bit,* you psycho!" I shoved past Underwood and slammed both my palms into Leo's bare chest. He stumbled back and raised his hands, but didn't try to defend himself. Some sort of macho crap, probably. I shoved him again.

"Lyssa!" My name sounded odd on his lips. I dropped my hands and glared at him. "That wasn't me, I swear."

"Tell it to someone who still believes you."

"Please."

He hobbled back towards me, and I might have been imagining it, but he seemed to be favouring his injured leg more than last time I'd seen him. Had his limp always been that pronounced? Come to that, surely it should have healed by now entirely. It had been two months since he'd got the injury.

"You're full of crap, Leo. I should have turned you in the moment we first met. Then maybe Paisley wouldn't be…"

I swallowed. I couldn't bring myself to finish the sentence.

"I didn't do th–"

"Stop lying!"

I slammed my palms into his chest again and he grunted in pain as he staggered back. When he straightened, I saw the twin palm-shaped burn marks glowing red on his chest. Bile rose up in my throat as revulsion warred with fury. I *burned* him. I used my powers to hurt him.

"Enough." Underwood's voice cut across us. He didn't need to raise it to stop us both dead in our tracks.

"I... I'm sorry," I gasped, staring at Leo's burns through wide eyes.

"He'll heal," Underwood said.

Leo squared his shoulders beneath Underwood's scrutiny, standing as straight as he could on his injured leg.

"This is it, then?" he said, a trace of bitterness in his voice. "You're taking me back to the alpha pack for judgement? Or will you just execute me here?"

Underwood shook his head once.

"My loyalty is to the druids. I'm a professor here."

"But..." Leo's forehead furrowed with uncertainty, and he shot a wary glance to me and back. "You're a shifter. I can smell it."

"A hybrid," Underwood said. "You broke the law on academy grounds. You'll answer to the circle. Put these on."

He pulled a pair of cuffs from his pocket and tossed them at Leo's feet. The cuffs were metal and engraved with dozens of symbols. Enchantments, for sure. Silver ran through them, and instinctively I knew that wearing those cuffs would hobble his supernatural powers and prevent him from taking his wolf form. The chain that linked them looked thin, but I felt sure the shifter wouldn't be able to snap it. Underwood would have taken precautions.

The blood drained from Leo's face as he stared down at the circlets lying in the mud at his feet.

"I didn't do it! You've got to believe me. Please. Don't put me in a cage. I'm innocent."

"That's for the circle to determine. Don't make this harder than it has to be."

Leo barked a harsh laugh but stooped to pick up the cuffs and stared at them in his hands, as if making a decision. No prizes for guessing what he was thinking. Two druid apprentices and two hybrids, against one shifter. His odds weren't great. And he was hampered by his leg.

"Why hasn't your leg healed?" I blurted. Underwood turned to me sharply.

"That's the same injury he had in your grove? You're sure?"

I nodded.

"Show me," he commanded Leo. The shifter scowled but rolled up his trouser leg, exposing the ruined skin.

And it was ruined. The burn had all but healed, but the grey-ish tinge had spread further, discolouring the skin in a patch at least twice as large as it had been before.

154

Jagged purple-grey lines traced the veins in his leg. Underwood inhaled sharply.

"Sit. Now."

Leo glanced up at him, then lowered himself awkwardly onto the ground, keeping the injured limb stretched out in front of him.

"You've had silver poisoning for two months?"

"Silver poisoning?" I asked. Underwood gave me a sideways glance, but it was enough for me to see the exasperation in his eyes.

"Silver is dangerous to shifters," Kelsey said. "It can kill us, if it gets into our bloodstreams."

"Which this has," Underwood said. "How are you still alive?"

"I convinced Lyssa to cauterise the wound. Figured it'd buy me some time."

"Crude. Stay calm, I'm just going to look, okay?" He raised his eyes at Leo, and when the other shifter nodded, Underwood moved closer and squatted down next to the injured leg. I wasn't so sure that was such a smart plan, given what he'd done to the bench in my grove last time I'd gone near the injury – before it had festered for two months. Leo had apparently reached the same conclusion, because he planted his hands on the ground behind him, and leaned his weight back onto them.

"It's badly infected," Underwood said. "If it's not treated, you'll be lucky to last another month. You'd be dead already if it wasn't for Lyssa."

Leo affected a shrug, as much as he was able while still leaning his weight back on his arms.

"I'll be dead sooner than that if the alpha pack gets hold of me." He shot me a look over Underwood's shoulder. "For something I didn't do."

I rolled my eyes but I didn't answer him. I'd saved his life according to Underwood – twice, by not telling anyone he was here. I was as much to blame for what had happened to Paisley as he was. Some small part of me wanted to believe he was innocent, because that would mean I was innocent, too. But that part was being crushed under the weight of logic.

"Don't move," Underwood said, and moved his hands towards the wound, watching Leo carefully through cautious eyes. Leo swallowed and jerked his head away, staring at the trees across the meadow. Underwood touched his fingertips lightly to the wound. Leo's reaction was instantaneous. His back arched and a howl of agony ripped from his lungs. His hands clawed deep gouges in the earth, and his other leg kicked out. The one Underwood was touching jerked and trembled.

"You're not going anywhere on this. I'm not a healer, but I can reduce the damage enough to get you to the castle."

"Why?" Leo's chest was heaving and his voice breathless. His forehead and torso were prickled in sweat. "Just... kill me here. Please. I don't want to be torn apart by the alpha pack."

"That's what they'll do?" I croaked. My throat was so dry I was shocked the words made it out at all.

"No," Underwood said. "His attack was on a druid. He'll face druid justice, not pack justice. And I'm not going to leave you to suffer until then. Lyssa, hold his leg."

I edged closer, and crouched down next to the pair.

"Remember what you said about inter-community relations?" I asked. "Try not to maul me."

"Scout's honour," he said with a grin that quickly faded to a grimace as another wave of pain rocked through him.

"Hold his ankle, here." Underwood positioned my hand, and the skin beneath it was hot to the touch, like he was running a fever. I wrapped my fingers around his ankle, gripping tight but trying to be gentle at the same time. The hitch in his breathing told me I wasn't successful. "Lie back. Sam, Kelsey, hold his shoulders."

Leo lowered himself into the damp grass, and Sam and Kelsey hurried round, kneeling by his head and planting their hands on his shoulders.

"This is going to hurt," Underwood warned. "I'll be as quick as I can."

A faint glow pulsed from Underwood's hands, and he laid them over the grey skin. Immediately, the leg jerked under my hand, trying to wrench itself free from my grip. Leo's guttural cry filled the air, and I could hear Sam's grunt as he fought to keep the shifter pinned down. I tightened my grip as the spasms ripped through him, gritting my teeth as I fought against his frenzied attempts to escape the pain.

Underwood moved his hands, but it was a long minute before the sounds of Leo's agony stopped. The purple-grey streaks of poison had started to recede, and there was a faint flesh-coloured flush pushing through the grey tinged skin. Belatedly, I released my grip on his ankle. Leo just lay on the grass, panting.

Eventually, he pushed himself unsteadily into a sitting position, and sought Underwood's eyes.

"Thanks."

I wondered if it was the first sincere thing he'd said since we met. He picked up the cuffs that lay abandoned beside him and weighed them in his hands.

"I won't fight you," he said. "I'm innocent, whatever you think."

He snapped the cuffs shut around his wrists with a cold finality.

"Let's do this."

Chapter Fifteen

True to his word, Leo went quietly, not putting up a fight when Underwood portaled him back to the castle. Sam and Kelsey were sent back to class, and I was ordered to Talendale's office to explain what a monumental lapse of judgement I'd suffered over the last two months. I went quietly, too. Talendale questioned me for hours before he let me leave, but I didn't complain. What right did I have to say anything, when Paisley was going through hell right now because of me? Madam Leechington said we'd caught it early, before the shifter virus had fully taken hold. Now all we could do was wait and see if she was infected. Talendale said we'd know at the next full moon – one week from now.

It was going to be a long week.

"Psst, Lyssa!"

I looked up from the gloopy mess brewing in the stainless-steel pot in front of me. It was supposed to be a light blue mix the consistency of single cream, but what I actually had was a greyish mess that was as thick as porridge, with twice as many lumps. No surprise: I'd been having a hard time focusing on the instructions in my textbook. Hard time focusing on anything, really.

"Lyssa!"

Sharna was working at the next bench along, and looking at me in between shooting glances at Professor Brennan.

"What?" I glanced over at Brennan too, but he had his head over Liam's vat and seemed busy trying to correct the contents. I hoped for his sake the lesson finished before he had to work on mine.

"Are you going to the Halloween party tonight?"

I started and frowned.

"That's tonight?"

The Halloween party was an annual Dragondale tradition. The students commandeered one of the dungeons, and the professors put their metaphorical fingers in their ears and hummed loudly, pretending they had no idea that the students were wreaking havoc two floors below. Truth be told, between Stormclaw's death sentence, Itealta practice, and everything coming to a head with Leo, I'd totally lost track of the date. The party had been the last thing on my mind. I shook my head.

"I'm not in the mood. Next time, maybe."

"You can't miss out again, not after last year. And you need more dandelion leaf in that potion." She tossed a handful on my bench and I threw them straight into the brew without looking, stirring absent-mindedly. "The party was amazing, Lyssa. And oh, my God, you should see the dress I bought. And I got these gorgeous new shoes…"

Her eyes glazed over for a moment and she all but swooned on the spot.

"Uh… I'll think about it."

"Ms Eldridge." Brennan's voice sounded from right behind me. "The only thing you should be thinking about is why on earth you felt the need to add toad spawn to this potion when the recipe quite clearly calls for toad*stools*."

With a sigh, I pulled the wooden spoon from my mix and tossed it on the bench.

"Sorry, Professor."

"A little less chat, a little more focus next time, please. We've only got a few minutes left, you might as well make a start cleaning up. Copy out that recipe correctly before next week."

Great. Just what I needed. More work. What I really wanted was to head over to the hospital wing and check on Paisley, but Leech wasn't letting anyone in, and it would look weird if I asked — it wasn't like we were friends or anything. The opposite, given her sycophantic adoration of Felicity.

I chucked my potion and cleared away the rest of my stuff, then ducked out of the lesson before Brennan could give me any more homework.

"Lyssa, wait up!"

I paused in the corridor while Sam and Kelsey caught up with me.

"Are you okay?" Sam's too-earnest eyes were fixed on me, his forehead creased in concern.

"Uh… yeah, I'm fine. I've got Itealta practice. I'll catch up with you guys later."

I turned and started along the corridor.

"Lyssa." I turned and arched an eyebrow at him. "It's not your fault."

Yeah, right. I just shook my head and left them behind. Any way you wanted to cut it, it was my fault. I saved Leo's life when I cauterised his wound. He hopped here on my portal. And then I kept his secret.

But I couldn't afford to think about any of that right now. Logan had been working all of us hard. The first practice game of the season was next week, and me and Stormclaw had a lot to prove if we wanted to keep our place. That was if he'd even let me take him out of the paddock at all – he'd become utterly obsessed with Redwing. Alden was convinced she must be pregnant, hence our little trip into the Unhallowed Grove before breakfast. Great. Another way it was my fault. We were foraging for snacks for my gryff's mate.

When I made it to the field, Stormclaw told me in no uncertain terms that he wasn't in the mood for being ridden — a beak snap at the face is pretty universal language for 'not today, thanks', so I groomed him out and left him to it. I didn't much fancy spending the next two hours with Kelsey and Sam watching me from the corners of their eyes and telling me it wasn't my fault, so I took off to do a lap of the academy grounds. Had to keep my fitness up for when Stormclaw eventually did let me back on him.

For a long time, I lost myself in the release of physical exercise — just one foot in front of the other, pounding my way round the beaten track I'd followed more times than I could count. Logan showed me this route when I first made the Itealta team; a less than subtle hint about my fitness level, although to be fair he made the entire team meet out here to run at least once a week. He was nothing if not a dedicated captain. The only trouble with running — aside from the burning agony in your legs, and your lungs trying to burst — was that it gave you way too much time to think. Thinking time was not my friend right now. A whole week until we knew if I'd ruined Paisley's life. What the hell was I supposed to do with that? And hanging out with Kelsey was hell right now, because I had to watch my every word. If I slipped up and made some reference to Paisley's life being ruined because she might be a shifter now, how was that going to look to my hybrid friend? Like I had a problem with hybrids, that's how, and I didn't. Kelsey was amazing. At the start of the year I'd even–

My stomach lurched, and I stumbled on the dirt track. At the start of the year, I'd jokingly wished I had her strength, her heightened senses, even at the expense of losing control of yourself every month. How had I even thought that? Even joked about it? Underwood was right. I was naïve.

I grunted and kicked up the pace, spraying a trail of mud and damp leaves in my wake. I pushed myself harder still, until there was no room in my mind for anything except the satisfying pain in every part of my being, and the single-minded focus of putting of foot in front of the other on the wet dirt track. The lake passed on my right, a wide expanse of rippling water, glinting unnaturally blue under the grey sky. I barely paid it any heed, nor did I pay attention to the occasional disturbance that broke the otherwise calm surface. Even in the summer, no-one wanted to swim in that lake. At least, not anyone who valued their limbs.

Darkness crept up on me and I greeted it with a frown. I had no idea what the time was, but there was a reasonable chance Itealta practice had long since finished and someone had noticed I wasn't back. I rounded a corner in the track and locked my sights on the castle, just visible in the dying light. Best not give anyone cause to panic after what happened this morning. Plus, I'd really rather not be expelled for being out after dark, even if the danger was gone now.

As I drew closer, my eyes picked out five cloaked figures. I slowed to a walk, breathing heavily. Running the grounds was much easier on the back of a gryff, that was for sure. I frowned at the figures, but something told me to keep out of sight. They didn't look like students, or professors. I edged closer, straining to pick out their words on the still evening air, but either they weren't speaking, or their voices weren't loud enough to carry.

I hung back as they approached the academy's huge oaken doors. The enchanted doors swung open without hesitation. Our guests were magical. No surprise there – how else had they gotten into the grounds if not by portal? Which meant Talendale had given them permission to be here: no-one could portal into the academy without clearance, not since he'd tightened up security after Raphael raised havoc last year.

Under the light of the entrance hall's fireballs, I could make out a figure step forward, and recognised the rigid posture of Underwood. He greeted them with a curt nod and an outstretched hand, and then glanced out into the darkness behind them. I gasped, and ducked back behind a tree, but I was pretty sure he hadn't seen me. Still, I waited a long moment before I stuck my head out again.

The figures had gone from the hallway, as had the professor. If Underwood was meeting them, it could only be for one reason. These were the council members. He was taking them to Leo. I forced my lips into a satisfied smile, but it didn't stick. He deserved to be taken away by them – if he was guilty.

"Ms Eldridge."

I jumped and spun around, almost crashing right into Underwood – as, no doubt, he'd intended. He glared down at me.

"Would you care to explain what you're doing wandering the grounds after dark, given that the headmaster has expressly prohibited students from doing so?"

I would not, so I went in on the attack.

"Who are those people? Are they here for Leo?"

He sighed, apparently resigned to the fact I was incapable of keeping my questions to myself.

"Yes, Ms Eldridge, they have come to pass sentence on the rogue shifter."

"If he's guilty."

He gave me a strange look that I couldn't quite decipher in the darkness.

"That is the one thing about which there is no question."

My mouth popped open.

"But... But there's going to be a trial, right? I mean, just in case?"

Underwood shook his head – in answer to my question, or in exasperation that I yet again hadn't managed to keep it to myself, it was hard to say which.

"I'd say the evidence speaks for itself, wouldn't you? Back inside now – you've broken enough rules for one day, even by your standards."

Harsh. Still, I didn't raise a complaint as I followed him back into the well-lit hallway. He was right: I'd pushed my luck enough for one day.

"Quickly, now," he said, with a glance over his shoulder into the darkness. If I didn't know better, I'd have thought he sounded on edge. But this was Underwood we were talking about.

"What's the hurry, Professor?" There I went, pushing my luck again.

"The hurry is I'm your professor, and I've told you to get inside. Now."

I narrowed my eyes at him and planted my legs. He was definitely rattled. But what the hell could rattle a druid half-werewolf professor? And then I got it.

"They're coming, aren't they? The... alpha pack?"

Underwood exhaled heavily and then nodded.

"Yes, they are. And it would be best if I wasn't the one to greet them."

"Because you're a hybrid? That's bull!"

"That's just the way it is." His smile was bitter and didn't reach past his lips. He glanced at the floor, hiding whatever was in his eyes, and then back to me again.

"You weren't raised in this community, Lyssa, but I think you're starting to understand the prejudice most druids hold against hybrids."

I nodded, and this time it was me avoiding his eye. None of the students, except me, Kelsey, and Sam, knew what he was – and me and Sam had found out by accident. I wasn't even sure if all of the professors knew. He was a good professor, a good man, and his loyalty had always been to the druids. Despite all of it, he'd still be an outcast if word got out.

"What you've seen is nothing compared to the way other shifters view us. For the packs, family is everything. Blood is everything. And half-breeds–" his lips curled in disgust around the words "–are a crime against nature. Kelsey is extremely fortunate that after nineteen years, her pack have permitted her and her mother into its outskirts. She will always be an outcast there, but her pack have shown more tolerance than most."

"But… I don't understand! Loads of shifters have one mundane parent, and they're not outcasts."

"*Loads*," Underwood said, and I could hear the inverted commas around the word, "is an exaggeration. A

169

small percentage of shifters mate with mundanes, but those mundanes are not permitted within the pack."

"But their kids are. How is this any different?"

Underwood gave me a tired smile, and his face seemed aged in the semi-darkness.

"It just is. Tradition is sacred in the packs. There was a time that druids and shifters were at war. They might have stopped openly fighting, but the prejudices and traditions aren't going away any time soon. Come on, let's get inside. I'm supposed to be escorting the council members to Professor Talendale's office, not chasing down students who are incapable of following the rules."

"Is there any news?" I blurted. "About Paisley?"

Underwood ran a hand over his face.

"It's too early to say. She's getting the best care possible, but there's no way to tell before the next full moon."

I nodded. I'd known that. I'd just hoped that he would have some answer none of the rest of us knew, some secret remedy that would spare her from becoming something else. As if reading my mind, Underwood placed a hand on my shoulder, and said,

"If I knew some way to prevent it, I wouldn't hesitate. But Paisley is alive. That will have to be enough, for now."

I nodded, and turned towards Dragondale's massive doors. Underwood looked relieved. It wasn't right, the alpha pack coming into our academy and intimidating one of our professors.

"Wait. Why are they coming?" I froze in place as the realisation hit home, but Underwood said it anyway.

"They're coming to stake a claim on Leo's life. He's one of theirs, they'll want to be the ones to punish him. The circle's council will oppose them because the attack was on one of ours."

"But... the truce! This could break it!"

I stared up at Underwood's face, truly stared at it, not avoiding his eyes, and saw that this wasn't news to him. He knew the truce could be torn down by Leo's actions, and the tentative peace that had lasted generations shattered. He said nothing.

"We can't let that happen, Professor. What can I do?"

"Leave it to the adults," he said gruffly.

"I'm nineteen," I said, my voice high with indignation. "I am an adult."

"Then act like it."

His words pulled me up short, and my objections died on my lips. He was right. I was acting like a kid. Lying, covering for criminals, sneaking around in the dark. If the truce broke tonight, it would be in no small part because of my actions. And making Underwood stand out here, chaperoning me, when he should be preparing for the conclave, was only going to make it worse.

His face softened slightly.

"Go to bed, Lyssa. I'll send word in the morning."

Chapter Sixteen

I t was a long night. Neither me nor Kelsey got much sleep – though we kept as quiet as we could. The last thing we needed was to have to explain everything to Ava. She seemed like a nice enough girl and all, but that didn't mean we could trust her.

The following morning when we stumbled bleary-eyed into the common room, we found Sam waiting, looking like he'd had no more sleep than either of us. At least we didn't stand out – most of the other students looked like death, too. It took me a moment to work out why, and then I recalled the Halloween party was last night. It seemed like so long ago that Sharna was telling me about her dress. That meant we only had two more days until the full moon.

We looked for Underwood at breakfast but there was no sign of him. We speculated in hushed voices, but none of us really knew what that meant, or what it meant that Talendale wasn't there, either. Of course, the professors had their own staff room in which to eat, but Talendale usually put in at least a brief appearance each morning.

"Do you think they're still in the conclave?" Kelsey said, leaning towards us over the table and keeping her voice low. I shrugged but Sam frowned.

"All night?"

"Do the three of you understand the concept of discretion?" Underwood's gravelly voice sounded from nearby, making me jump and slop orange juice all over the table. I dropped a napkin on it with a groan.

"Do you have to keep doing that?" I grumbled, then added with a vague stab of diplomacy, "Professor."

He was standing right behind me, but we'd been so caught up in our discussion that we hadn't heard him approach.

"Come," he said, turning and striding away from the table. I shared a quick glance with Kelsey and Sam, and then we hurried after him. He didn't speak again until he opened the door into a classroom, checked it was empty, and beckoned us inside. I shut the door behind me. Underwood took his time, perching on the edge of a desk before speaking.

"The council members and the alpha packs have been unable to reach an agreement."

"What does that mean? The truce...?"

"Still stands. For now."

"But..." Kelsey stared down at her feet, avoiding everyone's eyes. "What if they can't come to an agreement?"

Underwood grimaced.

"Let's just hope it doesn't come to that. They'll meet again in three days."

"After the full moon."

Underwood nodded. After the full moon, when we'd know what the stakes were – if Paisley had been turned or not. And if she had, the druids wouldn't let Leo go without a fight. They'd want their own brand of justice. I shuddered. Either way, the cocky rogue shifter's fate was sealed. Part of me wondered if it would be kinder to let the packs have him. At least it would be quick, unlike a life sentence in Daoradh.

"I imagine they'll want you to give evidence, Lyssa."

"Me?"

"It was your grove he invaded. They'll likely want to speak to you two, as well," he said to Kelsey and Sam. Kelsey went so pale she might as well have been see-through, and I remembered the quiet, composed Underwood's reluctance to be around the alpha pack. How much worse must it seem to the mousey hybrid?

"Gladly," Sam said, his voice full of animosity, but his eyes flickered with uncertainty.

"What happens to Leo until then?"

Underwood cleared his throat, and cast a glance around the empty room.

"I'm not sure you need to know that."

"He's staying here, isn't he?" Kelsey said, keeping her eyes firmly fixed on the spot between her feet.

"What?" Sam's jaw clenched.

"He has to," Kelsey said, lifting her eyes as far as Sam's knees. "Neither side is going to let the other move him, they don't trust each other."

I looked to Underwood for confirmation and he exhaled heavily and then gave a curt nod.

"He'll be confined to the dungeons, kept under guard until the conclave reach a decision."

"What about Paisley?" I blurted. Sam and Kelsey looked at me like I was talking jibberish — no surprise given my tendency to leap from subject to subject without warning. I'd have thought they'd be used to it by now.

"I mean," I added, maybe a touch defensively, "Paisley needs to be locked up on the full moon, just in case she shifts, right? You can't keep her next to the guy who bit her."

"Oh," Underwood said. "No, we won't be using that dungeon for Leo. There's another, deeper dungeon. It's more secure."

I couldn't imagine what would be more secure that the iron and silver barred dungeon Kelsey had been locked up in for half the full-moons last year, but I clamped my jaw shut before I could ask. Underwood was right. There were some things I just didn't want to know.

"Right. I've got work to do, and I'm sure the three of you have homework to catch up on."

Did I imagine it, or did his eyes linger on me when he said that? Seemed a little harsh. I mean, we were only a couple of months into the year, I wasn't that far behind. Yet. Anyway, it wasn't my fault if Stormclaw was taking up most of my time. I was trying to save his life, for crying out loud, because Talendale still hadn't lifted his death sentence, just suspended it, and with Redwing pregnant he was hardly getting more sociable by the day. The opposite, in fact. If he didn't loosen up a bit, I didn't even think I'd be able to get back on him by the new year, let alone ride him in the first proper game of the season and silence Talendale's doubts. Homework would still be there next year. Stormclaw wouldn't, not if I couldn't turn things around with him.

Our weekend passed in a knot of anxiety, alternating between strained silences and conversations spoken in hushed whispers. Around us, academy life went on as normal. I'd have thought Felicity and Cecelia would have been too busy worrying about their friend to pay us any attention, but if anything, Felicity got bitchier by the day. Hell, if there was a contest between her and Stormclaw to see who was doing their best to take lumps out of me, I'd have been hard-pressed to call the gryff the winner.

On Monday she managed to 'accidentally' blow my Law assignment half way across the classroom, leaving me snatching up the papers on my hands and knees (though, truth be told, if she'd blown them right out of the window I'd have been glad of the excuse not to hand in my pitiful essay). I spent the whole of intermediate elemental manipulation trying to tune out her theories about how a freak like me managed to manifest three elemental powers, interspersed with snide comments about my inability to exercise anything more than rudimentary control over any of them. And it wasn't like I could argue with that. Sure, I had good control of my fire element, most of the time, and I didn't tend to accidentally set stuff on fire any more – not much, anyway – but I still had almost no control over my other two elements, something I lamented when I met up with Swann after dinner for my extra tuition.

"You'll get it," Swann sympathised, removing the screwed-up sheet of paper I'd been trying to blow from the desk, and replacing it with a candle. "It's exceptionally rare for a student to have two powers so soon, let alone three. You shouldn't be so hard on yourself."

Easy for her to say. She didn't spend half her time comparing herself to the rogue druid – the same rogue druid who seemed to have an unhealthy interest in me – and worrying that if it came to it, she wouldn't stand the first chance of defending herself. Of course, I didn't say any of that to her. I wasn't even sure she knew about

Raphael and his third power. And anyway, it wasn't really relevant to my haphazard control of my air power.

She lit the wick on the candle, and nodded to it. I slumped further back into my chair and stared at it, willing it to flick and go out. It did. Swann tutted.

"With your air power, Lyssa. Not your fire power."

"It's not my fault," I muttered sullenly. "You know I don't have control."

"Nor will you with that attitude," she snapped. I lifted my eyes to hers, waiting for the rest of the lecture, but instead she pulled out a chair and sat opposite me.

"I know you've got a lot on your mind right now, but you've got to find a way to work past it." She raised a hand, forestalling my reply, and continued. "I know it's not easy, and you're not the first druid who didn't think elemental control exercises were a priority. But Lyssa, you are unique. Who else in our history has ever had control of opposing elements? I truly believe you wouldn't have been given these powers if you couldn't control them."

She rounded off what I'm sure was a very inspirational speech with a warm smile and a hand gently squeezing my shoulder, but all that my mind could focus on was her question. I knew of one other. He had control of three elements, too. By definition, two of those must have been opposing. Dammit. If Raphael could control his powers, why couldn't I?

"Let's finish there for today," Swann said, with a glance out of the window set high in the rootbound stone wall. Night had fallen, and the moon was starting to rise. I nodded my thanks and got out of there before she could change her mind. Kelsey was probably already making her way to the Unhallowed Grove – at least she wouldn't have to worry about Leo this time, since he was in Underwood's dungeon. And Paisley. In a few short hours, we'd know.

I was halfway there before I realised where my feet had carried me. The fireballs hanging near the ceiling were duller than the ones in the heart of the castle; each a little more wan than the one before. I followed the trail of encroaching darkness, feeling the air chill around me as I moved deeper into the academy's bowels. I drew my cloak tighter around myself and pressed on. There was no point in turning back now. Besides, I somehow couldn't imagine Felicity or Cecelia stooping to visit their potentially hybrid friend. There was no room for outcasts in their corner of society. My hands trembled – not from the cold – and I sucked in a lungful of the stagnant air, listening to my footsteps echo around me. Druid society was a mess. Shifter society was a mess. What the hell was the matter with people? We had magic, dammit. It was about the coolest thing on the planet, and people were getting hung up on whether someone could move fire or turn into an animal. Madness. Utter madness.

I shook my head at the absurdity of it, then slowed to a stop outside of the dungeon door. What if Paisley didn't want me there? It wasn't like we were friends – kinda the opposite after everything that had happened between us. Maybe she wouldn't want someone intruding on what could be the worst night of her life. Maybe she'd prefer her own company.

Maybe you're making excuses, Lyssa. Suck it up.

I raised a tentative hand and eased the door open. Inside were two figures, both turning to stare at me. Underwood, sitting on an old, dusty chair, and Paisley, separated from him by a row of iron and silver bars, each thicker than my forearm. I wasn't completely sure whether they'd been built to contain werewolves, or something far, far stronger.

When I found Kelsey in here last year, she'd been sitting cross-legged on the concrete floor, deep in a trance and looking completely at ease. The contrast could not have been more stark. Paisley looked tiny inside the huge dungeon, curled up in one corner of the cage with her arms curled around her knees. Her eyes were bright red like she'd been crying for hours – which she probably had. What else did she have to do down here but worry and mope?

"Lyssa," Underwood said, rising quickly from his seat. "I'm not sure it's appropriate for—"

"It's okay, Professor," Paisley said, and despite her red eyes and puffy face, her voice barely trembled. She fixed her gaze on me, with none of her usual sneer, but you couldn't have called the expression on her face friendly. "What do you want, Lyssa?"

Ouch. Her voice was colder than the dungeon air. I shut the door behind me and moved further into the room. The concrete beneath my feet was aged and grimy, with small cracks running through it, though the floor inside the cage was in perfect condition — no doubt reinforced with magic. Fireballs hung in the corners of the massive room, casting a dull, flickering glow, the sort that created more shadows than light. It was hard to imagine that a couple of nights ago this room was packed with partying students, celebrating Halloween with their friends, dancing and laughing and revelling in the joy of youth. Now it seemed exactly what it was — a prison. A barren place where hope came to die.

I shook off my lethargy. So what if Paisley turned? Sure, her life would be different, but no worse than what Kelsey had faced, and she'd handled it just fine. How could I condemn the druidic world for looking down on hybrids one minute, then stand here the next acting like becoming one would be an unspeakable curse? What a hypocrite.

"Came to see if you have any cool scars," I said, forcing a grin as I crossed the floor. I conjured a fireball in front of me, making sure it was chucking off plenty of heat, and pushed it through the bars, leaving it to hover in the middle of the cage. Paisley eyed it suspiciously, like she expected it to attack her at any moment, then held her hands out, warming them in its glow. She nodded me her thanks, and I fought the urge to give Underwood a reproachful look. Her hands were white with cold. She didn't have a shifter's temperature resilience, not yet at least. Maybe not ever. He should have thought of that. She was going through enough without freezing her ass off, too.

I didn't say anything else, just parked my backside on the cold concrete, and waited with her.

It was another hour before her scream of agony ripped through the air.

Chapter Seventeen

Within a week, it was round the entire academy. If I had to guess, I'd say from the looks Felicity and Cecelia were giving her, and the hurt ones Paisley was giving them in return, that she'd told her two best friends, hoping that somehow they'd stand by her. I could have told her how well that would have gone down.

She still wasn't back in classes yet, and we didn't see much of Underwood, either. No prizes for putting two and two together. Young werewolves were notorious for having little control over when and where they shifted. According to legend, hybrids struggled even worse. I could only imagine how hard it must be for someone who hadn't grown up with it, felt it inside them for their entire lives, to cope with the change, and control the inner beast.

The only time we ever saw her was at mealtimes, where she sat at the end of the air table, shunned by the rest of her house. She ate quickly and in silence, and then left again, spending no more than ten minutes with her fellow students, despite the mounds of food piled on her plate. She never looked in my direction, but then she never really looked at anyone. She kept her eyes downcast, and allowed her dark hair to spill over her shoulders, shutting out the outside world.

As for the one responsible for doing that to her – well, the one other than me – he was still locked in the other dungeon, while the circle and the alpha pack bickered over who would be the ones to mete out their own brand of justice. Talks continued deep into December, without either side convincing the other to yield an inch, and every day tensions ratcheted up, until students could be found whispering in every corner and every corridor, wondering when the truce would break and whether there would be an academy to return to after Christmas. Even the professors had given up trying to stop the spread of speculation.

"Do you think they'll keep negotiating over the Christmas break?" Liam asked Dean in a whisper that probably wasn't as quiet as he intended one Potions lesson the week before Christmas.

"If they don't," Alex said, tossing what looked like burdock root into her potion without bothering to measure it, "it'll be all-out war. I heard one of the pack shifted in the middle of the conclave yesterday, and threatened to turn one of the council members."

"And who did you hear that from?" Kelsey said, her voice tight with irritation. "Since there weren't any students there and the professors are hardly likely to be talking to any of us about it?"

Alex shrugged carelessly, and gave her potion, which had begun billowing greyish-green smoke, a stir with a long wooden spoon.

"It might have happened." She tossed the spoon aside and threw in some more of the burdock root.

"I don't think that's helping," I said.

"The rumours, or the burdock root?"

"Both. Try some dandelion leaf. And listen, if the–"

I broke off, staring at the door which had just eased open. Standing outlined in the door was Paisley, clutching a book in her folded arms, her dark hair hanging limply around her face, her shoulders slumped, and her gaze fixed firmly on the floor in front of her feet.

"Professor Talendale said I should come back to class," she muttered in the general direction of Professor Brennan, in the absolute silence of the room. She lifted her head enough to glance in Felicity's direction, then turned and made her way towards an empty desk at the back of the room.

"Paisley," I said. "Over here."

I shoved some books aside to clear a space on our table. She stared at me for a long moment, holding her book even tighter against her chest like a shield while her eyes darted to my face and away again far too quickly to have read my expression. Hopefully too quickly to have seen the wide-eyed looks I was getting from the rest of my table, too. After a moment of indecision, Paisley set her jaw and came over, carefully placing her textbook on the desk beside me, under the weight of thirty pairs of watching eyes.

"Alright, everyone," Brennan said, clapping his hands together. "Back to your potions before one of you manages to melt another hole in my classroom. Paisley, you can work with Lyssa for the rest of the lesson."

"Why did you do that?" Paisley said quietly, once the rest of the class went back to their potions. I shrugged easily, imitating Alex.

"I know what it's like to be an outsider."

"But... I was horrible to you. All of last year."

"That was last year. Pass me that willow bark, would you?"

She glanced over at the ingredients I'd piled up on the table, and pulled a cracked curl of bark from the middle of them.

"Does it... does it get any easier?" she asked as I chipped some pieces from the wood. "The stares? And the whispers behind your back?"

I hesitated, then tossed my handful of flakes into the pot.

"Just… give it time. You're back in class now. By the time Christmas break is over, they'll have something else to gossip about."

She didn't look convinced, which wasn't surprising, since I wasn't all that convinced myself. But what else could I say? That there was always going to be someone sniping at her, that this was her life now, better just get used to it? She was in no state to hear that, and I'd messed up her life enough for one semester. I wasn't going to be the bearer of bad news right now. Let her think this was the worse it was going to get. Consider it an early Christmas present.

None of us spoke much for the rest of the lesson, other than when one of us blurted something random at the top of our voices in an attempt to drown out a malicious whisper from another part of the room – mostly from Felicity's table – so that Paisley would be spared the worst of it. I don't think it worked, but I think she appreciated the effort.

After that, Paisley sat with us in every lesson we shared with Air for the rest of the week. I wouldn't go so far as to say we were friends, but we were the only students in the academy who weren't out to make her life hell, so she stuck with us. It was, for all of us, a long week before we broke up for the Christmas break.

Paisley was going home to her family in Suffolk, and Kelsey went back to her family to spend the holidays with her mother's pack. My parents had enjoyed their little two-person Christmas so much last year that they'd decided on a repeat this year. I didn't mind. Christmas at the academy was actually pretty fun, and anyway, Professor Alden needed me to be around to help out with Stormclaw. He was being really protective of Redwing – apparently that was pretty normal during the first trimester, but if Leech had to keep regrowing people's fingers after his outbursts, it was really going to make arguing his case with Talendale tricky. Not that the headmaster had much time to worry about gryffs right now – the conclave was still meeting daily, and so far as I knew, not getting anywhere.

Sam had offered to stay to keep me company – his family didn't do Christmas – but I'd told him not to worry about me. I had enough to be getting on with. I headed down to the main hall to grab some breakfast the day after everyone left, running through my plans for the day. I had a whole heap of homework to be getting on with, and much as I wanted to put it off until later, I figured I should do the grown up thing and get my History of Magic assignment done and out of the way, so I could spend the rest of my break working with Stormclaw.

It would mean paying a visit to my least favourite place in the academy: the library. That place was nothing but bad news. My last little visit there had resulted in me getting a dog tail. Alright, there was an argument that we shouldn't have been trying that spell in the first place, but let's not get into that. I mean, I hadn't envisioned winding up with a butt resembling a golden retriever, but we'd managed to get rid of it after a couple of hours, so all's well that ends well and all that.

I got some toast from Cora, the kitchen mage who was covering Aiden during his holiday break, and headed to the almost deserted Fire table. Most of the tables were pretty empty – less than a hundred students stayed over Christmas, and most of them were enjoying a first-day-of-the-holiday lie-in. There were a few people clustered on the Air table, and as I passed, I noticed the dark-haired figure sitting alone at one end.

"Paisley! I thought you were going home."

"Change of plan," she mumbled into her plate, but even that earned her glares from the rest of her house mates. I rolled my eyes at them, then picked up Paisley's plate, ignoring the low rumble that started up in her throat. Werewolves and food, it was always dicey coming between them.

"Come on," I said to her. "You're eating at my table today. You're an honorary Fire for the holidays."

"Can… can we do that?"

I could barely make out her voice, it was so quiet. I snorted loudly with amusement, startling her.

"I'd like to see anyone try to stop us. Let's go."

Truth was, I didn't think anyone on her table would be complaining about her leaving, and there was no-one at mine, since we were right at the start of breakfast and the Fires who'd stayed behind had been having a bit of a party last night. I wasn't expecting to see any of them any time soon.

I set Paisley's plate down, and sat opposite her.

"So how come you stayed?" I asked, trying to force some conversation from her. She didn't speak much anymore.

"I got a letter yesterday," she said, without looking up. "Just as I was getting ready to leave."

I waited while she chased a piece of bacon around her plate, but she didn't continue.

"What did it say?"

"They think it would be better if I stayed here this Christmas. My own parents." She jerked her eyes up and looked at me, long enough for me to see the hurt and anger she was trying to mask, then abruptly looked back to her food. "They don't want me. They're ashamed of me."

"They said that?"

"They didn't have to! No-one wants to be anywhere near me. I'm a freak!"

"You're not a freak. You're just… different."

She snorted softly.

"I'm a half-breed." She twisted her lips around the words as she spat them, like they left a bad taste in her mouth.

"So?"

"My life is ruined!"

I dropped my toast back onto my plate and took a leaf out of Swann's book.

"It is if you take that attitude. Alright, you didn't ask for this. But it's happened, and now you've got to deal with it. And you know what? It's not all bad. You're faster, stronger. You've got heightened senses. When you've got full control of your new powers, you're going to be able to change form whenever you want."

"You seem to know a lot about it."

Uh-oh, said too much. I took a hasty bite of my toast and swallowed.

"I've been, uh, studying."

She was still looking at me weirdly, but I didn't say anything else. I'd promised Kelsey I'd keep her secret. She'd been unhappy when we started spending time with Paisley, angry even, worried that people would start to see similarities between them. I sighed. If even the hybrids hated what they were, how were we ever going to convince the magic community to see them as something good?

"Is this seat taken?"

I glanced up at Ava, standing with a plate bearing half a dozen American-style pancakes in one hand, and a glass of juice in the other.

"Help yourself," I said, pulling out a chair for her. "You didn't fancy going home either then?"

"Home? Bit of a trek back to the states."

It wasn't, given that it was just a matter of stepping through a portal, and so far as I knew, international portals were just as fast as local ones, but I didn't pry. She didn't owe me an explanation, and honestly I was just glad that there'd be someone else around to help Alden with the gryffs so I could focus on Stormclaw. I plucked a stray feather from her hair and let it fall to the floor, then picked up my empty plate.

"No rest for the wicked," I said. "I'm going to hit the library. I'll catch up with you both later."

At least Ava didn't have any idea about the controversy surrounding hybrids, since she was raised by mundanes, like me. It was good; Paisley needed some people who wouldn't judge her right now. There'd be plenty of people doing that for the rest of her life.

Miraculously, I remembered the way to the library, despite my aversion to the place. Finding the books I needed was another matter entirely, though. I glanced at the assignment title, *The Influence of Magic in the first Roman Invasion of Britannica'* and stifled a reflexive yawn. I'd already been made to study the Romans once when I was at school, and it had been more than enough.

As I scanned the shelves, it quickly became apparent that there wasn't a book titled *Everything You Thought You Knew About The Roman Conquest of Britain is Wrong'*, but I did come across an old dusty tome whose gold lettering spelled out, *Defending Britain: A Historical Reference'*, and just for good measure I grabbed, *Military Magic'*, too.

I'd barely made a start on the first when a shadow fell across the pages. I looked up to see Professor Alden standing in front of my table, glancing down at my notes.

"Ah, Magic in the Roman Invasion?" she said. I nodded. "Professor Godwin was using that assignment when *I* was a student."

She shook her head while I sat pondering the fact that she'd studied here, which I guess made sense, and wondering how old that made Godwin. Seriously old.

"Anarevitos put shifter conscripts on the front line, and had his druids cast rage spells on them, which forced them to shift. Too bad some of the Romans had silver-tipped spears. So eventually the druids took things into

194

their own hands and conjured up some storms to stop the Romans sending reinforcements. Job done."

"O…kay?" I drew the word out, wondering why Alden was giving me the answers to an assignment that frankly had been about to take me the better part of the day to find.

"Great. Write that down, then head out to the paddock. Redwing needs a check-up, but I've run out of volunteers to distract your gryff while I do it."

I chuckled under my breath, and chucked my notes in my bag. The assignment could wait.

Chapter Eighteen

When Christmas day came around, I found myself at a bit of a loose end. I took Stormclaw the new headcollar I'd bought for him, along with a salmon I'd picked up at Fantail Market, which I happened to know were a particular favourite of his. He even deigned to let me hop on his back and go for a short ride around the academy's grounds, but he didn't stray far from Redwing's side for long, so by mid-day, I was wandering the academy, trying to decide what to do with the rest of my day. Maybe I'd head back to Fantail for a while – just to get out. I'd spent so much time at Dragondale recently that it was starting to feel like a cage.

A cage. I paused in my pacing, and frowned. Leo was in a cage and had been for weeks. Couldn't have been easy, not for someone who was used to being outside, able to roam wherever he wanted. On the other hand, maybe he should have thought about that before he attacked innocent people.

But did he, really?

That old niggle was back, that little part of me that wanted to believe he was innocent. If there hadn't been so much evidence against him, I might actually have listened to the little voice. Still, it was Christmas. It wouldn't hurt to pay him a visit, right? You know, just in case an innocent man *was* rotting away in a cage?

I'd made it down the first two corridors before I remembered the guard. Underwood had said he was being watched round the clock. Not much chance they were going to let me visit. Unless I had a little distraction.

I looped round, back to the main hall, and found Cora setting up for Christmas lunch.

"Sorry, Lyssa," she said, "You're a little early. Come back in half an hour?"

"Actually, I was going to take a dinner down to," I lowered my voice conspiratorially, despite the hall being deserted, "you know, the *guard.*"

She looked startled for a moment, no doubt because she wasn't supposed to know that someone was being kept under guard, but like everyone else round here, she couldn't resist a bit of gossip. I sweetened the pot.

"I'm not supposed to say anything, but, well..." I glanced over my shoulder again, and fabricated furiously. "They say the shifter isn't happy about having guard duty on Christmas, you know, being away from his pack and all. I thought if I could take him some food..."

I shrugged.

"But if you can't help, it doesn't matter."

"No, hold on!" She coughed, and wiped her palms on the white apron tied around her waist. "I mean, I'm sure I can conjure a little something. You'll be sure to come see me this afternoon?"

"Oh, you bet. I mean, I'm not really supposed to speak about it, but since you're helping me…"

That was all it took to see me armed with a plastic box ram packed with steaming food. When I reminded her that he was a werewolf and had a werewolf's appetite, it quickly became two boxes. I stashed one inside my cloak as soon as I got out of the hall.

Of course, I didn't know exactly where the second dungeon was, but I figured it had to be somewhere deeper in the castle than the first. It was supposed to be more secure than the one Paisley had been in, and that meant harder to get out of – or into. The halls were deserted. Everyone was probably getting ready for the Christmas feast. It was the last thing on my mind – I couldn't have been less hungry. Maybe I'd grab something later. For now, though, I made the most of everyone else being preoccupied, and stole past the first dungeon without anyone having seen me.

The corridors were darker here, cloaked in shadow and menace, and if you think that's melodramatic… well, you haven't seen them. The fireballs that flickered half-heartedly near the ceiling were few and far between, and the air was thick with the musty scent of disuse. I could feel a coat of grime beneath my feet, slick against the aged cobble stones that slanted on a slight downward incline, leading me deeper into the earth. Between each stone, roots erupted through the pack dirt and wove their way across the ground. Roots from the Tilimeuese tree, I was sure. There was nowhere in the grounds that the sentient tree didn't leave its mark. A reminder that we were all on borrowed time. The tree had been here before I was born, and would remain here long after my bones were dust.

I shivered and crept silently along the hallway, watching my breath form dense clouds in the air in front of me. It was cold down here. I wrapped my hands firmly around the food-laden plastic box, trying to glean some warmth from it.

I don't know how long I walked for, but each step took me into deeper, colder, darker territory, until I started to doubt the wisdom of this little trip. What if I wasn't even going the right way? I might make it all the way down here, not to discover Leo's prison, but something else. Something worse.

No. I wasn't turning back.

I thrust my chin out and took a deep breath of the dank air, forcing the melancholy from my lungs. Immediately, the uneasiness began creeping up my spine again, urging me to turn back. The sour air caught in my throat and my heart pulsed painfully in my chest. Something was down here. Something bad. *Turn back.*

No. I'd come this far.

I kept moving, until my legs started to tremble. This was a bad idea. A really, really bad idea. Anything could be down here. And even if I found Leo, I could get into serious trouble. This wasn't like before. I couldn't just pretend I'd taken a wrong turn. Students weren't meant to be here. I could feel it with every fibre of my being. The trembles travelled up my legs until they shook so much I checked to make sure it wasn't the ground beneath them shaking. It wasn't. Oh gods, I needed to get out of here.

No. I was doing this.

Abruptly, the band tightening around my chest eased, and the panic fluttering in my stomach calmed, so that I could draw in a proper, satisfying breath. My legs stopped trembling and I moved faster, more confidently. I'd made my decision, and nothing was going to change my mind. I would find Leo, and I'd face whatever came between us.

Which meant finding a way past his guard. The food suddenly seemed like a stupid idea. What was he going to do, take a stroll up to the main hall to eat it? He was hardly going to desert his post. Unless...

I pulled the lid off the box, and a cloud of steam erupted from it. I'd been pretty terrible at this spell in

Atherton's lesson, but then I was pretty terrible at everything when Atherton was around.

I took a slow breath, and held my hand over the box.

"Cadaileh," I muttered, and gave a soft pulse of energy. The food seemed to glow with a light of its own in the dull corridor for a second – or maybe the firelight had just caught my eye in a funny way. By the time I'd blinked, the food looked normal again. I fixed the lid back in place, and moved on.

After only a short minute, my eyes picked up a figure looming ahead, shrouded in the darkness.

"Halt," the voice commanded, and my feet stumbled to a stop of their own volition. "Identify yourself and your purpose."

"Lyssa. Lyssa Eldridge." Well, that was stupid. Now he knew who I was. There went my best chance of avoiding Talendale hearing about this. *Nice one, Lyssa.* I tried to keep the tremble from my voice as I spoke. "I, uh… I brought you some food. Turkey and stuff."

The hulking figure moved forward, so that the fireball hanging above him cast its light onto his face. There was nothing about him that marked him as different. No distinguishing feature on his face, no scar nor brand, and yet it was impossible to miss the feral energy pulsing from him. *Werewolf.*

I loosed an inward sigh of relief. That little spell I'd foolishly cast would have been like a red flag to a council member. A shifter, on the other hand, might not notice. I'd only been guessing when I said a shifter was guarding Leo, but it looked like I'd been right. At least one thing had gone in my favour today. Aside from the fact that being right meant I was face to face with six foot of hulking werewolf.

"You came all the way down here just to bring me some lunch?" He eyed me across the short distance between us, and I hoped I didn't look as guilty as I felt. "Through a fear spell?"

Fear spell? Huh. I guess that explained the illogical terror I'd felt in the corridor. I caught myself before I said anything to that effect. It was better that I at least appeared to have a clue what I was doing. And really, what the hell *was* I doing down here, visiting a condemned, and probably guilty, man? I forced a shrug and mustered as much nonchalance as I could.

"It's Christmas. Inter-community relations and all that, right?"

He gave a short, sharp laugh that was more like a bark, identical to Leo's. Maybe they all laughed like that. Maybe it was a shifter thing. Whatever. His eyes were on the box I held out in front of me and he stalked forwards.

A tiny tremor ran through my legs, and it wasn't because of any fear spell this time.

The shifter drew up short. Damn, these guys missed nothing. Then again, he had full on predatory shifter senses. He could probably smell my adrenaline.

He approached more slowly, and I thrust the box out to him.

"Never seen a shifter before, girl?"

"You're from the alpha pack, aren't you?" He caught my eye and I jerked my head away without meaning to. I tried to raise my eye to meet his again, but it was like trying to meet Underwood's eye – only a hundred times more intense. I physically couldn't do it. I gave up and let my eyes settle somewhere near his chin.

"Do you know what the alpha pack is?"

"The shifter council." My outstretched hand shook, and the box with it.

"The alphas of every major pack in the country," the shifter said. "Do I look like an alpha to you?"

I nodded. He *felt* like an alpha.

"Well, I'm not. Trust me, alphas don't get assigned guard duty in dank corridors. I'm just a dogsbody, and I'm not going to bite."

The flickering light fell across the slight curve of his lips, and he took the box from my hands.

"Thanks. I appreciate this." He pulled the lid off, and paused. "Wait, this isn't poisoned or some crap, is it? Inter-community relations, right?"

"You'd smell it if it was, wouldn't you?"

He shrugged, and started eating. After a few bites, he stretched out his shoulders and the tension dropped from his frame.

"Ah, this is good – too good to rush. I could use a sit down. Thanks, druid."

He brushed passed me and swung open a door I hadn't even noticed before. There went our inter-community relations – I must've just set them back a decade. But hopefully he wouldn't realise what I'd done, and I doubted he'd willingly tell anyone he'd deserted his post.

Speaking of which… I looked through the open door he'd been guarding. Guess he'd wanted to be able to keep an eye on Leo – who I could now see, slumped at the back of a small cage, furnished only with a bucket. Nice.

"Leo," I whispered as I stepped into the room, and my voice echoed back off the walls, amplified. The shifter's head jerked up to look at me.

"Druid girl?"

I rolled my eyes.

"I do have a name, you know."

"Yeah, remind me," he said, pushing himself to his feet, and stalking the half dozen paces it took to reach the front of his cage. "What is that? Betrayer? Traitor? Turn coat?"

He spat the accusations bitterly, glaring at me through the bars.

"Maybe you should have thought about that before you attacked people. And don't start with that 'I'm innocent' crap again, I'm not falling for it."

"What are you doing here, then?" he said sullenly, folding his arms across his chest. Yeah, good question. I diverted.

"I brought you this." I pulled the box from under my cloak, and slid it through the bars.

"What is it?" he said, picking up the box and opening it. "Turkey, sprouts, chestnuts… Shit, it's Christmas, isn't it? I've been in here for two months?"

For a moment I thought he was going to throw the box across his cell, but then he just slumped to the ground and picked miserably at the food.

"I should have just gone to the alpha pack and let them kill me."

"Don't say that!"

"Why?" He glowered at me over the top of the box. "Better than being locked up down here for a hundred years."

"A hundred years? Hyperbolic, much?"

"You really don't know the first thing about shifters, do you, druid girl? Considering you have a half-breed for a best friend, you really should make more of an effort."

He pulled a piece of turkey from the massive leg crammed in the box, and put it in his mouth. I blinked.

"What... what do you mean?"

He swallowed, and licked the juices from his fingers. Gross.

"Shifters have a longer lifespan than mundanes," he said, when he was finished cleaning his digits. "One of the many reasons we don't normally mate outside of our kind. A hundred-and-fifty is normal, two hundred isn't uncommon. You know, if you're not slowly dying in a fucking cage!"

I took an involuntary step back as he bellowed the last words, his face contorted into a snarl and his whole body shaking with rage. He raised a hand, and his breathing slowed as I watched, and then he shook it out. I scowled at him.

"You do realise I had to curse a guard to get in here, right? Are you trying to wake him up?"

"I *am* innocent," he said. "No matter what you think. You believed me, once. What changed?"

I diverted again.

"It doesn't matter what I think. It's up to the council and the alpha pack now."

"If I'd known that was going to be my last day of freedom, I'd have taken a moment to appreciate it more."

The food sat on the floor, ignored, as he stared off into one corner of his cage.

"I'm sorry," I said.

"Then help me. Please."

"I can't!"

"I'm losing my mind down here, druid girl. If you won't help me, then just kill me."

I shook my head. I wasn't getting roped into his mind games again.

"I've got to go. Enjoy your food. And hide the box before the guard gets back."

Chapter Nineteen

The rest of the holidays passed in a blur. I couldn't keep from thinking of the young shifter in the basement. Whether I was working on my assignment, working with Alden, riding Stormclaw – no matter what I was doing, my mind kept going back to him, and his insistence he was innocent.

Your fault.

Yup, no matter which way you cut it, it was my fault. Either I'd allowed a dangerous rogue shifter on the grounds to attack Paisley, or I'd condemned an innocent man to life – and death – in a cage, or at the hands of his peers who wanted to literally tear him apart. Bang up job I was doing of things this year.

When the first day of the new year rolled round, it found over three quarters of the students back in the academy. The new semester didn't start for a couple of days, but no-one wanted to miss the first Itealta game of the season. I was supposed to play winger, but Stormclaw made it perfectly clear he was in no mood for a rider. Logan looked like he might cry when I broke the news to him, but he nodded bravely and put up a reserve to ride in my place. The reserve had been training since the start of last semester, but we all knew his gryff didn't have even half of Stormclaw's speed. The rest of the team would have to pick up the slack, and we'd been pretty evenly matched as it was.

I slunk off towards the spectator stands, not entirely sure I wanted to watch the inevitable trouncing Earth were going to give us. I was just about to trudge up the steps, when a hand grabbed my arm from behind. I spun round, ready to give someone a piece of my mind, and found myself staring into a familiar pale face, framed in red hair.

"Kelsey!" I grabbed her and pulled her into a hug. "I thought you weren't getting back until tomorrow. You know," I lowered my voice, "because of helping your family with the… situation."

Kelsey shook her head, and glanced around.

"We need to talk. Come on."

Glad for the excuse not to watch the match, I turned away from the stands and let her lead me off towards the thicket of trees a few hundred metres behind it. It wasn't until we were deep inside the thicket and hidden by the tall oaks that she spoke again.

"There was another attack."

I stared at her, dumbstruck, for a long moment.

"Another attack… you mean…"

"Another attack. *Exactly* the same. On Christmas Day. We discovered the girl just after lunch. Leo must have–"

I cut her off.

"Leo was here. I saw him. I snuck down to the dungeon." She gave me a reproachful look, but I ignored her and continued, because this was too big to worry about whether my friend thought I had a thing for bad boys. "It can't have been him – I was with him."

"Then that means…" Kelsey shook her head again, sending her red mane flying around her face. "I can't believe I'm about to say this, but…"

I said it for her.

"Leo is innocent."

"But then who attacked Paisley?" she said. "How could someone have gotten onto the academy's grounds without anyone knowing?"

I thought about it for a moment.

"The same way Leo did. They jumped a portal." I recalled the kid who got stuck half-in, half-out of a portal when Alden had been taking me to the paddocks right at the start of last semester. "The third years have been practicing since the start of the year. There must be dozens of portals opening all over the place. He – or she – could easily have jumped in on one, attacked Paisley, then followed someone out over Christmas."

"We need to tell Talendale. You're Leo's alibi."

Crap. The guard hadn't reported me, but Kelsey was right – as soon as word got out that there had been another attack, he'd have to admit he'd deserted his post.

Everyone would assume that Leo had found a way to escape while he was gone, and come back to cover his tracks. I groaned.

"I'm going to be in detention forever."

*

Talendale didn't put me in detention. He did, however, make me stand in front of one of the alphas and admit what I'd done, and on balance I think I'd have preferred the detentions.

But it didn't matter. They had to let Leo go now, and that meant they could start looking for the person who was really behind the attacks. There was an academy-wide ban on portalling, and the professors personally supervised the portals bringing the rest of the students back over the following days. I think Paisley was the one it hit hardest. She'd gone from having someone to blame, and believing he was safely locked in the dungeon, to not knowing who'd attacked her, and jumping at every shadow.

On the first day of the semester, I ducked Atherton's spellcraft lesson (on the grounds that he'd probably have kicked me out before the end, anyway) and went looking for Underwood. I tracked him down in his office.

"Lyssa," he said heavily, looking at me standing in his threshold. "To what do I owe the pleasure?"

"Sorry to disturb you, Professor," I said, proving I was getting the hang of this diplomacy lark. "I was just wondering… about Leo."

Underwood stepped back, allowing me inside.

"You want to know what's going to happen to him now we know he didn't attack Paisley and the others."

I nodded.

"The alpha pack is leaving this afternoon. They're going to start looking for the real attacker. They don't have any more interest in him."

"That's great." Only, the look on Underwood's face said I was missing the obvious. "Isn't it? I mean, Leo can go free now."

"Leo entered an apprentice's grove uninvited, illegally jumped a portal, and trespassed in a sacred druid academy."

"So… they're not letting him go?" I ventured. "I don't care that he came into my grove."

"Not the point. You don't get a say in that until you're qualified."

"That's bullshit!" So much for my diplomacy.

"Be that as it may, Ms Eldridge," Underwood said firmly, "that is the law. And even if you were in a position to dismiss his infraction, he still has his other crimes to answer for. And they are grave. A shifter trespassing in

Dragondale… I cannot emphasise how serious this is, Lyssa."

"But…" The idea came to me in a flash. "He was seeking asylum. His own people were going to kill him for crimes he didn't commit. He was already injured."

Underwood rubbed his chin as he regarded me through hooded eyes. Encouraged, I pressed on.

"Surely, as one of the three magical communities, we had an obligation to provide sanctuary?"

"Is there any specific law you're citing, Ms Eldridge, or are you making it up?"

"Making it up," I admitted. "But that doesn't mean it isn't true. I mean, come on, you saw his wounds. They tried to kill him. They nearly succeeded. You said it yourself."

"Alright. I will speak to Professor Talendale. But I promise nothing. *If* the headmaster grants clemency, he will still have to make amends to the academy itself."

"He knows all about the Unhallowed Grove," I said. "He could help maintain it for the rest of the year, or he could–"

"Enough, Lyssa," Underwood said, but I could have sworn there was the trace of a smile on his lips. "Get to class before Professor Atherton forgets what you look like."

"I wish," I muttered under my breath, but slunk out of Underwood's office anyway. Better not push my luck too far today.

It wasn't until the end of the week that I saw him again. I was just heading back to the barn from the paddocks, wet, muddy, and with an abnormal amount of feathers in my hair, having just helped Alden turn out the Air team's gryffs after practice. It would not be entirely unfair to say it had not gone well; the beasts were in a particularly surly mood, and it was only by luck that neither of us was finishing the day with a trip to Madam Leechington.

"Well, that's the last of them, Lyssa. I appreciate your help. Ava's very keen, but she's not half the gryff handler you are. It sure would be good to have you helping out down here a bit more often."

I hid a smile at her ham-fisted flattery and ran the hose over the muddy headcollar I was holding.

"I'd love to, Professor Alden, but I have so much work right now."

"Hmph, well maybe when you have a little less on your plate," she said gruffly, scrubbing the clip on the lead rope in her hands.

I made a non-committal noise, then lifted a hand and scratched my nose – immediately regretting it when I realised just how caked in mud my hands were. If I hadn't already needed a shower before dinner, I did now.

I saw the two figures making their way towards us, and hung the wet headcollar on a hook next to the rest to dry. It wasn't entirely a surprise to see Underwood out here – I knew he came this way on occasion – but my jaw nearly hit the floor when I saw who was with him.

"Leo!"

"Hey, druid girl."

He gave me a wan smile and I looked him up and down. He was still wearing the same tattered pair of jeans he'd had on before, and someone, probably Underwood, had given him a white t-shirt. Despite the fact it was the middle of January, the cold didn't seem to bother him. His feet were bare, and now that I could see him in daylight, it was obvious he'd lost a lot of weight while he was incarcerated, and his fingernails were bitten to the quick. His hair was a little longer than it had been when I first met him, but his face still had only a smattering of stubble.

"What are you doing out here?" The light glinted brightly on something, and my eye caught the silver cuffs still locked around his wrists, albeit with no chain linking them. "And why are you still wearing those?"

Underwood coughed pointedly and I bit my tongue. Well, tried to, but the words slipped out anyway.

"And let the adults talk?" I rolled my eyes and heaved a sigh that wasn't entirely for the purposes of irony, but they were wasted on Underwood. Leo shot me a conspiratorial grin and a wink. Alden, however, seemed a lot less jovial than usual.

"Tom, please tell me this is not... this is the shifter who..."

"Who was found innocent, Janice," Underwood said, meeting her eye.

"Of the attacks."

"Of the attacks," Underwood agreed with a nod. "Professor Talendale feels it would be appropriate if he made reparations for the rest of his sins."

"And what has that got to do with me?"

Underwood said nothing, and I counted in my head. One, two, three...

"Oh, no, Tom. You can't possibly think that I... Not for one moment... No. He..." She locked eyes with Underwood – no mean feat – but he still didn't speak. Alden's head shook and her lips pressed together to form a thin, white line in her ruddy face.

"He's dangerous."

"He's not," Underwood disagreed.

"He is," Leo said. I elbowed him firmly in the ribs.

"Not. Helping," I muttered from the corner of my mouth. Alden turned her gaze on him for the first time, weighing him up like he was a gryff at the livestock market.

"Well, boy," she said gruffly. "What can you do? Are you any use to me?"

I could see his shoulders tense as she addressed him, and the fingers on his right hand twitched.

"Do you *want* to go back into a cage?" I hissed at him under my breath, and he rolled out his neck with an audible click. His fingers stilled.

"I'm strong," he said, his tone not quite achieving deferential. "I'm fast. And I can ride gryffs."

Alden snorted.

"Come near my gryffs? Not bloody likely."

"Professor Alden," I said. "Please, just give him a chance. He won't cause any trouble, I promise."

"Fine." She picked up a shovel and tossed it at the shifter, who snatched it from the air with deft hands. "You can start by mucking out the stalls. But stay away from the occupied ones. I meant what I said about my gryffs."

"What about these?" Leo held up one wrist and gestured to the cuff around it.

"You'll wear them until Professor Alden decides otherwise," Underwood said, in a tone that would brook no argument. "You do what she says, when she says, and you don't give her any lip. When you're not working, you'll be in your quarters. Food will be brought to you. And you'll stay away from the students, is that clear?"

Leo fired off a mock salute with one hand and twirled the shovel between his fingers in the other. He wasn't joking about being strong. Damn.

"At the end of the year, you can go back to your pack. I'm giving you a chance here, Leo. Don't blow it."

Chapter Twenty

Over the following weeks, Leo became a regular sight around the barn. By late March, Alden had even grudgingly allowed him to handle some of the tamer gryffs, and he proved surprisingly adept at calming the irate beasts. Of course, it didn't hurt that if any of them did take a swipe at him, he healed within minutes, without having to traipse all the way to a lecture from Leech, unlike the rest of us lowly druids.

He was taking Underwood's 'stay away from the students' order seriously, and he'd barely spoken a word to me, disappearing any time there was a lesson on near the barn. I didn't take it personally. He might look cocky, but he'd lived his own version of hell for weeks. He wasn't about to risk the limited freedom he had now. There were only two months until the end of the semester, but two months was a long time if you had to spend it locked in a dungeon. Still, I mean, surely he didn't think the no-students rule applied to *me*? I decided to find out one evening after my last class. The days were longer now, which meant Logan had the Fire team practising longer hours – not that there was much point in me trying to join in; Stormclaw refused even to leave his paddock anymore. So much for things getting easier after the first trimester.

I was on my way down to the paddock – because there was no harm in asking, right? – when I saw Leo heading in the same direction.

"Hey, wait up!"

He looked back over his shoulder at me, and slowed his long legs, with a worried glance around. I hurried to catch up with him before he changed his mind.

"I'm not sure we should be talking," he said when I reached him.

"Blame it on me if anyone asks," I said. "Where are you going?"

His brow furrowed and his eyes turned hard.

"Oh, you came to check up on me, did you? What, Alden not riding my arse hard enough for you?"

"Whoa, easy on the conspiracy theories." I held up the headcollar I'd brought with me. "I came to see if Sir Bite-a-lot felt like not being such a mule-headed idiot today. Apparently, it's going round."

"Sir Bite-a-lot?" He raised an eyebrow and his lips quirked.

"You're forgetting the mule-headed idiot part."

He exhaled heavily and stared at the sodden ground beneath our feet. The grass never quite recovered from all the feet that tramped up and down it every day. I wondered why Alden didn't have one of the Earth elements come and coax it back to life.

"You're right," he said after a moment. "I'm sorry. It's been a long few months. Want some company?"

"Sure."

We headed the rest of the way to the paddocks in silence, and it wasn't until the herd was in sight that one of the hundreds of questions racing round my mind made it out of my mouth.

"How did you convince Alden to let you near the gryffs?" Seriously. Out of all the questions, that was the one I asked. I mean, I could have gone for a conventional, 'How are you holding up?' or a nosey, 'What will the packs do now?' or even, 'Have you heard if there have been any more attacks?' But no, I had to ask about the most trivial thing I could think of.

To my surprise, Leo chuckled.

"Turns out there's this plant in your fancy haunted grove—"

"—Unhallowed Grove."

"Whatever. This plant she'd been after when that druid kid got attacked, and she hadn't been able to find it since. I'd seen a few when I was watching the half-breed's back out there. After that, Alden took a bit of a shine to me."

"Her name is Kelsey. Wait, you *protected* her?"

He looked at me askance as I clambered over the paddock fence, then planted a hand on it and sprung over easily.

"Of course I protected her. I'm not a monster."

"Could've fooled me," I muttered under my breath as I started striding across the field.

"Fooled a lot of people," he called, and then caught up with me. Right. Werewolf hearing. Crap. I risked a glance at him, but he didn't seem bothered. And why would he? People had called him plenty worse recently.

"Anyway," he said, brushing past me, "She's sweet."

He was already in front of me by the time the words registered so I couldn't see his face, but I wasn't going to let that deter me.

"She's sweet? As in, you like her? I mean, *like* like her?"

"What are you, twelve? Yeah, I like her. Don't tell her I said anything."

"Now who's twelve?" I teased, grinning from ear to ear. Leo liked Kelsey. And I knew she'd secretly been crushing on him; I'd never heard her insult anyone as much as she insulted the shifter – or talk about them as much.

"Shut up," he said, without malice. "Which one's Mr Bitey?"

"They're gryffs, they're all bitey. But that one's Stormclaw." I nodded to the massive black beast with gold outlined feathers, standing a little apart from the rest of the herd, grooming the feathers on his mate's neck with his porcelain beak.

"That one? You're going to try to ride that one?"

"Go big or go home, right?"

He chuckled.

"And you druids say *we're* nuts. Go on, then. At least I'm here to take your mangled corpse back to the castle."

"Thanks for the vote of confidence," I muttered. "Anyway, you've met him before."

"Well, I had other things on my mind at the time, like convincing you not to go screaming to your headmaster. Besides, that was before I knew how much of an attitude he had."

"Well," I said, covering the last few feet between me and the pair of gryffs, "that's not his fault. Is it, boy?" I crooned, rubbing a hand over his chest. He puffed it out and trotted a few steps on the spot, then dropped his head to nuzzle me. "He's got other things on his mind, too."

As I spoke, the gryff's head snapped up and his bird-like eyes fixed on Leo. He blinked twice, then screeched with unmistakable fury, shaking out his wings in agitation. I lowered my hands, which had clamped themselves over my ears of their own accord, and held them out towards him, patting the air in a placating manner.

"Easy, boy, it's okay."

Stormclaw ignored me, prancing again and tearing at the soft earth under his feet. I turned to suggest that Leo should get out of here, and saw the werewolf standing absolutely still, holding eye contact with the gryff. I stepped back, out of the space between them, and watched.

Stormclaw puffed up his neck feathers and swished his long tail, loosing another deafening screech as he did, but Leo just stood there, looking far too calm for a man who was about to be – at the very least – charged by a tonne and a half of over-protective hippogryff. How far would his shifter regeneration protect him? My breath caught in my throat, trapping my warning before it could escape, and I was reduced to a spectator.

And still, Stormclaw didn't charge.

I watched in amazement as he stopped clawing at the ground, and the feathers on his neck flattened. He flapped out his wings one last time, and then tucked them back against his sides.

"What… what just happened?" I asked, as Stormclaw turned from Leo as though he wasn't there, and continued nuzzling at my pockets, looking for snacks.

"One predator recognising another," Leo said. "Is that his mate?"

He nodded to the chestnut gryff lying in the damp grass, and started towards her before I could answer.

"I wouldn't do that," I warned him, rubbing a hand across Stormclaw's shoulder and waiting for the muscle to tense in response to someone approaching his mate. Only Alden had been able to get anywhere near her without Stormclaw charging, and even then she had to keep it quick.

"It's fine," Leo said. "He knows I'm not a threat to her."

He pulled a handful of leaves from his back pocket and crouched down beside her. Stormclaw paid him no attention beyond a quick glance. How the hell had he managed that? Redwing took the leaves from his hand, and he plopped down into the grass beside her, running his hands over the ruffled feathers on her long, muscular neck. She thrummed, and leaned into his touch. *Well, I'll be damned.*

"So, are you gonna stand there all day, or are you actually going to ride that beast?" Leo said, stretching out in the grass beside his new friend. I shook off my stupor and slipped the headcollar around Stormclaw's face. I would have been surprised that he allowed it so readily, if

I hadn't already used up my daily quota of being dumbstruck.

"How about it, boy? Shall we leave Redwing alone with the big bad wolf?

I expected him to pull the rope from my hands and go back to his mate at the first suggestion of riding, same as he had every day this month, but instead he lowered his withers and raised one scaly leg to form a mounting platform.

Carefully, I climbed onto him, and perched on his withers, allowing my legs to hang down on either side of his neck, resting on the front of his massive shoulder muscles, and staying out of the way of his wings. I could feel him shivering with anticipation beneath me. A grin crept onto my face.

"Alright, Stormclaw. Let's go."

I pressed my hands to his neck and he leapt forward into a rocky canter which lasted all of four strides before he launched into the air with a flap of his massive wings. The ground fell away beneath us and I settled into the steady up and down motion as his wings bore us through the sky with effortless grace.

At first, I didn't pay any attention to where we were going – no, despite how well that had ended last time, I hadn't learned any lessons – and it wasn't until I saw other gryffs wheeling through the air in the distance than

I realised where he had taken us. We were nearing Logan and the rest of the Itealta team. My heart thudded in my chest as I watched Mason snatch the ball mid-air and swoop away, racing through the sky towards the hoop at the far end of the field. I could feel Stormclaw's excitement through my legs as he took us closer, and closer.

He wanted to play.

Not only was he letting me take him away from Redwing, he actually wanted to play Itealta. My grin doubled in size, and I urged him down towards the paddock. A cry went up and I saw Darren pointing at us as we cut through the clear grey sky.

"Lyssa!" Logan touched his white gryff, Dartalon, to the ground seconds after we landed, and trotted over. He waved enthusiastically, running an appraising eye over Stormclaw. "How did you get him out?"

I shrugged, leaping down from his back. Best not to mention Leo, I didn't want to get him into trouble. There was no way Alden had given him permission to be anywhere near the pregnant gryff.

"He just wanted to come. Where's my saddle?"

He pointed into the barn – because clearly, he'd had about as much expectation of Stormclaw making it out here as I had – and jumped off Dartalon to give me a hand hauling the heavy leather tack from its rack.

"Keep practising the liotus," he called back over his shoulder to the rest of the team, who had landed and were chattering excitedly.

"Do you think he's ready to get back on the team?" Logan asked, reaching up to grab Stormclaw's bridle. I grabbed a spare pair of reins and fitted them to the large brass hoops.

"I think so," I said. "He couldn't wait to get here today. That is, if you still want us."

Logan almost choked on air, so enthusiastically was he nodding, which was kind of flattering.

"Look," he said, setting the bridle aside and fitting some fresh stirrup leathers to Stormclaw's saddle, which shone with fresh oil despite its long disuse. "We've got one game left this season, against Water. We're tied with them for first place in the academy elemental tournament. If we beat them next month, we'll win. Please, *please,* tell me you'll be ready to ride by then."

I grinned, and scrambled up the tacking up steps beside Stormclaw, holding my hands out for his saddle.

"I like our chances." So long as Leo kept showing up, that was. "Stormclaw was born ready."

"Good. Then let's check you haven't forgotten how to catch a ball."

Chapter Twenty-One

There were just three weeks until our last game of the season, and Logan was on some sort of personal mission to make sure we didn't squander a single minute, despite my protests that end of year exams were looming, and that seeing as this was his third year, he ought to spend more time studying. Every day he had me practising until darkness fell, until I was considering lying and telling him Stormclaw refused to leave Redwing's side. Truth was, he seemed happy enough to be away from her as long as I wanted, so long as Leo was guarding his mate. Guess it came down to that predator thing. Which was great, because it felt amazing to be back on Stormclaw again. I'd missed riding. My aching muscles, on the other hand, had not.

"This is it, guys," Logan announced to the team as we all led our gryffs into the training paddock. "In half an hour, we're going to be playing our final match of the season. Win this, and we win the cup."

Like we hadn't already known that. It was all he'd talked about for the last three weeks. No pressure, right? I stifled a groan, and walked Stormclaw into the circle that was forming up in the middle of the paddock, for Logan to deliver his last pre-game pep talk of the season. His last one ever, actually, since this was his final year – although rumour was that the Essex Hornets had sent a talent scout out to watch him play today. There was more than just the cup riding on this game for him.

When we rode out onto the pitch a short while later, I couldn't keep my eyes from the roaring crowd that greeted us, wondering if one of them was the scout. I couldn't see anyone who looked like they didn't belong, but there were hundreds of people packed into the stands. I hoped he was out there, for Logan's sake. But whether he was or whether he wasn't, there was one thing we *could* control. We were going to go out there, and give it everything we had.

I caught sight of Professor Talendale in the stands with the other professors, and blanched. There was more than just the cup riding on this game for us, too. Talendale still hadn't lifted Stormclaw's death sentence – and nor would he, with the number of people he'd sent to Leech's office throughout the year – not unless I proved to him that he was reformed, and an asset to the academy.

I scratched his withers as we flew a lap of the stadium, leaning forward along his neck to whisper to him.

"Don't blow it, boy. Just show them what you can do."

His ear flickered back to me and then forward again as his wings carried us through the air with effortless grace.

"Welcome to what is bound to be the Itealta game of the season. I'm your commentator, Finn Seddon, and I'm joined by Adam Wharton. Adam, are you as excited about this game as I am?"

"You bet I am, Finn. There is literally everything to play for, and– Do my eyes deceive me, or is that Lyssa Eldridge riding out onto the green?"

"Yes it is, and she's riding Stormclaw in her first game of the season. Of course, we all remember the only game she rode in last season, and you've got to think Logan Walsh is hoping she can pull off the same stunt again and win them the cup."

"You sure do, Finn. But let's not forget there are eight players in a team, no-one likes a glory hog."

I groaned. Adam had commentated on my only game last year, and taken every opportunity to heckle me. Looked like he didn't plan to change his approach this year. The last thing I needed was for someone to call out our every mistake for Talendale to hear.

"Looks like there are no changes to the rest of the team since their last game – a reminder for anyone who hasn't been paying attention, that's Walsh, Wilcox,

Saunders, Fuller, Armstrong, Locke, and their keeper, Foster."

"And it looks like Turnell for Water is putting up the exact same team he played in the last match – Mundie, Suthers, Perkins, Hayden, Monroe, Carthy, and Keeper Gillick. But you know what they say – if it ain't broke, don't fix it."

"I don't know about that, Adam – let's not forget Hayden on the left wing is on probation for dangerous play after his last match."

Well that sounded like fun – Itealta was a fast and furious game, dangerous enough without my opposite number having a reputation for flouting the rules. Having access to near-instantaneous healing at Leech's hands was only useful if you weren't dead before she reached you. There were some things even magic couldn't fix.

I tuned out the commentators before they could psych me out completely, and focused on what I was here to do. My mouth pressed into a grim line, and I guided Stormclaw to fly up onto one of the eight raised rocky platforms around the edges of the long, rectangular pitch. At one end of it, I could see our goal – a vertical hoop high atop a metal pole. Behind me was another, but if luck went our way, we wouldn't spent too much time in that end of the field.

There was a clatter of hooves and a scratching of rock beneath taloned feet as Hayden guided his gryff to land beside us. The beast was big and heavy, making up for his lack of elegance through sheer bulk and power. His feathers were a dirty-white, and dark patches adorned his hide. I knew him: his name was Greybeak, and he was mean. His rider, perched easily astride him despite his size, looked a perfect match in both shape and temperament. He gave me a nasty sneer and edged his mount closer to mine.

A flash of movement caught my eye from the middle of the field, and I jerked my attention that way as Professor Alden, our umpire, lifted the ball high into the air. The Itealta ball, if you've never seen one, is about the strangest type of ball imaginable. Picture a beaten metal cage the size and shape of a basketball, but with four handles welded onto it, left and right, top and bottom. These gloves we were wearing weren't cosmetic – I doubted there was a single person on the pitch who hadn't broken a few dozen fingers fumbling a catch, or mistiming a grab.

The whistle blew, and Alden tossed the ball high into the air. Something thudded into my leg, and I felt Stormclaw's bulk lurch sideways as Greybeak barged into him and took to the air. With Stormclaw off balance, I did the only thing I could think of, and urged him to leap from the platform before we both fell. His wings flared as soon as we jumped, and his back levelled out. I glanced at Alden but she hadn't seen – her eyes were tracking Turnell as he snatched the ball from the air and raced towards his hoop, with Suthers on his flank.

So it was going to be like that, was it? Fine.

"Let's go, boy," I urged Stormclaw, and aimed him at the action.

"Water are off to a flying start," Finn said. "No pun intended."

"They sure are, Finn. Turnell is streaking towards the hoop, he's got his eyes set on scoring a goal in the first minute of the game. Looks like Fire are lagging behind the pace – once again proving having the fastest gryff isn't everything – there's no-one between him and the hoop, he shoots…"

"Oooh! Denied by Locke – where on earth did he come from?"

"I've got no idea, Finn, but he's streaking up the right wing. He's got a long way to go…"

Stormclaw wheeled effortlessly to race alongside the pair. Devon Locke was hunched over his gryff's neck, one hand on the reins, the other clutching the ball as he urged his animal on. He glanced right and saw me on his wing, pressed his lips together and gave me a curt nod. He took the ball into both hands and I dropped my reins, ready to catch. There was only about ten feet between us. I risked a glance forward, there were just two defenders between us and the hoop, but Stormclaw could outfly them both. I snapped my head back just in time to see Devon raise the ball, and Hayden appear on his flank. I opened my mouth to shout a warning but Hayden slammed Greybeak's shoulder into his mount just as he released the ball. It plummeted downwards and Devon was thrown sideways. He gripped his saddlehorn, his gryff flying out of control, and I hesitated for a split second, torn between chasing the ball and making sure Devon didn't fall.

A shrill whistle pierced the air, and Hayden's grin turned into a snarl that quickly vanished as Alden rode up to us.

"What on earth do you think you are doing, Hayden?"

"Sorry, Professor," he said, looking suitably chastened. "Lost control."

She eyed him for a moment then nodded.

"Try to be more careful before you cause an accident."

"I will, Professor," he said, shooting me a smirk behind Alden's back that left me in no doubt – we were going to have to watch our backs around him.

Alden restarted the game, awarding a throw-in to Fire.

"It looks like Walsh will take the throw-in," Finn said as Alden's whistle sounded. "And the ball is safely in Wilcox's hands, Lightning is living up to his name and they're flying towards the hoop. But the defenders have seen him coming, and–"

"What a steal by Monroe! The ball is back in Water hands, no, wait, that's a steal by Walsh, not the worst I've seen. Intercepted by Carthy... Fire have got to be wondering where their winger is."

I gritted my teeth and pushed Stormclaw harder, but the bigger, heavier form of Greybeak was between us and the action, blocking us from getting involved. I feigned asking him to fly higher and Greybeak rose up to block us again, but at the last second I told Stormclaw to go low, and we ducked under Greybeak's belly. I plastered myself flat to Stormclaw's neck, narrowly avoiding taking a talon to the back of the head, and then we were clear, and streaking towards the action.

"Here's Eldridge, she's coming out of nowhere – Saunders has offloaded the ball to her."

"She's got Monroe and Carthy right in front of her, will she go for the gap?"

"No, she's offloaded the ball to Walsh – rookie move."

"Walsh's at the hoop, just Gillick to beat, he shoots… he scores!"

The crowd erupted in wild cheers at the ball sailed cleanly through the hoop and plummeted to the ground on the far aside.

"A lucky shot puts Fire one-nil up as we enter the last ten minutes of the first half."

I guided Stormclaw back to our starting plinth, and Hayden glared at me as I landed.

"I'd like to see you try that again, Eldridge."

"Pfft," I waved him off. "You didn't see me the first time."

His lips curled back in a snarl, but before he had chance to retort, Alden's whistle blew and Stormclaw leapt into action. He was faster than the heavier gryff – faster than probably any other gryff in the field, and I locked eyes onto the ball. It had landed on the floor in no-man's land – I would have to touch down, lean out of the saddle to scoop it up, and take off again before anyone could snatch it from us. But we'd trained that manoeuvre to death. I could practically do it in my sleep.

The other riders were racing to the ball, but we were going to get there first. I knew, and I saw the same realisation flash across Logan's face. He turned Dartalon, pulling up just as I started my dive, ready to support us. My path clear, I dropped the reins and hooked one knee over the saddle horn, preparing to stretch my entire body down from the saddle, at speed. I felt Stormclaw's front talons slam into the ground, and a split second later, his back hooves thudded down behind them. I threw myself sideways from the saddle, only my knee around the horn holding me in place, and stretched out my hand. My fingers closed neatly around the ball's handle.

"Up!" I urged Stormclaw, but he was already rising, propelled into the air by the force of his bounce. The motion threw me back and I gripped the saddle horn with my free hand, using it to haul me back into the saddle, raised my head and suddenly there was a flash of grey in front of us. We were going to crash. I swore, still not completely back in the saddle, and dropped the ball in panic as I lunged for Stormclaw's reins to haul him round. We passed so close I felt my leg brush against Greybeak's flank, and saw Hayden's grinning face.

A flash caught my eye from below; Turnell had caught the ball and was thundering towards the hoop, unopposed by my team who'd been caught up in the dive. I raced after him, but I knew before we were even halfway there that it was no use. We were never going to catch him.

"Turnell scores for Water!" Adam shouted in glee. "One all heading into half time."

I circled Stormclaw down to the ground, breathing heavily.

"You okay?" Logan asked as I landed. I nodded.

"Yeah. I'm sorry." I dismounted and let the big beast drink his fill from one of the troughs at the edge of the pitch.

"Don't be. Hayden's playing dirty. Everyone, listen in!" He waited until he had the entire team's attention.

"That was good work. They know they're not going to beat us by playing fair, and they're getting desperate."

"Great," Darren mumbled.

"Stick to the game plan. Hold your positions, and mark your men. Watch your space. By the book, guys. Let's do it!"

We mounted up and flew back to our plinths, and Hayden was already waiting for us.

"You wanna be careful, Eldridge. It'd be a real shame if you fell and broke something."

"The only thing that's about to break is your ego."

Alden's whistle blew before either of us could get any more jibes in, and the ball flew up in the air.

"That's an impressive take by Saunders for Fire," Finn said. "Looks like they're not going to take this half lying down."

"And nor are Water – Turnell is hot on his heels, they're shoulder to shoulder, flank to flank, looks like Turnell's going for a snatch."

I watched the tussle helplessly as Turnell's brute strength overcame Josh's, and Turnell ripped the ball right out of his arms, then offloaded to Mundie heading in the opposite direction. I swung Stormclaw round to intercept, but yet again found Hayden blocking my way with that cocky grin. I tried to duck low, but he mirrored my move. I went high, and still found him in my way. Grunting in annoyance, I tried to find a way past him, but everywhere I turned, Greybeak's off-white hide was blocking my path. Fortunately, while he was tied up marking me, Mundie had no support. He made a desperate pass back to Turnell, but with a flash of shining white feathers, Logan steered Dartalon between the pair and snatched the ball right out of the air. He raced down the pitch, swerving left to dodge Carthy, right to dodge Monroe, then streaking straight for Gillick and the hoop. Dartalon pinned his wings to his side and dived for the goal, brushing straight past Gillick to give Logan a clear shot at the target.

"Logan scores again!" Finn whooped. "He is *unstoppable* today! Two-one to Fire."

Hayden made it his goal to keep me out of the action for the rest of the game, and I had to grudgingly admit that he was up to the task – if only because Greybeak snapped and clawed at Stormclaw every time it looked like we might edge past him. And, of course, he made sure that every time he took a swipe at us, it was when Alden was caught up watching the main action.

240

"We're heading into the final few minutes of the game, and Water have everything to play for. Can they equalise with Fire and force the game to go into extra time?"

"Not if Wilcox has anything to do with it," Finn replied. "He's snatched the ball... but he's got nowhere to go. Monroe and Carthy are flying in from both sides, it looks like they've got him boxed in."

I glanced around and saw they were right – then I glimpsed Logan flying just below Wilcox on his left flank. I grinned, and took Stormclaw down low, catching Hayden unawares and ducking under Greybeak's claws for the second time, touching down to the ground below Logan and off to his right flank. We'd practised this move a dozen times over the last week. Logan had designed it himself. Darren would swing across so he was almost directly above Logan, then drop the ball into his hands. Logan would do the same to me – and I would gallop Stormclaw along the ground, under the defenders, and then take off and make straight for the hoop.

That's what was meant to happen. That's what should have happened – what would have happened if we weren't playing the dirtiest team in the history of Dragondale.

Darren dropped the ball. Logan caught it and zagged right, making straight for the airspace above me. I watched his shadow on the ground, waiting for the moment it would pass almost right over my head – and suddenly there were two shadows. I looked up, and with a sinking feeling saw Greybeak racing towards Dartalon. I saw Hayden lean up Greybeak's neck and whisper something in his ear. The ear twitched back, and then the gryff banked hard, kicking out with his hind legs. One of the hooves smashed into Logan's shoulder, and there was the sickeningly loud crack of breaking bone, and a cry of pain that carried right across the pitch. Then Logan was falling, thrown from the saddle by the force of the blow, and Greybeak was swooping towards him, neck outstretched and sharp beak wide open.

Terror flooded me as I watched the falling druid and the pursuing gryff. Hayden wasn't just trying to win, he was trying to give Logan a career ending injury. Alden's whistle was giving one continuous blast, but I could barely hear it above the roaring of the crowd, Logan's shouts, and the wind rushing past my ears. I dropped my reins and threw my hands up, one at Logan, one at Greybeak. My palms glowed yellow and two gusts of air blasted out of them. The first caught under Logan, slowing his descent. The other thudded into Greybeak's chest, halting his forward progress. He screeched and flapped his wings, but the air blasting out of my palm kept him at bay while Logan drifted the rest of the way to

242

the ground, and touched down gently, safely, to the soft earth, face still creased in agony.

I lowered my hands and stared at them in shock, mouth agape.

"Lyssa Eldridge!" Alden's whip-sharp voice cracked around my ears, and I blinked her furiously into focus. "Dismount immediately! You are disqualified from competing in this match!"

"But Professor Alden–" I protested.

"No. I don't want to hear it. The rules are very clear. You do not use magic on this pitch." She glanced down at Logan, lying on the floor gripping his shoulder, and then the timer around her wrist. She put the whistle between her lips and blew it three times, signalling full time, then sighed. "Let's get Mr Walsh to the hospital wing."

Chapter Twenty-Two

Lessons with Swann went more easily after my accidental use of magic in the match – which was just as well, because with exams less than two months away, the professors were piling more work on us than ever, and I was falling so far behind in Spellcraft that I was genuinely in danger of failing, and having to repeat this year. I so did *not* want to have to repeat this year.

Officially, I was suspended from playing Itealta, but only for the rest of the semester, and since we had no more matches to play this season, I didn't even bother appealing it. I mean, I'd broken a pretty serious rule, and sure, it had been by accident – and in response to a pretty horrific foul by Hayden, at that – but I'd still broken it. If I appealed, Alden had said, it'd get escalated to the National Itealta Committee, and if it didn't go in my favour I could walk away with a ban for next season, too. There was no way I was risking that. I mean, assuming… well, Talendale hadn't made his decision yet. Assuming Stormclaw was still alive.

I tried not to pester him – if only because I figured breaking down and begging him wouldn't help our cause. It hadn't at the start of the year. Anyway, the way my luck was going, he'd probably end up expelling me for using magic on another student. No. Hard as it was, I had to accept that it was out of my hands, for now at least, and try to put it out of my mind, too. Easier said than done. That same mind was busy thinking of ways I could smuggle Stormclaw out of Dragondale, and where exactly one could hide a hippogryff in the mundane world.

"Ms Eldridge, if you're not going to pay attention, there really is no point in your taking up space in my class."

My cheeks reddened and I lifted my head from the gryffs I'd absentmindedly been doodling on top of my Botany notes to see Professor Ellerby regarding me with a look of exasperation. There were a couple of muted chuckles and I let my pencil slide through my fingers.

"Sorry, Professor," I mumbled.

"Yes, I'm sure you are," she said, shaking her head slightly in defeat. "Mr Devlin, perhaps you could tell me what the primary uses of Solerium Sithum are."

"Uh, counter-balancing Belladonna-based potions, determining sunrise, breaking emotion-enhancement spells, and, uh, as an ingredient in healing tinctures."

"Excellent, Mr Devlin," Ellerby said, and I shot him a dark look, mouthing the word 'traitor'. He just shrugged with a grin and nudged his notes towards me. I waited until Ellerby turned her back on us before I furiously scribbled them down.

"Excellent idea, Ms Eldridge. The uses of these plants will almost certainly be in your exam next month."

Damn, that woman had eyes in the back of her head. Wait, next month? I dropped my notes and started counted back on my fingers. It had been almost a month since the game – only four short weeks until our exams. Crap. I needed to study.

And yet, when Ellerby finally dismissed us, the first thing I did was make for Talendale's office. A month after the game was long enough. I climbed the ancient yet immaculate stone steps to his office. The massive wooden door was open, and I knocked once on it before entering without being invited. I'd waited long enough for Stormclaw's reprieve.

"–expect you to honour the trust I'm placing in you," Talendale was saying. "Professor Alden tells– Lyssa, what are you doing here?"

"Professor Talendale, I'm sorry, I didn't– I mean, you're busy, I should come back…"

My eyes widened as I took in the person standing in front of his desk. What was Leo doing in here? I took a faltering step toward the door. Whatever was going on was none of my business.

"Nonsense," Talendale said, rising from his seat. "I'm sure whatever you came barging into my office for is of the utmost importance."

His grey eyes searched my face, freezing my legs and pinning me in place.

"Um, well…"

"Come now, girl, speak up."

Leo shot me a wink and a grin tugged at the corner of his lips. Trust him to be amused that I was about to get a dressing down from the headmaster. Oh, well. At least I could count on him to be on Stormclaw's side.

"I was wondering if you'd made a decision about Stormclaw, sir."

"The aggressive hippogryff?"

"Stormclaw isn't aggressive!"

Leo gave the slightest shake of his head and I winced as I realised I was on the verge of shouting. Talendale had a real hang up about manners. Losing my temper was not going to help.

"I mean, sir," I said, moderating my tone and trying to look reasonable with my hands clasped in front of me, "Stormclaw's *former* aggression was part of his mating behaviour. Since Redwing has reached the final trimester of her pregnancy, his temperament has returned to normal. And I know I was stupid in the game, but Stormclaw was amazing, he did everything I asked and he wasn't aggressive to anyone. He's been an asset to this academy for years, he deserves a second chance and–"

Talendale raised a hand and I clamped my mouth shut, cutting off the tumult of words tumbling from it. I chewed my lip as I searched his face, looking for some hint, some clue that would tell me what he was thinking.

"As it happens, Ms Eldridge, I agree. On my desk is an order rescinding Stormclaw's destruction warrant – which you would have seen in the morning had you waited to hear from me as you were instructed."

"Oh." My cheeks reddened. "Um, thank you."

"Good. If that is all, I suggest you return to your studies. Professor Atherton tells me he has deep concerns about your level of competence in his subject." His attention snapped from me to Leo as though I was no longer standing there, with all of his usual brusqueness.

"As I was saying, Professor Alden has agreed that your restraints are no longer necessary. Please hold your hands over my desk."

"You're getting your cuffs off?" I blurted. "That's great."

"Are you still here, Ms Eldridge?" Talendale asked dryly, without raising his eyes from the wrists Leo had stretched over his desk.

"Um. No. Thanks, Professor."

I hurried for the door, crashing straight into a large vase and almost sending it flying. I steadied it with a hasty hand and muttered an apology, then slipped out of the office. The grin erupted all over my face before I'd made it ten steps. We'd done it! Stormclaw was going to be fine. And Leo was getting his cuffs off. Could this day get any better?

The answer to that was a resounding 'no'. I was halfway to the common room when Kelsey and Sam found me, spun me around, and directed me to the library, where she proceeded to dump about twenty books in front of me while he crammed me into one of the most uncomfortable chairs on the planet.

"What did I do to deserve this?" I said, as I stared at the mountain of textbooks on the table in front of me.

"We're not going to let you fail," Kelsey said firmly.

"Yup," Sam agreed, perched on the edge of the table and twirling a pencil in his fingers. "Third year would suck without you. Besides, whose notes would I copy for Supernatural Zoology?"

If you've never experienced a month-long academic intervention, can I just suggest you do whatever you can to avoid one? I mean, Kelsey was my best friend and all and I loved her, but damn, that girl was a slave driver who made Atherton look like an amateur. And either I was becoming crankier by the day, or she was – it was hard to say. Either way, most days ended with one of us snapping at the other, and then having to make it up again when we finally ditched the books for the night. Sam practically had a pulmonary each time one of us lost our temper, proving that he had literally no experience with women outside of us, poor man. But he soldiered on with my tutoring sessions, and probably saved one or both of our lives by making sure we both had plenty of chocolate handy. Between class and all my extra studying, I had less than an hour a day to spend with Stormclaw, which was killing me because Redwing was getting huge now. She was going to drop that foal any moment, and the closer we got, the more time I spent staring out of the library window, wishing I could be down there with her, Stormclaw, and Leo – who was basically inseparable from her outside his work duties. Even Alden had recognised how good they were for each other and permitted him to spend time around the pregnant gryff long after everyone else had been banned from going anywhere near her.

Last week, my daydreaming had annoyed Kelsey so much she'd cast a darkness spell over the window – which I would have countered, if I'd been paying enough attention to know which spell I needed – and started berating my lack of gratitude. Sam stopped our fight before anyone got hurt, but it was the full moon and we didn't get a chance to make up until the following morning. We were both a little more careful with our tempers after that. I hadn't liked going to bed with the argument hanging between us – and judging by the amount of blood she'd come back wearing, neither had she.

And then it was over. Exam week was on us, and there was no more time for studying. As usual, written exams came first: Gaelic, in which I remained half a dozen years behind most of the other students, Druidic Law, and of course History of Magic, in which I may or may not have invented the dates of a few rebellions, and made a few guesses on which wars had been influenced by the use of magic. I got a little creative on the industrial revolution, too, because that had definitely got a mention in one of the books Kelsey had practically rammed down my throat.

Things picked up after that. Practical work had always been more my thing than theory.

This year, Zoology had both theory and practical elements. I breezed through the practical stuff – most of which revolved around handling the gryffs, and even the theory test wasn't too horrific. It was harder than last year; we were expected to identify pictures of over two dozen different native creatures, put them in order of most to least dangerous, and justify our decision.

"What did you put for the shug monkey?" Sam said, as we all shuffled out of the exam hall, some of us looking more traumatised than others. "More dangerous than the gilled antelope, or less?"

"Depends how you feel about poison barbs," I said, a little absent-mindedly: I was watching Paisley, who'd been edging closer to Felicity all day. So far, the blonde had steadfastly ignored her – looking straight through her former friend as though she wasn't there, and Paisley was becoming increasingly desperate.

This time, Felicity turned her back with a swish of her long hair, almost hitting Paisley in the face with it. The hybrid ignored the snub and reached out with a hand to touch her on the shoulder.

"Get away from me, you freak!" Felicity shrieked, turning to glare furiously at Paisley, who went bright red.

"Felicity, please! It's still me, I haven't changed."

"If you touch me again," Felicity said, her mouth contorted in a snarl that made her face look as ugly as her soul, "my father will demand Talendale has you expelled. You shouldn't even be here. You could infect anyone with your filthy disease."

Paisley's face fell and Felicity brushed straight past her, making sure to knock her shoulder into the girl hard enough to make her take a step back. Unfortunately for Felicity, her little tirade took her in my direction.

"Hey, airhead," I said, stepping out and blocking her path. "You've been spreading your filth all over the place for the last two years, and no-one's banned you yet. What gives?"

She looked me up and down, and her face took on its customary sneer that she reserved for us lesser mortals.

"The academy exists for druids like me. It's not here for half-breeds and the likes of you. How much of an education to you really need for a future of cleaning out stables?"

"As opposed to rolling around in them with every guy who looks at you?"

I know, I know, slut-shaming is a low blow, but dammit she makes it so *easy*. What's a girl supposed to do?

"Careful, Felicity," I said, as her face turned bright red and her hands curled into fists at her sides. "That colour really doesn't match your hair, and what have you got if not your looks?"

Her fists curled and a nasty smile spread over her heart-shaped face.

"Only good breeding, money... and a future. What's your breeding like? Oh, you still don't know, do you? Your mother must have been an alley cat."

For a moment, I allowed myself the deeply satisfying image of smashing my fist into her perfectly straight nose. Still, tempting as it was, it would probably get me expelled, which seemed like a waste of the torture I'd been through over the last month, so I forced a relaxed smile onto my face.

"The future? Look around, Felicity. The alley cats and the nobodies outnumber you, and that high horse you're riding has an expiry date. The future belongs to us."

"Hmph, in your dreams," she said, but she couldn't quite hide the uncertainty in her eyes as she stepped around me. I let her go – I'd made my point.

"Hey, Paisley," I called – because half our year group were watching, and I felt like I should do something to undermine Felicity's snobbery. "Wanna join us for lunch before Spellcraft?"

Or, you know, turn me into a shifter so I had an excuse to ditch this afternoon's exam. But I figured it wasn't the moment for that sort of joke, so I kept it to myself, and a large group of us headed off to the main hall, and no-one objected when Paisley sat at our table.

Spellcraft was a nightmare. I think I'd actually rather have faced down the zombie Raphael raised last year all by myself than sit in front of Atherton, attempting the half-dozen spells that made up the exam – but sadly it turned out that wasn't an option. My hippogryff illusion looked like a squat donkey with wings, my serenity spell had resulted in a seriously pissed off wasp dive-bombing my face, and although my fog spell *seemed* to work, Atherton scribbled down a whole lot of notes, which made me think I'd probably overlooked something important.

The following day was Elemental Manipulation with Swann. Since I now had three elements, I had to sit three exams, which seemed a bit like victimisation to me. I mean, I hadn't *asked* for all these extra powers. No-one else had to sit three exams. Deeply unfair.

For Fire, we had to hold a sheet of paper in one hand, and then conjure a fireball in the same hand, without burning the paper. I noted a couple of singed sheets behind her, and one that was nearly completely charred – probably a student who had Fire as a second. My sheet, I noted with maybe just a little smugness, was completely white and undamaged.

My other elemental exams weren't so good. Same trick, but with a water ball. Let's just say that my sheet got a little on the soggy side... as did my hand, my shoes, and somehow, Swann's sleeve. I think I was focussing so much that it all just kinda... exploded.

Air was a little different. A circle of eight small pillars, each with a pile of tiny feathers on top of them. I had to blow all the feathers off, leaving one feather on the first pillar, two on the second, and so on. Let's just say I didn't envy the person who had to clean up after the exams, and leave it at that.

Friday was our final two exams – Botany and Potions, and they were to be a combined exam. In the morning, we would have to harvest all the herbs and ingredients required to make a specific potion, whilst explaining in what conditions they grew, and how they should be harvested to maximise their magical potential. In the afternoon, we would have to use those ingredients to create the potion.

"Right, Lyssa," Professor Ellerby said, rolling herself up onto the balls of her feet and back down again, whilst tapping a pen against the clipboard in her hand. "Today you will be brewing the Dathanium potion."

Well, the good news was, I'd actually heard of the Dathanium potion. The bad news was, I'd never made it before, and had only a vague notion of how it was done.

"When you're ready, you may enter the greenhouse. Once you step inside, you'll have twenty minutes to gather everything you need. I cannot identify any of the plants for you, however if you cannot find something you require, I can give you the row number on which you'll find it. Please explain the properties of each ingredient you collect. Do you understand?"

I nodded. Twenty minutes. That wasn't long, not when I still wasn't completely sure what I needed. Hopefully I'd find some inspiration inside. I looked up at the massive greenhouse, which I knew to cover about half an acre. It had just about anything a druid could ever want inside – you know, if said druid had an idea of what it looked like.

I took a breath and placed my hand on the door. Dathanium potion. Hallow Flax, Dusk Grass, and Climbing Gilliflower – I definitely needed those. Solerium Sithum, maybe? Or was it Thecreptum? Behind me, Ellerby coughed into her hand. I took the hint, pushed the door open, and stepped inside.

The heat and humidity hit me immediately, momentarily driving my shopping list from my mind as I took in a lungful of the heavily scented air. Ellerby clicked the door shut behind me and I forced myself to focus. Solerium Sithum was an embryophyta, and if I remembered correctly, that meant it should be pretty near the front, somewhere over on the left. I scanned the tall rows and benches until I picked out a cluster of leafy green plants, squatting low to the floor, with their segmented leaves splayed around them. I made right for them, trying to ignore Ellerby as she followed in my wake.

There were over two dozen of the plants, and to me they all looked identical. Too bad I didn't have an earth power – sure would be nice to be able to sense which of the plants was most ready to be harvested. I was sure there was something about the underside of their leaves... or was that Creeping Milkweed? I considered it for a moment, but if I wanted to get all of the ingredients I needed, I didn't have time to examine each plant for something that might not even be on any of them. I plucked a couple of leaves from one, and glanced around for something to put them in, which was when I remembered the harvesting sacks that were generally kept just behind the door. Crap. This was shaping up into the worst game of Supermarket Sweep ever.

I shoved the leaves into one of my cloak's pockets. I had to head back by the doors for the Hallo Flax anyway, but I wanted to get the Climbing Gilliflower first, and I was going to need both my hands for that.

Belatedly, I remembered Ellerby, and turned to see her watching me expectantly, pen poised above the clipboard.

"Uh, Solerium Sithum leaf, used for healing tinctures, breaking emotional-enchantments, and counteracting nightshade. Best harvested under a full moon, with, um..." Oops. "A silver blade."

Good job the Solerium Sithum was pretty hardy. I moved on, scanning the rows as I went. The Gilliflower should be somewhere round here, I saw it when I was in here a couple of weeks ago. I paused at the head of the next round, then went down it.

"Five minutes gone," Ellerby said.

Five minutes? How the hell had five minutes passed already? I picked up my pace, talking as I went.

"I'm going to get Climbing Gilliflower, used for... Well, used for the Dathanium potion." I heard the scratching of Ellerby's pen, and muttered under my breath, "I hope."

I spotted the plant – a creeper – stretching along one of the glass panels, from floor to ceiling, and about eight feet wide. Arrow-shaped leaves sprouted from green vines that varied in size from the width of my finger to the width of my forearm, and were studded generously with thorns. Here and there, small yellow flowers grew, protected by the protrusions. I reached out to pluck one, then paused.

"The most potent flowers," I recalled aloud, "grow between curved thorns, not straight ones. The bigger the thorns, the better – too much sunlight damages the flower."

Huh. I guess all that studying Kelsey made me do had paid off. Ellerby grunted in what I took to be approval, and made a note of something. Wishing I'd had the foresight to bring gloves, I carefully worked my fingers between a trio of thorns, each longer than my thumb, reaching for the small yellow flower behind them. One of the thorns scratched my finger, scoring a red line. A drop of blood leaked from the wound and onto the flowerhead. Dammit. Well, I sure as hell wasn't going to try to grab another one. I'd just have to hope that the blood didn't royally bugger up my potion.

Aware of the clock ticking, I spun on the spot, and doubled back the way I'd came, past the entrance where I snatched up one of the harvesting sacks – a hessian sack that was made up of five separate compartments inside. I dropped the yellow flower into the smallest one, and sealed it inside with a quick binding spell at the top of the pouch, then skidded round the next corner. Behind me, Ellerby's booted feet struck the floor at a slower pace, but if I was going to get everything I needed, I couldn't afford to wait for her. I snatched a few leaves from a Bregon Lotus plant as I passed, calling some mostly made-up details back to Ellerby, crammed them into the sack, and as an afterthought, pulled open one of the propagation drawers stacked up by the wall. I couldn't remember if I needed toadstools or not, but it couldn't hurt to have them. They went into the bag, too, along with some Faux Bark, the Hallow Flax, a few blades of Dusk Grass, and a handful of the soil that a Weeping Dewberry was growing in.

"Time is up, Ms Eldridge," Ellerby said as I rattled off some facts about the ingredients – some of which might actually have been true. I exhaled heavily, and handed over the bag for her inspection. She walked with me back to the entrance, then bent her head conspiratorially towards mine.

"Nice work blooding the Gilliflower. Not many people would have thought of that. I didn't know you were a fan of Zenna Sephiran's work."

Chapter Twenty-Three

I could tell you that I breezed through the Potions portion of the exam – but I'd be lying. I'm pretty sure my potion wouldn't have killed anyone, though, which was more than could be said for Liam's.

Still, by the end of the day I was beyond exhausted. I'd planned to go and hang out with Stormclaw, but the light was already starting to fade and Talendale's ban on moving around the grounds after dark was still in effect. Which was ridiculous, of course – with portalling being banned, there was no way the rogue shifter could get back into the academy. But rules were rules, and it didn't pay to get caught breaking them. I headed up to the common room, but Sam had turned in for an early night, along with most of our year, and Kelsey was nowhere to be seen, and I didn't much fancy sitting still, so I took a wander round inside the castle.

And then I got lost. Obviously.

I'd thought I was past that. I'd thought that once I ceased to be a lowly first year, I'd somehow magically know my way around the castle. I'd thought that it would just kinda fall into place. In short, I was an idiot.

I don't know how long I *stayed* lost, but it was long enough that the castle had that peculiar stillness to the air, the one that falls over a place in the thick of the night, filling it with silence and unearthly tranquillity.

There were no professors patrolling the cold stone corridors, no students sneaking along them with hushed whispers or excited giggles. It would have been eerie, if not for the fireballs flicking near the ceiling, casting their comforting light and shadows across the barren walkways.

No, scratch that. It *was* eerie, eerie as hell, and if someone had grabbed my shoulder as I crept along, I'd have screamed like a little girl. I know, because they did, and I did.

"Easy, druid girl, jumpy much?"

"Jesus Christ, Leo!" I slapped both of my palms into his chest, covered by a thin white t-shirt, then when my heart slowed to something south of two hundred beats a minute, I peered up at him, narrowing my eyes with suspicion. "What are you doing creeping around down here?"

Wherever the hell down here was.

"Right back at you, druid girl," he said, then raised his hand to cut off my reply. "Actually, forget it, we don't have time. I was tracking you."

A cold dread started at the base of my spine and crept steadily upwards. Leo, as ever, seemed oblivious.

"Why?"

"You're not going to want to miss this, trust me."

"Miss what?" My dread turned to confusion, and I didn't budge when he tugged on my elbow. He rolled his eyes.

"Redwing's in labour."

"She's having the foal?"

"That's what in labour means, isn't it? Come on, or we'll both miss it. Only, let's go back the short way, yeah?"

"How the hell do you know your way around the castle better than I do?" I cocked a hip and put one hand on it, but he totally ignored me and set off at a jog. I didn't want to be left behind here – still having no idea where 'here' was – and I sure as heck didn't want to miss the birth, so I caught him up and stayed alongside him as he ran along the corridors, up a set of steps and through the lobby, out into the grounds. It was just as well I'd stuck to Logan's brutal fitness regime, or I'd never have kept up with Leo, what with him having shifter stamina and all.

It was dark outside, with only a sliver of moonlight to guide us in its fleeting glimpses from behind the clouds, but of course that sort of thing didn't bother Leo, so I just followed in his footsteps and hoped there were no potholes or protruding tree roots. Through luck or divine intervention, we made it to the paddocks intact, with the notable exception of my lungs. I bent over, hands on my knees, and tried to catch my breath.

"No time for that," Leo said, grabbing the back of my cloak and hauling me upright. As he did, what little moon there was cast its light across the field, which was empty except for two figures, one prone, and one standing. Redwing and Stormclaw.

We climbed the fence and headed over to them, moving more cautiously than before, because nothing spooked a gryff like a human and a shifter running full pelt towards them, and spooked gryffs tended to bite first, and ask– Well, no, that was pretty much it.

"Hey, boy," I called, as we neared the pair. "It's me."

He lowered his head in greeting, then Redwing writhed on the floor, letting out a noise that was half-grunt, half-squeal.

"Do you think she's okay?" I asked, my voice thick with anxiety.

"How would I know? I'm not a hippogryff midwife!"

"And you didn't think it might be a good idea to get Alden?"

"Do you think either of these would have let her anywhere near them?" he countered. He had a point. The pair of them had been increasingly moody over the last few days. Even the other gryffs had been moved to another paddock, to prevent a fight breaking out.

Redwing loosed another braying squeal and I could see her flanks heaving with exertion. I gasped.

"Is that… Look, it's a foot!"

It was. One scaly foot had been pushed out, surrounded by a white amniotic sack. The talon was pointed downwards, which was a good sign. Up would have been dangerous for Redwing, and would mean that the foal was in the wrong position – and I didn't like anyone's chances of getting close enough to help if she got distressed.

I watched in fascinated silence as a second foot pushed its way out, and then a curved beak edged out between the foal's knees. Redwing grunted again, and Stormclaw clawed at the soft earth under his feet, snorting loudly. The mare gave him a glare that needed no interpretation and he backed off a pace, eyeballing her and shaking out his wings.

"Ever the gentleman," I muttered under my breath.

Another push saw the foal's shoulders emerge, and then Redwing stretched out, panting heavily.

"What's wrong with her?" Leo tensed to push himself out of his crouch and I grabbed his wrist before he could get himself kicked, trampled or bitten.

"She's resting," I said, keeping my voice low. "It's not easy giving birth, you know."

"Got much experience of that, have you?"

He had me there, so I ignored him and kept my eyes on the chestnut gryff as she steeled herself, and pushed again. The foal was almost out. Just a few more pushes… My breath caught in my throat as a tiny pair of wings emerged, pressed flat to the foal's sides, and then its hips, and then finally, with one last heave, Redwing pushed the foal's back legs out, and lurched to her feet, trembling and sweating with exertion.

Stormclaw took a tentative step towards the tiny heap in its sack, watching Redwing, but she had eyes only for the foal. Between them, they tore at the amniotic sack with their sharp beaks, and I waited for the foal to take its first breath.

And waited.

"Something's wrong," I said, my voice trembling with fear. "Why… Why isn't it moving?"

Beside me, Leo shook his head, but I could hear him muttering under his breath.

"Come on, come on, breathe, dammit…"

Redwing nuzzled the foal, then butted him harder with her beak, but the small, dark shape didn't move as it lay on the wet grass, flanks still.

The mare let loose a long, low keening wail that sent a shiver through me. I'd never heard such a sad, haunting sound in my life, and hoped I'd never hear it again. My eyes burned hot, and when I looked at Leo, I had to blink several times before I could see him properly. He turned to me, his face solemn. We both knew what that sound meant. It was a sound of mourning.

His lips pressed into a grim line, and he shook his head fiercely, once, and pushed himself to his feet. He took a step towards Redwing and she spun to glare at him, shaking out her wings and screeching in rage. She took a step, planting herself firmly between him and her foal's body.

"Shh, easy girl," he said, and Stormclaw locked an ear onto him, puffing out his chest in the semi-darkness.

"Uh, Lyssa?" Leo said, his voice not quite calm. "Little help?"

"What are you doing?"

He answered without taking his eyes from the chestnut gryff.

"I spent a bit of time on a farm last spring. Sometimes when lambs are born, they get fluid blocking up their airways. If the farmer got there in time, he could usually save them."

"That's not a lamb," I said dubiously, getting to my feet.

"I know," Leo said, his eyes tracking the massive red gryff's movements.

"And you're not a farmer." I took a step closer, but her attention didn't leave the werewolf.

"I know."

"But you still think this will work?"

I could just about make out the small shake of his head.

"I don't know. Maybe. What've we got to lose?"

"Aside from our lives?" I muttered, but I started towards Redwing, hoping to get her attention on me for long enough for Leo to do whatever he could. She snorted, and shifted her weight back onto her haunches. Her neck snaked forwards and her sharp beak snapped at the air in front of my face. I froze.

"Hey. Hey, girl," Leo said, drawing her attention back onto him. "Come on, stay with me."

She twitched her ears, looking from me to Leo, and she took a tentative step towards him.

"Leo, what are you doing?"

"One of us has to keep her busy, and she doesn't seem too keen on you right now. Get to the foal."

"But I don't know what I'm doing!"

He didn't answer me, which was all the answer I needed. He was right. We were going to get one shot at this, and I couldn't afford to waste time panicking. I crept round her, staying out of reach of her claws and hooves, until I could see the dark form lying on the remains of the amniotic sack. A loud snort made me jump, and I flicked my eyes up to see Stormclaw watching me reproachfully.

"Steady, boy, I'm going to help." *I hope.*

A few seconds passed without him trying to remove any of my limbs, so I took a shaky breath of the cold night air, and crouched down beside the foal. *Poor little thing.* I could make out every detail; the tiny yellow talons and scaly front legs, jet black feathers plastered flat to its small frame, and wet hair covering its back end, with a small tuft of tail hair. It was so perfect. But utterly still.

"Okay," I said, my voice a breathy whisper. "Leo, what do I do?"

"Pick the foal up," he said. "By its back legs. Have you got it?"

Pick it up? I shot him an incredulous look that was wasted because Redwing was still between us. He obviously hadn't taken into account that this was a gryff foal, not a lamb. Even newborn, it was the size of a Great Dane, and not all of us had werewolf strength.

"Lyssa? You need to get its body higher than its head, have you done it?"

Body higher than its head. But how? I glanced at Stormclaw and narrowed my eyes. *Got it.*

"Stormclaw." I clicked my tongue softly a couple of times and patted the floor beside me. He quirked his head, blinking one bird-like eye at me, then sank to the ground.

"Good boy. Wait there."

I gave his withers a quick scratch, then yanked the cord from my cloak, and hastily tied it around the foal's back feet. *I hope to hell this works.* I grabbed the other end of the cord and hauled it over Stormclaw's back. He snorted softly and rolled an eyeball at me, but stayed where he was. I wrapped the cord around my wrists and planted my feet firmly on the ground.

"Alright, boy. Stand."

With a rustle of feathers, he lurched to his feet. I grunted as I felt the foal's body lift up from the floor, and leaned back, putting all my weight onto the cord.

"Alright," I grunted. "Now what?"

"Open its mouth and clear its airway."

"What? How the hell am I supposed–"

I cut off as an idea hit me.

"Stormclaw, lift your leg."

He craned his neck round and squinted at me. I rolled my eyes. I swear he knew more than he was letting on.

"Come on. Like when you help me mount. Mount up."

He exhaled in a sharp white cloud, then lifted one front leg, tucking it up behind his body and balancing on the other three. I wrapped the cord around his thick leg and was about to tie it off when he clacked his beak at me in disapproval, and gripped the rope in his talon.

271

"Smartass," I grumbled, then ducked under his neck to the foal. How long did we have if this was going to work? It had to be at least two minutes since the foal had been born, maybe three. I tilted the foal's head and then worked two fingers into the corner of its beak and pulled it open, pushing my fingers inside its still-warm mouth. A trickle of fluid dribbled out and onto the floor. Its chest stayed unmoving.

"It didn't work!"

"Try swinging it. And hurry up, she's getting restless."

Right. No pressure, then. I slid one hand under the foal's head and the other around its shoulders, and started swinging it backwards and forwards. The cord creaked loudly under my efforts. I had no idea how long a standard cloak cord could support the weight of a Great Dane-sized hippogryff foal, but hopefully a bit longer. I pulled the foal higher up and tried another, faster swing. The foal's beak popped open and a stream of fluid gushed out and splashed on the floor. Its whole frame shuddered as it dragged in a wheezing breath, and then its eyelid twitched, and opened.

"It worked! Leo, it worked!"

"Alright, no need to wake the neighbours. Lie it back flat."

Right. I was trying to work out how to ask Stormclaw to open his talon when the foal crashed to the floor, trailing a frayed piece of cord. Luckily it hadn't had far to fall. I loosened the loop around its back legs and slipped it off past its hooves, which were already starting to kick weakly.

A rustle of feathers interrupted the air and then Redwing was towering above me, staring down at me with her chest puffed out and wings held aloft. She screeched, and then something caught her eye. She quirked her head and blinked, then clacked her beak softly and stretched her neck down to the foal.

I backed away a dozen steps back to Leo, and squatted down in the grass beside him as Redwing nuzzled her foal onto its feet.

"Do you think it'll be okay?" I asked. He nodded.

"He's a fighter, and he's got tough parents."

"He?"

"Or she," he said with a shrug.

We settled back and watched as the baby hippogryff stumbled around, growing more confident with each step. The two adult gryffs plucked worms from the soft each and fed them to the young foal, who devoured them greedily and let out a high-pitched screech, demanding more.

"Come on," Leo whispered, tugging lightly on my sleeve. "Let's go."

I glanced at the three gryffs, and back to Leo. He was right. This was a time for them to be alone. We rose slowly and backed away from the small family, and climbed out of the paddock.

"That was amazing," I said, my face splitting into a grin.

"Yeah, it was pretty cool," Leo agreed with a shrug that I could just about make out in the pale moonlight.

"Pfft, pretty cool. I saw your face back there."

"What can I say – I'm a werewolf. I have to remain manly at all times."

"Then you probably shouldn't tell anyone about how you squealed when it took its first step."

"Let's get one thing straight, druid girl. I do not squeal."

"Oh, it must have been one of the other werewolves then. Maybe—"

"Shut up."

"What, the manly werewolf can't take a bit of banter?"

"Sshhh!"

He held his arm in front of me, blocking my path, and the urgency in his tone finally caught up with me.

"What is it? What's wrong?" I hissed, scanning the darkness. And then I heard it; a single, high-pitched note in the night air. "Was that... Is someone screaming?"

"Well, I might be able to tell if you'd stop talking." He rolled his eyes, and cocked an ear into the darkness. "This way, come on."

"Wait!" I grabbed the back of his t-shirt. "That could be anything out there."

"Don't worry," he said, giving me a cocky smile. "I'll protect you."

"Please," I snorted. "I was just worried your ego might never recover if you have to be saved by a girl."

I took off at a sprint, trying not to fall over any stray rocks, or tree roots, or frankly my own feet. Leo easily outstripped me and I followed as close behind him as I could, until I could make out the faint outline of a person, no, two people... No, a person and... an animal?

I skidded to a walk and tried to process what I was seeing. On the floor, scrambling backwards, was a person; a girl, her face white with terror. Stalking towards her, a large wolf, its body covered in slabs of heavy muscle, not quite concealed by its shaggy coat, monochrome in the moonlight. Triangular ears were pinned flat to its skull, and its lips were pulled back into a snarl, revealing a row of razor-sharp canines.

A werewolf. And not just any werewolf. I'd seen that werewolf before.

It was Kelsey.

Chapter Twenty-Four

One look at Leo told me he recognised her, too. There was no mistaking the reddish tint to her coat.

"I don't get it," I said, glancing up at the sky and back again. "It's not a full moon!"

"Does she look like she's in control to you?" Leo said, not taking his eyes from the feral beast that was my best friend. No, she didn't look in control, no more than she had that day all those months ago, when she'd shifted in the storage room, and Underwood had saved us. But Underwood wasn't here now.

"What do we do? She's going to kill her!"

"Pl… Please," whimpered the girl on the floor, and I recognised her vaguely as one of the third years from Earth – I'd seen her in the main hall a couple of times, her blonde hair framing her face, high cheekbones accentuated by expertly applied make-up. Now her hair was in disarray, and her face was streaked with dirt. Tears reddened her eyes as she begged, "Don't let it bite me."

A flash of movement caught my eye; Leo was pulling his t-shirt off. I stared at him.

"What? It's not like I have a whole lot of clothes."

"Leo, she'll kill you."

"Honey," he said, tugging his trainers from his feet, "She's not the only big bad wolf round here."

I rolled my eyes. The 'honey' comment was enough for me to let him get shredded, but he was right. He was bigger, more powerful, and better trained. If any of us could stop her, he could.

"Get the girl out of here," he said, unzipping his jeans. "As soon as Kelsey's attention is on me."

I didn't waste time arguing. The moment Leo started his shift, Kelsey's head whipped round, her yellow eyes locking onto the new threat. Leo's wolf form was a full two inches taller than hers, his coat jet black and shorter than her shaggy red fur, revealing his more-defined muscle beneath the pale moonlight. Where she moved with pure aggression, he moved with pure intent. Every step was careful, controlled, as he stalked towards the she-wolf. She snarled at him, warning him from her prey, but Leo didn't so much as flinch.

Her prey.

Oh my God. The realisation struck me like a physical blow, knocking the air from my lungs. All those attacks, they'd been Kelsey. On the mundanes. On Paisley. Kelsey had been the one creating new werewolves. She'd broken the ancient laws. She'd destroyed people's lives.

I shook my head, trying to scatter the fog that had settled inside it. She hadn't known what she was doing.

Look at her, she wasn't in control. I doubted she'd even remember any of this in the morning. Kelsey would never intentionally hurt anyone. Wolf-Kelsey, on the other hand, clearly had no such reservations, as she advanced on Leo, hackles raised, lips pulled back to reveal those gleaming white fangs.

I beckoned frantically to the third year on the floor, but she didn't move, frozen with terror. Dammit. She'd probably never even seen a werewolf before, and now two were about to fight it out in front of her. *Dammit!*

I edged towards her, keeping my eye on the pair of feral beasts. No, not pair... Kelsey was feral, but Leo was still careful, controlled. No less deadly. For the first time, I was starting to understand why most druids feared shifters.

As soon as I reached the girl, I stretched out a hand to her, taking hold of her arm. A startled scream burst from her lips, and Kelsey's head snapped back round towards us. Shit. Leo loosed a growl that chilled my blood, but the she-wolf ignored him. Her attention was fixed on me now. I froze, still holding the girl's arm. If I ran, she would chase. But if I stayed still, I was as good as dead, anyway.

Sensing my indecision, the wolf reacted instinctively, launching herself at us. I threw my hands up, and a gust of air burst from them, smashing into the wolf mid-air,

278

and sending her tumbling backwards. She was on her feet the second she hit the ground, and she rounded on us again. I kept my hands outstretched, wondering how many times I could do that before I was completely drained. I didn't get the chance to find out.

A dark shape smashed into the she-wolf from behind, colliding with her hind quarters and spinning her round. The momentum of the attack brought her head round to face her attacker, and her teeth had started snapping at him in the same split-second. I heard a grunt, unmistakably of pain, from Leo – one of her bites had landed.

The fight was fast and furious, punctuated by snarls, grunts and yelps, with teeth and claws flashing in the dark mass of aggression as the pair locked together in combat; a raging ball of fury.

I ripped my eyes away and tugged again on the girl's arm.

"Come on, we've got to move. Now."

I pulled her to her feet and started to tow her away. Her eyes were blank, still dazed, and she stumbled over her own feet. I snapped my fingers in front of her face.

"Hey!"

She blinked several times rapidly.

"What's your name?"

"Kendra," she said, darting looks between me and the pair of wolves. I couldn't even tell who was winning anymore, and I was torn with indecision all over again. What if Leo needed my help? I set my jaw. I couldn't help him and protect Kendra at the same time. I had to get her out of here.

"Listen to me, Kendra. We need to get back to the castle. I'm going to help you."

"How? They'll attack us!"

Her voice was bordering on hysterical and I sucked in a breath of the cold night air, forcing myself to stay calm. We couldn't afford to both lose it right now.

"The black one is on our side. He'll protect us."

"But… it's a werewolf!" She clutched at my arm, her fingers digging into my skin.

"You *know* Leo. You saw him shift to save you."

Her eyes snapped back to me, and she nodded, getting some sort of grip on her terror.

A yowl of pain erupted from the fighting pair, and my legs weakened. Which of my friends had been hurt?

I couldn't afford to think like that… but I couldn't leave them, either. Change of plan. I spun Kendra round to face me.

"I'm going to stay here and help. You need to get back to the castle, as quickly as you can. Get the professors."

What blood was left in her face drained, leaving her pale as a corpse as she stared at me in horror.

"Alone? I... I can't."

"Yes, you can," I told her firmly, turning her shoulders again so she was pointing in the direction of the castle.

"You're going to run, and you're not going to look back, and you're not going to stop running until you find help. I'll make sure no-one follows you. Go!"

I shoved her between the shoulder blades, hard, and she took off like a greyhound, racing across the dark grounds of the academy. I heard a snarl of fury from behind me; Kelsey had seen her prey escaping.

Leo wasted no time punishing her distraction. His teeth snapped shut around her shoulder, gripping the muscle in his powerful jaws. She howled in pain and tried to spin around, but his bulk held her pinned in place. Her feet kicked out at him but her claws couldn't find any purchase. He'd done it! He had her under control. He just had to hold onto her until Kendra reached the professors. I hoped she was a fast runner.

Maybe Kelsey had the same thought, or maybe her feral rage was so consuming that she was oblivious to the damage Leo's teeth were inflicting on her hide, and incapable of submitting. She threw herself sideways, this time *into* the male wolf, sending the pair of them crashing to the ground. There was a grunt as the impact knocked the air from Leo's lungs, and his grip loosened. Red fur slipped through white fangs, and then she was free. She regained her feet in a flash, while Leo lay still, stunned. The pale moonlight gleamed on the dark wet patch slicking her fur, but she paid it no attention as she snapped and ripped at the prone wolf's body.

"Leave him alone!" The words burst from my lips with no solid plan – born of panic, not intention.

Her head lifted, blood dripping from her muzzle. Amber eyes locked onto me, and her lupine face contorted with feral rage. A cold terror flooded my limbs as she broke away from the fight, and started to advance on me. Behind her, Leo growled and struggled to his feet. There was no mistaking the way he was favouring his right hind leg. Blood slicked his pelt in at least a dozen places, and each step seemed to pain him. He was injured and moving more slowly than she was. A lot more slowly.

I threw up my hands, aiming another gust at her… and nothing happened. Shit, shit, now was *not* the time for my powers to fail me! I tried again. Still nothing. I started backing away, fighting the deep-seated instinct that was screaming at me to run, because there was no way I could outrun a werewolf. Without my powers, I was finished.

A flash of light caught my periphery, and I risked a glance in its direction. Was that… was that a *portal?* But…

how was there a portal? My mind raced, trying to understand what my eyes were seeing. Kendra! It had to be. She must have reached the professors. One of them had sent a portal. I backed towards it, waiting for Underwood or one of the others to step out of it... but no-one came through.

Maybe whichever professor Kendra had found had gone to look for the others. That had to be it. They'd sent the portal to get us out of danger, while they got enough people together to contain Kelsey. We needed to escape through it.

"Leo!"

His eyes broke from Kelsey, snapping to the portal, and then to me. His head dipped in an unmistakable nod. I would go through the portal. He would follow. He'd damn well better follow, or I'd come right back for him. I wasn't leaving him here to fight alone. I tried to put all of that in my expression, and then glared at him. If wolves could roll their eyes, he would have. As it was, he managed to put all his amusement and cockiness into a single look, and directed it at me.

I would just have to trust him not to do anything stupid. It was a stretch.

I took another step towards the portal, and then I realised that Leo staying behind wasn't an issue... because Kelsey was going to follow me through. What if I led her into the middle of a crowded corridor? What if she attacked someone? I risked another glance back over my shoulder at the portal. Relief rushed through me. The floating doorway didn't show me a crowded corridor. It showed a stone room with chains and bars, bars just about wide enough for a small human to squeeze through, but not a werewolf. It was one of the academy's dungeons. The professor had set the portal to take us away from the rest of the students. They wanted us to lead Kelsey into an ambush. Okay. I could do that.

"Hey, Kelsey," I said, locking eyes with the beast as I took another step towards the portal. It was only a few feet behind me now. Four steps, at the most. "Here, puppy, puppy."

I turned, and sprinted with everything I had. One step. Two steps. I could hear her pounding after me, hear Leo's injured gait lumbering behind her. Three steps. She snarled with fury and her teeth snapped at empty air. One more step. I lunged for the portal, aiming myself at the wide doorway, and hoping like hell she didn't land right on top of me.

My feet hit the ground on the far side, and I raced forward, towards... nothing. There was no cage, no dungeon, no castle, just a crumbled set of ruins, and a single cloaked figure standing amongst them.

The figure pulled back his hood, and my heart sunk. I'd just walked into a trap.

Raphael's trap.

Chapter Twenty-Five

A thud sounded behind me and for a second I forgot about Raphael – I had more immediate problems. I dived left, hitting the ground hard and rolling. I twisted over onto my back and threw up my hands, praying my air powers would return in time to stop my best friend shredding me into confetti. Tingles rushed through my hands as I braced myself for the attack.

Several things happened at once. Kelsey launched herself through the air towards me. Leo landed on our side of the portal, snarling and dragging his injured leg behind him, and immediately collapsed. Raphael raised one hand and spoke a word I didn't hear. Glowing blue bars made of pulsing energy sprung into existence and encircled Kelsey, trapping her in a small cage. Leo changed back into his human form. And the portal blinked out of existence, trapping us all with the most powerful druid Dragondale had ever seen.

I scurried to Leo's side, staring at him in horror. His body was a mass of wounds, blood pumping from his thigh, his arms, his torso. I crouched over him, and stretched my fingers tentatively to his neck. He still had a pulse. Just.

Raphael lowered his hand, and took a step forward. I twisted my head round to look up at him.

"Lyssa. I'm so glad you could join me."

"What do you want?" My voice shook with fear or fury; I could no longer tell one from the other.

"To talk." He waved a hand dismissively, and a pair of ornately carved tree trunks sprang into existence, pushing up through the soft earth. He sat on one of them, and beckoned to the other. I looked at him like he was insane. He must be. I said the first thing that came into my mind.

"What's wrong with picking up a phone?"

He laughed. I was right. He was crazy.

"Ah yes, sometimes I forget you were raised by mundanes. Please, sit."

I shook my head, and tried to put pressure on Leo's wounds, but there were just too many; I didn't know where to start, and he'd lost so much blood already. If I didn't get him out of here soon, he was going to bleed to death. Unless I could convince the crazy druid to save him.

"Help him first."

Raphael raised an eyebrow and looked at Leo as though seeing him for the first time.

"The shifter?" He sounded genuinely confused by my concern.

"My friend," I growled.

"Oh. Well, I'm afraid I have no skill in the healing arts. Not really my thing, you see. But… Yes, step back."

I hesitated a moment, then shuffled back a few steps. Raphael raised one arm again, palm towards Leo, and uttered something I didn't quite catch. Green light erupted from nothing, surrounding Leo's body, and whirled around him. Raphael clenched his fist.

"Reòth!"

The green swirling pattern froze mid-air, and as I looked closer, I could see the blood had stopped flowing from Leo's wounds, and the shallow rise and fall of his chest had stopped. My heart stuttered in panic, but then I saw even the swirling dust motes had frozen where they were. I looked over my shoulder at Raphael.

"What did you do?"

"A simple stasis spell."

Simple. Right. And I couldn't even remember the counter spell to a blacked-out window. I was so screwed.

"You just want to talk?" I said, glancing at Kelsey, who was pacing her energy-constructed prison. One friend caged, the other frozen, and yet again I was at Raphael's mercy. He inclined his head.

"As I have told you once before, I have no interest in harming you."

I edged towards the tree trunk chair, hesitated, then lowered myself on the floor a short distance away. The two chairs were far too close for my liking. The corner of Raphael's lip twitched, like he was amused by my delusion that a little distance would keep me safe from his magic, but he made no comment on it. I looked up at him warily.

"There," he said, settling back into his seat. "Much better. No-one will interrupt us this time."

"Why are you so interested in me?"

Kelsey snarled and threw herself towards the bars of her cage, then leapt back again with a yelp, and resumed her frantic pacing.

"What's wrong with her?" My brow furrowed. "How did you know what was happening tonight?"

"So many questions. Though of course, intelligence always breeds an inquiring mind. The half-breed is under the influence of a rage spell. Messy, I'll admit, but effective."

"You did that to her? I don't understand. Why?"

"There is much you do not understand. Where to begin?"

I didn't care that this man could obliterate me with a snap of his fingers. I didn't care that he was some sort of super druid. He was a smug prick, sitting smiling down at me, and right at that moment I wanted nothing more than to wrap my fingers around his neck, and squeeze.

"How about you start with why you ruined my friend's life?"

He was calm in the face of my fury, but then I suppose it was nothing compared to Kelsey's fury, and that hadn't fazed him. Of course, mine wasn't something he could turn on or off with a wave of his hands.

"That was not my objective. Such a mundane goal." His eyes glittered dangerously and his voice deepened, became darker. "You do me a disservice."

I swallowed. I'd gotten away from this lunatic once before, because the professors had interrupted us, and he'd chosen to run. I was on my own this time. If I wanted to get out of here – get all of us out of here – then I had to act smarter. I couldn't take him in a fight, not even close. But maybe if I kept him talking, I'd find some way to escape, or some weakness I could exploit.

"Then why did you do it?"

"Do you know how close we came to being wiped out, two centuries ago, by–" He eyed Leo, and his lip curled in disgust, "–a bunch of curs? They'll do it again, it's just a matter of time. The only thing they respect is power, and for too long the council – fools – have allowed them too much. They needed to be taken in hand before they became a threat."

"You were trying to start the war." My head spun as I looked up at him, understanding churning in my gut.

"You made Kelsey illegally create werewolves. You made her turn a druid, and you set Leo up to take the fall. You knew the council and the alpha pack would never be able to agree who had the better claim on him. You wanted them to break the truce."

"Yes."

I glanced around the clearing we were in again. The stubble of a few old walls jutted out from the earth here and there – an old cottage, maybe, or some sort of bunker. An old track led away from them, mostly overgrown now. It looked like it went towards a wood, maybe we could hide in there… if Leo wasn't in stasis and Kelsey wasn't in a cage, and the crazy druid wasn't staring right at me.

"Why?" I asked.

"Haven't you been paying attention?" His voice was raised, not quite shouting, but not far off. I flinched, and turned my eyes back onto him. He composed himself, took a deep breath and gave a quick shake of his head. His eyes remained brighter than they had been, almost fanatical. "They cannot be allowed to threaten our existence. Someone has to stop them."

"And that someone is you?"

"Us." His voice softened again. "It's your destiny, Lyssa. You're the only one who can help me, I knew it the moment I first met you, and nothing I've seen since has dissuaded me."

I took a moment to process what he was saying. In her cage, Kelsey snarled and raged. I snatched my eyes from her back onto Raphael.

"Why are you so interested in me? Is it because I'm... like you?" I choked on revulsion as I said the words. I didn't want to be like him, not in any way. I clarified. "Because of my powers?"

"Lyssa, you're like me in more ways than just that."

"What are you talking about?"

"How frustrating for you, I am sure, to have been raised by mundanes, away from our world. I assure you, it was not what I intended."

My blood ran cold.

"What you intended?"

"Your mother would not see reason. It is my greatest regret."

"What do you know about my mother?" I was on my feet without realising it, my hands balled into fists at my sides.

"She was just as passionate as you. You remind me of her, a lot."

"Was?"

"I do not know for sure, of course, but I must assume she is dead. There is no other way you would have been left in mundane hands. I certainly would never have left you to such a fate."

"You?" I blinked twice, stared at him, blinked again. "What did it have to do with you?"

"You see," he continued as though I had not spoken, "I had no idea what your mother intended. Leaving me was one thing, but she never even told me of your existence. It was many years before I learned I had a daughter."

"Your…" My legs felt too weak to support me. I staggered, reaching out for support against the tree stump chair he had conjured. I forced the words from my mouth. "Your daughter."

"As soon as I found out, I set about tracking you down, but you were well hidden. Outside of our world, raised without magic, like some sort of common mundane. But of course I knew you must come of age soon enough, so I created Toby, a convenient disguise, and planted myself inside Dragondale. It is amazing what information you can uncover when the world believes you to be a harmless cat."

"But don't you see?" he'd said last year. *"I did all of that for you."* All this time, I'd wondered what he'd meant. Wondered why I was the *second* druid in our history to control more than two elements. Why he'd gone to such

lengths to protect me when he was tearing down everyone around him. Because he was my... my father?

"You need not return to the academy," he said, while I still clung to the back of the chair. "I can teach you everything you need to know, and when the war begins, you will be by my side. We will return the half-breed to the academy. It is a shame her victim escaped unscathed, but no doubt the girl will be able to identify her attacker. The council and the alpha pack will each hold the other responsible. All that remains is to dispose of the other shifter."

He cast a glance at Leo in his stasis cell.

"What? No! Leo's my friend. Kelsey's my friend. You can't do this to them!" I straightened, taking my hands from the chair, and met his eye. "I won't let you."

He frowned at me, like me having some basic tenet of humanity hadn't been part of his plan. A forced smile stretched across his face.

"Lyssa, I know you became friends with this... abomination before you knew her true nature, but you've been a part of our world long enough by now to understand that simple sentiment is not justification enough to allow the corruption of everything for which we stand. And to have any reservation about the disposal of the shifter is absurd. Even without my influence, he is arrogant and abrasive – why else do you think I selected him to take the blame? Not even his own kind questioned his guilt."

"Then they're as stupid and arrogant as you!"

Shit, did I just say that? Absolute silence reigned for a heartbeat as I could see the same question flash through his eyes, and then his jaw set. I recognised something of myself in the gesture and recoiled away from him.

"I'm nothing like you. I'll never be anything like you. You're evil."

One day I was going to learn how to keep my mouth shut – if I lived that long. From the look on his face, the odds of that were getting slimmer by the second. The air thickened around us – literally – and the sky darkened. I could feel the first drops of rain in the air. How the hell powerful was this guy?

"I'm your father," he said stiffly, his eyes boring into mine.

"No. My father is George Eldridge. He's a lawyer and a good man."

"He's a mundane. He's not even your blood."

"He's ten times the man you'll ever be. I'm not going to help you hurt people, Raphael. Not ever."

He rose to his feet, towering over me.

"That's your decision?"

I swallowed hard, and nodded, trying to banish the quiver that I knew would be in my voice the moment I spoke.

"It is."

His carefully composed face twisted into a snarl.

"Fine. You *will* regret this."

He raised one hand, and a portal appeared behind him. I breathed a sigh of relief. That had gone better than I hoped.

He started towards it, then turned and locked eyes with me over his shoulder.

"You care so much about your precious curs? You can die by their hand."

He lifted his hand again, and the green swirling stasis spell fell away from Leo. He gasped in pain and writhed on the floor, blood pumping freely from him. I raced to his side, but before I could get there, Raphael twisted his hand towards Kelsey's cage, and clenched his fist. The bars disappeared as though they had never been there. She froze, and then locked her eyes onto me.

Oh. Crap.

Chapter Twenty-Six

I didn't see Raphael step through his portal, but I felt the change in the air when he left. If I'd hoped that his leaving would break the rage spell on Kelsey, I'd have been disappointed.

On all fours, with her hackles raised, she started to stalk towards us. I slapped my hands over Leo's wounds, half trying to staunch the bleeding, half hoping to bring him round. How the hell was I going to get us out of here if he couldn't move? I glanced back over at the tree line, wondering if I could pull him up one. But he was too heavy for me to drag him, and there was no way I could outrun the werewolf, hybrid or not.

"Kelsey? Kelsey, it's me."

She didn't falter. She didn't so much as blink. Leo groaned and I pressed down harder on the bite on his thigh. It was a mess.

"Kelsey, listen to me! I know you're in there somewhere."

I searched her eyes, trying to find some truth to my words, but the yellow orbs held no trace of human emotion.

"I don't want to hurt you!"

I conjured a fireball and propelled it into the air between us. Her eyes flicked to it and back to me again.

She bared her teeth and kept coming, until only a dozen feet separated us, until I could see the saliva dripping between each fang.

"Lyssa…" Leo's rasping voice came from beside me where he lay on the floor. I didn't dare take my eyes from the wolf advancing on me, or the fireball I'd hung in the air between us. I pushed it towards her, but she didn't give it so much as another glance. It was like she could focus on nothing but her rage and her hatred of me.

"Lyssa!" Leo's voice was weak, but more urgent. "Get… out of here. Run!"

"Not leaving you," I grunted, pushing the ball closer to Kelsey, until it was almost touching her reddish fur.

"Do it," Leo said, and I didn't know if he meant use the fireball, or run.

"Kelsey, please…"

She sank onto her haunches, preparing to launch herself through the air. I twisted my hand and the fireball thudded into her side. The smell of burning hair and flesh assaulted my nostrils, and my stomach churned. Kelsey lunged.

With a gasp, I threw myself aside, then immediately realised my mistake as she landed between me and Leo. He growled at her – but it was just a human imitation of the sound, he was too injured to shift. Her head snapped down to the prone form.

"Hey!" I shouted, and my words came out in a breathless rush. "I'm over here!"

She hesitated, looking back and forth between us, and then a furious snarl burst from her and she snapped at the empty air. I tossed another fireball in her direction, landing it squarely on her shoulder. She twisted round and started stalking towards me again.

Great plan, Lyssa. Now what?

I backed away as she advanced, glancing left and right, but we were in the middle of the clearing and there was nowhere to hide. I couldn't make a break for the treeline and leave Leo behind, and instinctively I knew if I broke into a run, so would she.

"Come on, Kelsey," I pleaded. "Snap out of it. You can fight this!"

Her claws cut into the ground beneath her as she kept coming, giving no sign she'd even heard me speaking. I wasn't going to break Raphael's spell that way. There had to be something I could do, there just had to be! If I didn't do something, she'd kill us both and then be murdered by the council. I couldn't allow that.

I rooted desperately through my pockets, hoping for something – anything – to get us out of here. Why the hell didn't the academy allow us to carry phones? Or some other way of contacting them? I wished I'd paid more attention in Atherton's lessons, there had to be some sort of spell that could stop her. Right now I'd have settled for a taser.

But all that my hand closed around was some crushed leaves, left there from my Botany exam. Wait, that was it! Solerium Sithum leaves. They could break emotional control spells. My heart sunk as quickly as it rose. If I could get her to ingest them.

She threw herself at me and I dived aside again, narrowly avoiding her teeth, but her claws caught my arm, opening three long gashes. I cried out in pain and spared a glance for the wounds. They were deep, and blood pumped freely from them, dripping down my hand. I gritted my teeth and tried to push the pain from my mind, because if I didn't find a way to get her to eat the leaves, that was going to be the least of my problems.

I glanced over towards Leo, and took another backwards step. If I could just keep circling round, I could get back to his side – and do what, I didn't know. But I needed to get some pressure back on his wounds, tie a tourniquet, or something. I had to keep him from bleeding out until his shifter powers could heal his injuries, but I had no idea how long that would take. Too long. Too long for him to help in this fight, and without his help, I didn't know how I was going to get the leaves inside Kelsey.

She leapt at me again, snapping her teeth around empty air as I dived. I hit the ground hard, jarring my injured arm on impact. Her head swung round towards me, sensing my weakness, and I scrambled forwards through the dirt. Leo was just a few feet away… and I was starting to get an idea.

My heart pounded furiously as I watched Kelsey, waiting for her next attack. She leapt again, but this time between me and Leo, trying to herd me away from him, whether by design or coincidence I had no idea. I didn't think she was capable of that much logic anymore, yet she seemed determined to stay between us.

With a cry of pain and frustration, I launched a fireball through the air at her, and another, and another, each of the balls striking her massive body, trying to drive her back, make her lunge, just make her *move,* I didn't care where.

I got my wish.

She threw herself right at me from just half a dozen feet away. I froze, staring at her as she leapt through the air, half formed fireball still in my hand.

"Lyssa!"

Leo's shout snapped me from the horror-struck stupor and I dived forwards into a roll, right beneath the werewolf's extended claws, crushing the fireball to nothing in my hand. I came up right next to the injured shifter. Kelsey roared with anger as she closed on thin air again, and then she whipped around to face us.

"Listen," I said, looking down into Leo's dirt and blood-stained face. "I've got a plan. Do you trust me?"

He searched my eyes for a moment, then cracked a weak grin.

"Sure. You can't... let me die, right? Bad for... inter-community relations."

"Why else would I bother keeping your cocky ass alive?" I forced a smile, then squeezed his hand. "I need you to distract her."

He nodded, so weak he barely moved more than a fraction.

"Help... help me sit."

I slipped a hand behind his back, flicking my eyes to the shifter, and back. She was advancing on us slowly, cautiously, placing each paw with deliberation as she sized us up. Leo swayed and I held a hand behind him, ready to steady him, but he shook his head.

"Get out of here, druid girl."

The air around him rippled and a thin line of fur started to coat his arms, not quite covering them, so that I could see the muscles bulge and ripple, and then bones... *change shape* beneath his skin. He roared in pain, but the transformation continued to creep slowly over him, gaining momentum as it went, fuelled by his agony.

Kelsey's attention immediately switched from me to him as she took in the new threat.

He tried to take a step towards her, and stumbled. Her eyes moved back to me, and Leo loosed another roar, ferocious and furious, and Kelsey could not ignore it. She leapt towards him.

I didn't stick around to watch what happened. Leo was risking his life, and I couldn't squander a second of the precious time he'd bought me. I ducked my head and sprinted straight for the treeline, my eyes locked onto a fallen branch as thick as my arm. I skidded into the cover of the woods, and grabbed hold of the stick. Not much of a weapon, but it didn't need to be. As long as it could hold her off for just a second, that would be enough. It would have to be.

I sucked in a deep breath, shutting out the loud yelps and squeals of pain, rose to my feet, and stepped out from the scant protection of the trees.

"Hey, Kelsey, I'm over here!"

She lifted her bloodstained maw from Leo's chest – Leo's shredded chest – and glared at me. My stomach clenched. Leo wasn't moving.

"Get over here, you big, dumb animal," I screamed, swinging my stick like a battle axe.

She abandoned her downed prey, and started towards me.

"Come on!" I bellowed. "Come and fight me!"

She broke into a run, eating up the ground between us in a dozen strides. Ten feet from me, she leapt through the air. I locked my eyes onto her gaping jaws, and kept them there, trembling where I stood, stick held out between my hands, and the leaves crushed up in one palm. She hit me hard, front paws smashing into my shoulders. With a scream of pain, I thrust the stick forwards, jamming it right to the back of her mouth where there were no teeth. The force of her attack threw me to the ground and her weight pounded me into it, shoulders first. I felt something break, and searing agony raged through my left shoulder as my hands fell away from the stick.

She shook her head back and forth, trying to dislodge the branch, but her first attempt to bite me had wedged it into her gums. I lifted my right hand, and conjured the strongest terror I could. The blast of wind carried the leaves straight into her open maw, and down her throat, and I collapsed back to the ground, spent.

Looking up from where I lay, I saw the manic fury fade from her eyes. I must've hit my head because I started hearing voices... and it sounded like they were calling my name. It was a nice thought, so I pretended they were real, and smiled to myself as I leaned my head back in the dirt, and lost my grip on consciousness.

Chapter Twenty-Seven

When I woke, I was in a soft bed, covered by warm blankets. There was the quiet buzz of hushed conversation around me, and I could smell warm food, disinfectant, and magic. All of this I discerned without opening my eyes. My lids felt heavy, but after a moment of lying in the bed, listening to feet brush against the stone flooring, I forced them to part. Brilliant light scorched my pupils and my lids blinked shut, protecting my eyes from the searing brightness. Cautiously, I prised them apart just a fraction, and squinted out. The light hurt less this time, and I recognised where I was immediately. And why wouldn't I? It seemed like I'd spent half my time in Dragondale getting patched up in the hospital wing. It was practically my second dorm.

"Welcome back, druid girl."

I rolled my head to my left and saw Leo sitting up in the next bed along, blanket pooled around his waist.

"Where'd I go?" I slurred, blinking him into focus. The memory punched into my skull with dizzying force – it was a good thing I was still lying flat on the bed. "Wait, you're alive!"

The shifter chuckled, and then winced, holding a hand to his ribs. As my eyes adjusted to the light, I could make out the crisscross of wounds all over his torso – long, straight lines, and smaller jagged ones in circular patterns. Even from here, I could see that those ones, the bites, were deep. And I knew that wasn't the worst of it. Under the sheets, his right leg was stretched out. That was the bite that had nearly killed him.

"Where's Kelsey?" I asked, and the levity fell abruptly from his face. He chewed his lip a moment, then nodded and exhaled heavily.

"She's okay, but… They know what she did. They've got her under guard. Sam's trying to convince the alphas and the council that she's innocent."

He hung his head.

"Wait, I don't understand," I said, struggling to sit up, and failing.

"I'm not sure you want to do that," Leo said, leaning back against his bed's headboard and regarding me with an amused look.

I gritted my teeth, grabbed the side of the mattress with my right hand, and hauled myself up, because I refused to be defeated by a damned blanket. I swore as a lance of pain shot through my shoulder.

"Told you."

I ignored him, because there was no way I was letting the alpha pack or the council have my best friend. None of it was her fault. Leo knew that.

"You were there," I said. "You saw everything. You *know* that none of it was her fault."

He shook his head.

"I didn't see anything. I can't remember a damned thing after going through that portal, your healer thinks I hit my head or something."

"The stasis," I blurted, and he frowned at me. "He put you in stasis while we talked. Hold on, you don't remember anything that happened before or after that?"

He was pretty beat up after Kelsey's attack – her first one, I mean. Maybe he did hit his head. He was barely conscious for a lot of it, too.

"Ms Eldridge." The stern voice came from my right, and I turned to look at its owner, immediately regretting it when the movement sent pain lancing through my shoulder. Leech was staring down at me with a look of disapproval on her face. Nothing new there, then. "You absolutely should not be sitting up. You were very badly injured. I must insist you lie down at once."

Leo gave me a smug, 'told you so' look as Leech moved in to help lie me back down. I shrugged her off.

"I'm fine."

"You are *not* fine," she snapped. "Your shoulder was broken in five places, and the magic holding it together has not yet fully set."

"Five? Wow." Guess that explained why it hurt like a bitch. "Please, Madam Leechington, it aches when I lie flat."

She narrowed her eyes, then gave a curt nod.

"Very well. You may remain sitting. But absolutely minimal movement, do you understand?"

"Yes, Ma'am," I said with a nod. See? I was getting the hang of this. I shot Leo a smug look of my own.

"Professor Talendale will want to know you're awake," Leech said. "Meanwhile, try to eat something. It will help hasten the spell along."

She lifted a tray of food from the bedside locker I hadn't even seen beside me, and placed it across my lap. A quick flick of her hand sent a wave of heat across the food, and steam rose from it. Roast beef, mashed potatoes, carrots and broccoli. It smelt amazing. My stomach clenched, and I waited until Leech had bustled off before I pushed the food away from me. Eating was the last thing on my mind.

I had to tell Talendale what had happened. If Leo hadn't seen any of it, then Raphael was out there, working on his plan, and no-one was any the wiser. He could be putting the plan in motion right now, just waiting for the war to erupt. Did he even know I'd escaped alive?

"Hey, are you eating that?"

Leo was looking at my tray, practically drooling. Werewolves. I shook my head.

"Knock yourself out."

He gestured to his leg, which I suspected was heavily bandaged beneath the blanket.

"Uh, little help?"

"Pfft, you know how much control I have over my air power, right?" He was more likely to end up wearing the food than eating it. He looked mournfully at my plate and I rolled my eyes, then, after a quick glance to make sure Leech hadn't come back, shuffled to the edge of the bed and held the tray out with my good arm. Leo grabbed it and dug in like a man who hadn't seen food in a month. I'll say it again. Werewolves. We sat in silence while he ate, and I leaned back against my headboard – because there was no way I was going to admit that just *sitting* was taking it out of me.

"How long was I out?" I asked.

"Two days," he said.

Two days? Huh. Must've been pretty mashed up. My jaw hardened. Two days Kelsey had been locked up, waiting for the packs and the council to decide her fate. Just as well they couldn't agree on a single thing, otherwise– I cut that thought off before it could take root. Kelsey was fine. Well, maybe not fine, but alive, and that was as much as could be hoped for. If I'd died,

FERAL MAGIC

there'd have been no-one alive left to speak for her. The packs and the council would have come to blows arguing who would be the one to deliver her sentence, and Raphael would have got his wish. War. A shudder ran through me. He'd come so close. Too close. And the danger wasn't over yet, not until I convinced Talendale what had happened.

As if on cue, the door behind Leo swung open, and the headmaster stood outlined in the doorway for a long moment, before his eyes came to rest on me. He crossed the room and stood at the foot of my bed, ignoring the shifter. If Leo took offence, it didn't show – but then he was still eating, so he probably hadn't even noticed Talendale. I looked up at the professor, and one glance at his stern face told me I was in trouble. His shoulders rose and fell, and then he shook his head, exhaling heavily.

"I suppose there's no point in telling you that what you did was extremely reckless?"

"I'm sorry, Professor."

"That portal could have led you anywhere. From what Madam Leechington tells me, you were very nearly killed. Had Kendra not raised the alarm, you most certainly would never have been found in time."

"Sorry, Professor," I said again. There was no point in trying to explain I'd thought the professors were the ones who sent the portal.

"Must we end every year having this conversation?"

"Would it help if I tried not to get caught next time, Professor?"

I could have sworn a fleeting look of amusement crossed his face, but it was gone before I could be certain it had ever been there. He was right. This was no time for jokes. Before I could say anything, the door opened again, and two more men entered the room. One I recognised immediately as the head of the council – an old, greying man with deep-set frown lines in his face, and a stooped gait. I'd seen his image in textbooks, and his portrait hanging in the academy's entrance hall. Authur Cauldwell. The other man I hadn't seen before, but even from here it was impossible to mistake the aura of power surrounding him. He had to be one of the alpha pack. The two men clamped eyes on Talendale and approached. Despite his stooped gait, the councilman moved with an air of authority. The alpha wore the same air, but with a whole lot less civility. There was something predatory about the way he moved, the sort of stride that would make other people step out of his way.

Leo looked up from his plate at the sound of their approach. He hastily rid himself of his sheets, and as they reached the gap between our beds, he threw himself onto the floor and dropped into a crouch, wincing with pain as his injured leg – I was right, it was heavily bandaged – momentarily took his weight, and bowed his head.

"What are you doing?" I hissed at him.

"Showing my respect," he said in a low voice, without raising his head. I glanced at the two men, and a flash of hot anger flooded through me. My voice probably wasn't as quiet as it should have been.

"To *him*? They wanted to have you killed a few months ago."

"He is the alpha of the alpha pack." Leo kept his head bowed as the words rumbled from him, low and calm. "His word is my law."

"I see you," the alpha said, only the way he said it made me think there was more significance to the words than just seeing with his eyes. "Rise. Return to your bed."

Leo rose unsteadily, and edged back until he was perched on the edge of his bed. He took the weight on his arms and lifted himself back. The blood drained from his face as he stretched out his ribs, but he seemed determined not to make a single sound of pain, biting down on his lip. The alpha avoided looking at his face, either to allow Leo the privacy to hide his pain, or because he simply didn't care. It was hard to say which – his stoic expression gave nothing away. Talendale, on the other hand, was not wearing his poker face, and he was most definitely not happy to see the pair of visitors.

"Authur, Draeven, Ms Eldridge has just regained consciousness. I do not think this is the appropriate time."

"We must speak to her urgently," the councilman said. "She is the only witness."

I raised a hand before Talendale could refuse him.

"It's okay, Professor," I said. "I want to speak to them."

"Very well," he said, and to the councilman, "Keep it brief."

He looked like he had more to stay on the matter, but even he had to acknowledge the authority of the Grand Council. Cauldwell cleared his throat and turned his attention to me.

"You are addressing Head Councilman Cauldwell, representative of the Grand Council of the Druid Circle. Your words will form part of the official record of the matter of Kelsey Winters, the druid-shifter hybrid. Do you understand?"

I nodded, and swallowed.

"Yes. I… I understand."

"You need not be afraid," Draeven said, in his deep, rumbling voice that did nothing to dispel my instinctive wariness. "Tell us what happened two nights ago with the half-breed."

The way his lips curled around the words 'half-breed' rankled, like her very existence offended him. Hell, who was I kidding? That was exactly the case. This mighty 'alpha of alphas' was just as bigoted as the rest of them. My eyes hardened, and I jerked them up to meet his. I heard Leo's sharp intake of breath beside me and knew I was breaching some serious etiquette. I didn't care.

"Don't call her that. Kelsey is my friend, and she's innocent."

The alpha's jawline went rigid and his shoulders stiffened. He probably wasn't used to people contradicting him, or telling him what to do.

"Lyssa's still groggy, Alpha," Leo said quickly. "She doesn't know what she's—"

"She knows exactly what she's saying," Draeven said, cutting across Leo, who instantly fell silent. The alpha's eyes stayed locked on mine. Great. I was in a staring contest with the most powerful werewolf in the country. No way was this going to end well. But I wasn't backing down.

"Lyssa," Cauldwell said, and my eyes snapped to him without my permission. *Dammit.* "We have Leo's testimony of the events before you entered the portal. That is to say, you came across Kelsey in her wolf form, about to attack another student. Leo shifted and fought her. You opened a portal, and escaped through it, pursued by Kelsey, who was followed by Leo. Is this correct?"

I shook my head.

"No. I mean, yeah, right up to the portal, but I didn't open it. Raphael did."

"Raphael?" Talendale cut in, his voice sharp. "You're sure?"

"Yes, I'm–" I took a breath. My shoulder was really starting to throb, but no way was I taking this interrogation laying down – literally or figuratively. Still, some diplomacy wouldn't kill me. Probably the opposite. "Yes, Professor. He sent a portal from some other place. It was a trap. And he was the one who made Kelsey attack all those people. He used a rage spell on her."

"You have proof?" the alpha asked, narrowing his eyes at me. I shook my head, not bothering to lift my gaze higher than his chin this time.

"No, but he told me. Sir."

The werewolf snorted with what might have been amusement.

"I can smell your defiance, druid."

"Then you can smell my honesty, too!" I wasn't sure if that was true, but at the very least he could probably tell that I didn't reek of guilt. "I used Solerium Sithum leaf to break the spell."

"Clever," Cauldwell said, with a curt nod. "If you're telling the truth—"

"I am."

"—then a simple spell will detect the presence of the leaf in her bloodstream. It takes several days to dissipate."

"Unless you want to amend your story?" the alpha said.

I shook my head again.

"It's the truth."

I crossed my arms, then hissed as a bolt of pain stabbed my shoulder.

"Councilman, Alpha Draeven," Talendale said, "I think it's time we ended this. Lyssa clearly needs to rest, and you have your information."

"No," I said, through gritted teeth as I waited for the pain to fade to a manageable level. "You need to hear this. All of you."

The three of them waited, four if you counted Leo, who was surreptitiously watching me from his bed.

"He did all of it. He cursed Kelsey, and he set Leo up to take the fall. He wanted to start a war between you. He knew you'd fight over who would be the ones to kill Leo."

I glared at both the alpha and the councilman, because despite my best intentions, diplomacy had never been my strong suit.

"Then why the attack when the shifter was imprisoned?" Cauldwell asked.

I shrugged, cursed under my breath, and waited for the pain to fade again.

"Maybe he lost control of his rage spell. Maybe he thought you'd each blame the other for letting Leo out for long enough to attack. I don't know. When you let Leo go, he tried to frame him again, setting Kelsey on another student, assuming you'd blame him. And it would have worked, wouldn't it? Except I stumbled across the fight, and Leo shifted in front of Kendra, and he had to move up his plan. So he sent the portal, knowing I'd have to escape through it."

"Why did he care what happened to you?" the alpha said. He sounded genuinely perplexed, but then, he didn't know much about me. I was just another druid apprentice to him.

"He wanted me to join him." I looked away then, because I didn't want to see the expressions of revulsion and curiosity on their faces, or see them trying to work out why he would want *me*. I didn't look away quickly enough.

"When I *refused*," I said, before they could vocalise their questions, "he set Kelsey on me and Leo. He figured he'd have his war one way or another. Without any witnesses, you'd have been arguing over whether to kill Kelsey, or throw her in Daoradh."

Neither man spoke for a moment, telling me they'd spent the last two days doing exactly that.

"That doesn't explain his interest in you."

"It's because..." I looked away again, staring at my hands folded in my lap. "It's because he's my father."

Noise erupted as the three of them all started talking at once. I tuned them all out. Every time I said it, it became more real. I didn't want it to be real. I wanted to bury my head under this duvet, and wake up in my own dorm, with Kelsey telling me I'd had some crazy dream, and she'd never hurt anyone, Paisley wasn't a hybrid, and my father was a lawyer from Georgia.

The noise died down, and when I looked up again, all three men were staring down at me in silence. The alpha wore a look of pity on his face, the councilman a look of consternation, and Talendale a look of understanding.

"It seems we have much work to do," Cauldwell said. "But I will talk to you further when you recover."

Oh, joy. I'd look forward to that.

"We must make our preparations," Draeven agreed. He glanced over at Leo. "Your sentence here is almost served. You will leave with me, and return to your pack."

"If you will it, Alpha," Leo said in a solemn voice that didn't suit him. "Only..."

The alpha raised an eyebrow, and Leo immediately ducked his head.

"Speak," the alpha commanded. Leo kept his eyes down, but obeyed.

"I was hoping…" He risked a fleeting glance at Talendale. "I was hoping to stay here this summer, and help with Redwing and Stormclaw. If, you know, if you want me…"

I'd never heard him sound more uncertain. Personally, I thought it was a great idea. Who else could handle Stormclaw while I was gone for the summer? And who else stood a hope in hell of getting close enough to that foal to make sure it was healthy, if neither of us was here?

Talendale rubbed his hand across his chin, appraising the shifter with his eyes.

"Professor Alden speaks very highly of you, and your familiarity with the Unhallowed Grove would most certainly prove an asset. I have no objections."

All of us turned back to the alpha, though Leo's eyeline didn't reach higher than the man's knees. These wolves took the dominance thing to a whole new level. I'd never seen Leo so careful not to cause offence or appear insubordinate.

"Very well," the alpha rumbled his consent. "You will remain here, on the condition that you do so as a free man, and as an emissary to the packs."

Draeven locked eyes with Talendale, who appeared completely uncowed by the dominant man's stare. Talendale gave a curt nod, and extended his hand. The two men gripped hands, and I winced, because even from here I could see the strength of the alpha's handshake. Remind me never to do that. My bones broke too easily, and I'd spent too much time in this hospital wing already.

"Then it is done," the alpha said. "I will make my preparations to leave."

"And Kelsey?" I said, looking between the alpha and the councilman. "You're going to let her go, right?"

The two men shared a look.

"It wasn't her fault!"

"If the spell shows she was indeed under the influence of Raphael's curse," Cauldwell said eventually, "then the council will not hold her accountable for her actions."

"Nor will the packs," Draeven said.

"Good," I mumbled. My eyelids were getting heavy, and the pain in my shoulder was worsening by the moment.

"Gentlemen, Lyssa needs her rest," Talendale said. "Let us leave her in peace. We have all the information we need."

"For the moment," the councilman agreed, and I knew he wasn't going to let my relation to Raphael drop. Like it was my fault he was my father. He'd made it pretty damned clear he'd disowned me back in the ruins when he'd tried to have me killed. Whatever. I needed to sleep.

Chapter Twenty-Eight

Madam Leechington kept me in the hospital wing for another three days before she reluctantly agreed that I was well enough to leave. Leo had been discharged the day before, and I was so bored that I'd even started co-operating when Draeven and Cauldwell visited me to bombard me with more questions about what I knew – which didn't amount to very much, but that didn't stop them coming up with new ways to ask the same half-dozen questions anyway.

I wasn't sure whether my premature release from purgatory was because Leech was sick of them disrupting her ward, or because Sam's antics grew more raucous with each visit. Kelsey visited too, once, but she didn't say much. Her crimes, even though they weren't really hers, weighed heavily on her shoulders. Or maybe Leech let me out because tomorrow was the last day of the semester and she wanted me gone so she could take a break over the summer. Whatever her reason, I wasn't planning on sticking around long enough to question it.

I was mildly surprised to discover that Ava hadn't moved out of our dorm room – apparently druid-shifter hybrids weren't a big deal to her, but then again she'd been an outsider like me – this whole damned world was weird, and what difference did one little hybrid make?

That girl could grow on me – if I lived long enough to get to know her. Which seemed less likely by the day, because by now Raphael had to know that his plan had failed, and I doubted he intended on letting it go.

But that was a problem for another day. I had enough to worry about – like my guilt-wracked best friend, and my exam results that were due in the morning.

"Hey, Kels, are you okay?" I know, tactful, right? But no sense beating around the bush.

She lifted her head and looked at me across our dorm room. Ava was working late tonight, helping bed down the gryffs and prepare them for their long summer break. I'd offered to help, but Alden had turned me down flat, pointing out that one good barge from a gryff was all it would take to shatter my shoulder again. I hated it when she was right.

"I'm fine," Kelsey said, flopping her head back down onto her pillow so I couldn't see her face. I didn't need to.

"Since when do we lie to each other?"

"Apparently," Kelsey said, her voice taut, "I've been doing it all year."

"But that wasn't your fault," I protested, propping myself up on one elbow – not the one that was attached to my recently un-broken shoulder. Kelsey didn't need to see that break all over again. It was obvious she was feeling guilty enough.

"Tell that to Paisley."

Paisley had been waiting for Kelsey when they let her out, Sam had told me on one of his visits. It hadn't been pretty – not least because Kelsey refused to defend herself.

"I'll tell it to the whole damned academy if I have to," I said. "You were under a spell."

"Exactly," she said, sitting up and staring at me. The anger and self-loathing in her face were almost more than I could bear, but I didn't look away. "My temper has been getting worse and worse all year. I should have known something was wrong."

"No." I shook my head, biting my lip, and despite my shame, I still didn't look away from her face. "*I* should have noticed. You're my best friend, and you're the kindest, most patient person I know. If you want to blame someone for not seeing what was going on, blame me."

"I think you've been punished enough," she said, eyeing my shoulder meaningfully.

"And so have you," I said. "Except in your case, you didn't do anything to deserve it. Raphael attacked those people, using your body. It wasn't you."

She sighed.

"Maybe you're right. I don't know."

"Of course I'm right. Besides, the council and the alpha pack all agree, and let's face it, those guys don't agree on anything."

She made a noise that might have been a chuckle, and then waved a hand, extinguishing the fireball hanging above her bed.

"We should get some sleep."

I watched the fireball above my bed wink out of existence, removing the last of the light from the room, except for the faint glow of the moon coming through the window. I stared up at the ceiling in the near darkness, listening to the sounds of my own breathing for a long while.

"Kelsey?"

"Yeah?"

"I'm sorry everyone found out you're a hybrid."

"I'm not."

"You're not?" That was weird. Nearly the whole academy was shunning her, and it was as much to do with what she was as what she'd done. It seemed like she was all anyone could talk about, and I knew first-hand how crappy that felt.

"I'm tired of being ashamed of who I am. I can't change it, and I don't want to hide it anymore. Hybrids exist, whether the magic community likes it or not, and they're going to have to accept it. There's nothing wrong with what I am, and I'm not going to let other people tell me that there is. I'm a good druid, and a good shifter, and I'm trying my best to be a good person. If anyone doesn't like that, then it's their problem, not mine."

"Kelsey?"

"Yeah?"

"I love you."

*

There were no alarms at Dragondale – not any conventional ones, at least, but we were still awake not long after the sun rose. Well, alright, in my case 'awake' might have been an exaggeration, but Ava and Kelsey made up for it. Not only were they awake, they were both out of bed, dressed, and talking in excited whispers. Honestly, they were like a pair of kids on Christmas morning, waiting to see what Santa had brought them. Except in this case Santa was the bringer of grades, and I'd been a very bad girl all year. I didn't want to get out of bed.

"Do you think we should wake her?" That was Ava's voice.

"Probably not. She's really not a morning person."

I rolled over to hide my grin. She had me there.

"But it's the end of the semester."

"Well, maybe she wants to stay here forever. You know how much she loves Spellcraft."

"Alright, alright," I grumbled, sitting up. "I'm awake. How long have you known?"

"Since you stopped snoring." Kelsey grinned at me.

"Ouch. Okay, give me five minutes." It was hard to be cross – the last thing I'd expected was to find my best friend smiling again. Then again, if anything was going to make her smile, it was the prospect of getting another perfect 4.0 – I mean, who wouldn't like getting results if they were practically an academic genius? I, on the other hand, was just hoping I'd scraped a pass so I wouldn't be held back a year.

I cleaned myself up in the bathroom and threw on my robes for the last time this semester. By the time I came out, Kelsey was all but bouncing from foot to foot by the door, and Ava had started to pace.

"What's eating you?" I asked the American. "I thought you were doing alright in your classes."

"I am. At least, I think I am. But you never really know, do you?"

I grunted my agreement, and pulled open the door before Kelsey self-destructed. We headed out into the common room, where a few dozen students were already clustered, Sam amongst them. He waved us over when he caught sight of us. We left Ava with some of her year group and went over.

"You're looking happy," I accused, eyeing him suspiciously.

"Are you kidding?" His grin widened. "One more morning, and then weeks of glorious freedom. What's not to be happy about?"

"Uh, I don't know," I said, rolling my eyes. "Exam results?"

"Ignore her," Kelsey said, grabbing the back of my cloak and towing me towards the common room door. "Apparently she's forgotten that she had two excellent personal tutors for weeks."

"Yeah," I grumbled, letting her shove me through the door with poor grace. "And apparently I forgot everything they taught me the moment I sat down for my exams."

"Last meal for the condemned woman, then." Sam grinned, so I aimed a slap at his head on general principle, which he dodged with ease. Bloody morning people.

We reached the main hall and grabbed some breakfast from Aiden the kitchen mage, then claimed a couple of seats on the end of the Fire table, and pretended not to notice the looks some of the other students were giving Kelsey.

All around us, the hall was filled with the excited chattered of several hundred nervous students, and the scraping of knives and forks. It wasn't until the latter sound had died away, and most of the plates had been collected up, that Professor Talendale stood and cleared his throat. At once, silence descended on the hall.

"Good morning, students," he said, his voice carrying easily through the hall. I glanced behind him to the professors' table, where piles of neatly stacked envelopes sat. This was it. Professors Alden, Ellerby, Swann and Atherton each collected a stack of envelopes, and moved to their house tables. My eyes tracked Alden as she moved towards us.

"Your exam results await you," Talendale said. "First, I congratulate you on a productive year here at Dragondale. For some of you, your first. Others, your last. All of you represent this academy, whether further study lies ahead of you, or whether you are ready to make your contribution to the magic community. Your actions reflect on us all."

He paused for a moment, his silence underscoring his words.

"Second years." He paused again and a shiver ran the length of my spine. "You have some important decisions to make before you return to us next year. Those of you who progress, that is."

Gee, thanks Professor. He was right, though. Next year we'd have to start choosing our specialisations, and thinking about our careers, and honestly I wasn't even close to ready for that.

"For those of you who did not pass all of your exams, resits will be held as usual at the end of the summer. The rest of you, enjoy your break, and return ready to embrace next year's challenges. I assure you, there will be many."

He glanced at each of the four head of houses, and nodded to himself.

"Once you have received you results, you are free to begin your preparations to leave the academy. Portals will be opened from mid-day onwards. Your heads of elements will inform you of your assigned portal times. Now, without further delay, your results."

He raised his hands, and the envelopes flew out of the professors' hands, racing the length of each table. One skidded to a halt in front of me, my name emblazoned on its front in shimmering red letters. I stared at the stiff white card, my mouth suddenly dry. I glanced at Kelsey on my left, and Sam on my right. They both had their envelopes, too. Kelsey was the first to flip hers over.

"I predict," Sam intoned, rolling his eyes up into his skull and holding his hands out, "that Kelsey's a swot."

Kelsey pulled out her results card, and I looked at it over her shoulder, then winked at Sam.

"If only your potions were as good as your predictions."

Kelsey, as we all could have predicted, had passed every exam, and earned a perfect 4.0 to match last year's.

"Who's next?" she said, grinning from ear to ear. I shared a resigned look with Sam, and raised an eyebrow.

"Rock, paper, scissors?"

He nodded, his face a mask of seriousness, and we both raised our right hands and chanted.

"Rock... Paper... Scissors!"

I held my hand flat as his curled into a fist. I wrapped mine around his with a touch of smugness.

"You're up, Devlin."

He flipped his envelope open and pulled his card out, scanning it rapidly. His face fell.

"What?" Kelsey asked.

Sam slumped his head forward onto the table, and held the card up. I plucked it from his hand.

"Druidic Law. You missed out by two marks."

"I'm going to be stuck studying all summer," he groaned.

"Open yours," Kelsey urged me, and I was sure I didn't imagine the trepidation in her voice.

"Well at least if I have to re-sit, I'll have company, right?" I forced a grin as I opened my envelope, and plucked out my results, trying my best to ignore the

331

butterflies fluttering in my stomach. Sam raised his head a few inches to watch me.

"Oh. My. God."

"What?" Kelsey said.

"I don't believe it."

"What?" Sam echoed.

I slapped my results down on the table in front of me, and a grin spread across my face. Sam squinted at it.

"How the hell did you get a perfect score in Botany?"

"Beats me," I shrugged, a huge weight lifted from my shoulders. "Too bad my Potions score didn't match."

I didn't really care, though. I'd passed all of the other subjects, even Spellcraft – somehow – and that meant in just a few months, I'd be entering my third year here at Dragondale, and preparing for a future I'd never even dreamed might exist.

"We'll get together in the summer," Kelsey was saying to Sam. "We'll help you study."

"Yeah," I agreed. "I mean, you guys managed to tutor me to a pass in Spellcraft, how much harder could it possibly be?"

"Anyway," Kelsey reasoned, "It was only a couple of marks."

"You know what?" Sam said after a moment. "You two are a pair of trouble magnets. Hanging out with you all summer is going to be way more exciting than hiking through the Lake District with my family. Something interesting is bound to happen."

I looked at Kelsey, and we both burst out laughing.

"What?" Sam protested.

"Well," Kelsey said. "It's just…"

"Well, I mean," I said. "Don't you have a habit of sleeping through all the action?"

"Next year I'm turning over a new leaf," he declared, clamping one hand over his heart. "Where there's danger, I will venture. Where there's adventure, I will go. And where there's action, I will… act."

He frowned as he trailed off, and Kelsey laughed at him. It had been a rough year for her, but she had finally stopped running from her demons. Her journey might be an uphill one, but at least she'd decided to face it. As for me, I didn't have a clue what to do about Raphael, about the war he was trying to start, or about the fact that the most powerful druid I'd ever met wanted me dead.

Sam was right. Where I went, trouble followed. Werewolves, rogue powers, dark druids… One thing was for sure: life at Dragondale was never dull. And as for next year, who knew what it would bring?

I knew one thing though, looking left and right at my two best friends. Whatever was waiting for us, in the academy, in the world, we would face it together. Because no matter what happened, we were family, and this was our   home.

A note from the author

Thanks for joining me for Lyssa's second year at the Dragondale Academy of Druidic Magic. I hope you enjoyed it as much as I did. Be sure to come back for her final year in Primal Magic, book 3 in the Druid Academy series.

Meanwhile, if you enjoyed this book, I'd be really grateful if you would take a moment to leave me a review.

Sign up to my newsletter by visiting www.cschurton.com to be kept up to date with my new releases and received exclusive content.

There's one thing I love almost as much as writing, and that's hearing from people who have read and enjoyed my books. If you've got a question or a comment about the series, you can connect with me and other like-minded people over in my readers' group at

www.facebook.com/groups/CSChurtonReaders

Printed in Great Britain
by Amazon